C000151933

The Pink Elephants

Sam Harris Adventure Series Book 4

PJ Skinner

Gemma Louise
Happy Reading
PJ Skinner

Cover design by: Self Publishing Lab

ISBN: 978-1-9996427-2-3

For My Parents

Chapter 1

Dirk Goosen surveyed the chaos on his desk with a sigh. *Mess expands to fill the space available for it.* He gathered files in a pile and put them on the floor out of sight. He buzzed for his personal assistant, Miriam, whom he shared with the chairman of Consolidated African Limited, Morné Van Rooyen.

'Miriam, please, help me out. I'm meeting Morné in fifteen minutes and the place is a tip. I haven't had time to tidy it this week.'

Miriam rolled her eyes to heaven. Dirk's desk was always inundated with files, and receipts and dirty coffee cups. She bustled around straightening the mountains of paper and removing the remains of various lunches eaten at his desk. He stood back against the wall getting in her way instead of moving. She tutted.

'I won't steal your precious papers. Why are these on the floor?'

Her sharp tone betrayed her irritation. As an experienced executive secretary, she was efficient enough to look after both Dirk and Morné, but she did not suffer fools gladly. Dirk shrugged and moved into the doorway.

He lit a cigarette and ran his fingers through his salt and pepper thatch of hair, watching her busy

1

hands reducing the maelstrom to tidy piles. She picked up the files he had placed on the floor and marched over to the filing cabinet where she dropped them in their rightful positions with a thud and banged the drawers shut.

'Right, that's better. I'll call him,' she said, and knocked on the door of Morné's office, which was on the opposite side of her room to Dirk's. She popped her head around it and said, 'he's ready for you, sir.'

'Thanks, Miriam.'

Morné limped through Miriam's office and entered Dirk's now tidy sanctum. Dirk glanced up and smiled.

'What's up?' said Morné.

'Masaibu,' said Dirk.

'Again? That project is jinxed.' Morné tugged at his ginger moustache. 'What's happened now?'

'Jack Oosthuizen resigned while you were at Richard's Bay,' said Dirk.

'No. What a pain! Do you want me to talk to him?'

Dirk shook his head. 'He won't talk. He's burnt out with the constant firefighting.'

'Do we have any candidates?' said Morné.

'We have lots of replacements, in theory, but no-one wants Masaibu on their resumé.'

'I don't either, but we're stuck with it. The Lumbono government won't favour our other projects if we dump this one. Where can we find a manager?'

'Someone desperate enough to take an impossible job?' Dirk shrugged. 'Damned if I know. I'll call my friend Carol Downey in Australia. She's an expert head-hunter. If there's a candidate out there, she'll find them.'

Sam Harris reclined in the rocking chair with the baby on her lap. She peered out at the starless night which hung over London and pondered her situation. Jack guzzled milk from a bottle that threatened to run out before his appetite did, his little face crimson with effort as he sucked the dregs from the bottom. The smell of the baby made her sleepy. *Maybe I should make up more formula for him.*

They both jumped as the phone rang on the table in front of them. She tried to grab the receiver and almost threw the baby onto the floor. The child wailed as the teat popped out of its mouth and hovered just out of reach. Sam manoeuvred the chair from side to side, inching it forward until she could reach the telephone and shove the bottle back in Jack's mouth. She picked up the telephone.

'Hello? Gloria?' said Sam, assuming it was her nutty friend calling from Sierramar. She never remembered about the time difference between South America and London. But it wasn't Gloria.

'Hello, my name is Carol Downey. I'm calling from Sydney. What time is it there?'

'It's early. Three o'clock in the morning,' said Sam.

'Sorry, I've mixed up the time zones. Aren't you in South America?'

'No, I'm in London. Can you hang on a minute, please?'

Jack's bottle had finished and he wailed again in fury. Sam put the receiver on the table and heaved herself out of the rocking chair. She slipped into the bedroom and placed the baby on the mattress beside her sister. Jack burped up milk, which trickled across to Hannah's mouth. She wrinkled her nose and screwed up her face in disgust.

'Yuck! What are you doing, Sam?' said Hannah. 'Bored with being an auntie?'

'It's an emergency. Someone's calling me about work. I'll be back for Jack in a tick.'

Before Hannah could protest, Sam hurried out to the sitting room and picked up the receiver.

'Hello? Carol? How can I help you?' she said.

'Can I speak to your husband, please?'

A job inquiry. She tried to damp down her annoyance at the presumption but failed.

'My husband? You've got the wrong number. I'm not married.'

'I'm looking for Sam Harris,' said Carol, doubt in her voice.

'You've found her.'

'Oh, I see. I'm not sure, I mean...'

'Oh, the baby? It's not mine. My sister is visiting me. It's her child.'

'The baby? No, it's not that. I'm sorry to have disturbed you.'

The woman hung up. Sam sank back into the rocking chair. So close and yet so far.

'Who was it?'

Hannah stood in the doorway with Jack on her shoulder burping on a terry nappy.

'A recruitment agent who wanted a man for a job.'

'But you are the best man for any job.'

'Thanks. I wish other people realised that.' She reached out to Jack, who grabbed her finger with his fat hand. His resemblance to Simon was so strong that her heart lurched. 'It's nineteen-ninety-three but even Jack's got more chance of work in exploration than I have.'

Hannah tutted in sympathy, but she didn't comment, being accustomed to Sam's travails in the industry.

4

'I'm going back to bed. Thanks for feeding him.'

Sam rocked in the chair for a while before returning to the sofa bed. She had sacrificed her bedroom for Hannah and the baby, Simon's baby. It was difficult to accept that Hannah had a child. A selfish being, the image of her as a mother clashed with Sam's lifetime of experience of her sister's self-centred ways. Even stranger was the concept of Simon as a father. She'd had a lucky escape, despite the circumstances.

She shook herself and dismissed the memories of Simon that threatened to make her nostalgic. He'd always been a bastard and now he was someone else's bastard. She slipped under the sheets. It was a pity about the work; she needed the money.

To Sam's surprise, Carol Downey rang again the next day.

'Hello? Is that Sam?'

Sam recognised the South African accent.

'Yes. Carol, isn't it?'

'Sorry about yesterday. I was expecting you to be a man, and I didn't have instructions from the client whether they had a preference for this role. I needed to check with them before I spoke to you and wasted your time.'

'That's okay. I'm used to it. I presume they're desperate if you've called me back?'

Carol laughed. 'In a nutshell,' she said. 'They need someone straight away. Are you available?'

'It depends on the job.' Sam bit her lip. She wasn't good at lying. She kept her voice neutral even while her heart rate had mounted. 'Where is the position based?'

'In Lumbono, near the border with Ruanda. My client needs a general manager for an exploration project.'

'Can you tell me who it is?'

'Consaf.'

'Consolidated African? Wow. Why haven't they filled the job internally?'

'They didn't say, but I got the impression they were looking for new blood.'

Fresh blood more like it. If no-one in the company wants the position, that's a red flag in any language.

'So how did you find me?'

'Alex Simmonds recommended you.'

'That was nice of him.'

'He said you were perfect for it.'

Sam made a mental note to thank her ex-boss.

'We worked together on a project that got cut short.'

'Shame. This is not a prime position, but it's a great opportunity to work for a major company and get that on your CV. Shall I tell them you are interested?'

Sam fought her inclination to self-deprecation and say 'if they'll have me'. *This is my chance to work for one of the big boys. I've got to toughen up and act as if I believe in myself. No-one knows how I feel inside except me.*

'That'll be great.'

'I'll let you know if they want to interview you. Can you fly to South Africa next week?'

꙳꙳꙳ ꙳꙳꙳

Consolidated African paid for a business class ticket on the overnight flight, but even that luxury didn't prevent Sam from feeling exhausted by the time she arrived in Johannesburg. She fell asleep in the car that picked her up, waking only when it stopped outside her hotel, an identikit member of a global chain with box hedges lining the turning circle outside the front entrance.

'They've asked me to pick you up at two o'clock, Miss Harris. Will that be okay?'

'Yes, thank you. What time is it now?' said Sam.

'Nine thirty.'

'Okay. See you then.'

She entered the lobby of the hotel and approached the reception.

'Good morning, madam.'

'Good morning. My name is Sam Harris. You should have a reservation for me in the name of Consolidated African Limited.'

'Ah yes. Consaf. Let's see. It's right here. Can I have your passport, please?'

Formalities over, Sam got into the elevator and pressed the button to the ninth floor. The label beside it read 'executive level'. Five-star accommodation. *Did every interviewee get the same treatment?*

The room was both palatial and claustrophobic with a wealth of uncomfortable looking furniture and lacy covers. The windows had safety catches on them so they could only be opened a crack. She dropped her luggage and walked into the bathroom where she turned on the water in the shower. Leaving her clothes piled on the floor, she slid into the shower and stood under the hot stream trying to release the tension in her back.

Afterwards she sat swathed in towels looking out over the suburbs. She tried to get her interview head on but something nagged at her. It had been such a rush to get ready to travel; she had not asked herself why Consaf were so keen to interview her. It was a large conglomerate made up of mining companies with thousands of staff members.

Why couldn't they find anyone suitable for the position from within their own ranks? What was wrong with the project? It couldn't have been a lack of funds or they wouldn't have flown her business class from London for an interview. That must have been expensive. And then there was this hotel suite.

Finding no answer, she set her alarm clock to wake her in time to change and have a cup of tea before going to the interview. Like a lot of British people, tea occupied an essential place in her armoury, a cure-all that merited first place in the queue when she packed for a trip. She got into bed and dozed off, the air conditioning acting like a lullaby with its even hum.

The alarm sounded too soon and she made tea which tasted of coffee in the coffee maker provided in the room. She used three of the little pots of milk to cool it down and take the edge off the coffee flavour.

As she sipped the reviving brew, she pondered what she already knew about the offer and worked out her tactics for the interview. The circumstances of her arrival suggested that she was the only person in line for the job. Somehow, she would cover up her insecurities and present a confident front. It would be a fitting test of the changes she had made to her attitude since her sister Hannah had announced that she was pregnant with Simon's baby.

Simon had been Sam's boyfriend all through university, and despite the ups and downs caused by his inability to stay faithful, she had stayed with him until she started to work abroad. While she was away in Sierramar searching for a missing friend, Simon had seduced her sister and finally killed the relationship. It seemed obvious to her Simon would break her sister's heart too and she waited with metaphorically outstretched arms to receive the prodigal sister. Instead, her sister had found a harmony with him that she had never achieved, and it culminated in the birth of a child.

This event induced an emotional crisis for Sam. She couldn't deal with all the feelings that assailed her, giving her the sensation of drowning in a sea of sorrow. On the advice of a friend, she went to talk to a therapist who was patient and kind, and gave her coping strategies. She also sent Sam to a life coach to bolster her confidence.

'You shouldn't allow people to walk all over you. You are well-educated, capable and able-bodied. While they force you to suck up a certain amount of abuse to keep your jobs, you need to be more resilient,' said the life coach.

'But how? How do I stop everyone treating me like shit?' said Sam, staring at her feet to prevent tears of self-pity from leaking out.

'It's your perception that is the problem,' said the coach. 'People believe in you. You've had good results in an industry that is ninety-nine per cent male. You are successful on your own terms. You need to stand up for yourself.'

'It's hard to get over the habits of a lifetime,' sniffed Sam.

'I recommend you pretend to be confident. Pretend and keep pretending. Soon, you won't have to pretend any more. Trust me. Trust yourself.'

It was time to play hardball. No more Mr Nice Girl.

Chapter 2

The Consaf building loomed over the road, putting most of the others in the shade. It had a smart marble façade that reflected the shabby tenements occupying the majority of the road. Broken windows and cracked wooden doors bore testament to the neglect common to this area of town. There was no obvious reason for plonking such an opulent building in the middle of such poverty. Perhaps they were trying to gentrify the area and return it to former glories.

Whatever the thinking, the Consaf edifice stood out like a sore thumb on the battered street, which had a high population of vagrants, perhaps because it was shady. They had done their own decorating in the overhang of the building across the street. Old newspapers were stacked up in alcoves with folded cardboard boxes and ancient blankets.

Sam jumped out of the taxi at the entrance to Consaf. One of the ragged men congregated in the shade stood up when he noticed her hesitating on the pavement and began to stagger over the road to her. The driver leaned out of the window and gesticulated at the entrance.

'Don't stand around outside. It's not safe,' he said.

Then he gunned the engine and shot off, leaving her standing in the swirling rubbish whipped up by the car. Awoken from her reverie by the approaching peril, she pushed the revolving door and shuffled into it, trying to assume the same speed as the panels. A security guard approached the door and put his foot against it to prevent it revolving, trapping her inside.

'ID please,' he said.

Overcoming her surprise at being trapped in such a way, Sam reached inside her bag and pulled out her passport. She waved it in the air, but his foot stayed planted on the ground.

'Open it at the photo page and put it up against the glass, ma'am,' he shouted.

Sam couldn't believe her ears.

'Are you kidding?' she said, throwing her hands out in supplication.

He folded his arms, his boot pressed up against the bottom of the door where she could see some pink chewing gum stuck between the tread.

Sam fumbled with her passport and opened it at the photograph page. She pressed it against the door, level with his face. He peered at it, his forehead wrinkling as he narrowed his eyes. Claustrophobia caused her to break out in a cold sweat, but she pretended to look out at the street where several vagrants had now gathered to leer at her. *Jesus. Imagine if he revolved her back out again.*

The guard nodded and ran his pen down his clipboard until he located her name. He ticked it with a deliberate action that made her feel like screaming. At last, he moved his foot away from the door with the speed of a crippled snail. It seemed to Sam that his reluctance was due to the thrill he was getting from keeping her trapped like a butterfly in a glass jar.

He leered at her as she emerged and put his hand on his crotch in a reflexive gesture that disgusted

11

her. Worse was to happen. He then offered it to her for shaking.

'Miss Harris, welcome to Consaf.'

No way would she shake that. Instead, she dropped her passport on the floor and grovelled at his feet, pretending to have difficulty picking it up. Thwarted, he withdrew his hand.

'They're waiting for you on the seventh floor,' he said. 'The lifts are at the back.'

'Brilliant. Thank you,' she said.

She hurried past him, avoiding the hand that stretched out to guide her back, and pressed the lift button with her elbow. The left-hand lift doors opened and received a grateful Sam into its leather-clad interior, which smelt of cigars and male cologne. She selected the seventh floor and leant back against the side of the lift as it shot upwards. Her hands dripped with sweat. She wiped them on a tissue and sprayed a dash of cologne on her palms.

Sam emerged out into a panelled passageway almost Victorian in its formality. A tall thin woman in a bright yellow dress was sitting in a chair opposite the lifts. She stood up and glided across to greet her.

'Sam? I'm Miriam, PA to the chairman, Morné Van Rooyen. They're waiting for you in the boardroom.'

'The boardroom?' Sam's heart rate shot up. She glanced back at the lift.

'Nervous?' said Miriam. 'Don't be. They need you more than you need them. That position has been vacant for six months.'

Sam took a deep breath and smiled.

'Thank you. I'm ready.'

The clinking of a spoon in one of the expensive porcelain coffee cups littering the table was the only sound to break the embarrassed silence. Sam waited, hoping for the answer she wanted. She examined the all-male board, resting her gaze for a moment on each face. The emerald-coloured silk shirt she was wearing accentuated her piercing green eyes.

Most of the board members avoided her scrutiny, looking down at their copy of her resume and fiddling with their pens, waiting for someone to break ranks.

'No-one will take the position. Our employees consider it to be a poisoned chalice, a job nobody wants,' said Dirk Goosen, the operations director.

Sam turned to face him, trying to keep her face neutral.

'And you imagined that I might fancy it?'

His face registered astonishment.

'Well, um, help me out, someone.'

A gurgle escaped from Sam's throat. She scanned the tense faces around the boardroom table. She'd never been in this position. In the past, employers had held her to ransom with the hope of a job. These people were gagging for her to accept it. This would be fun.

She pierced him with a stare, unflinching.

'What made you think that?' she said.

Dirk shrugged like a man who had met his match. An awkward silence reigned. Sam leaned forward in her chair and placed her arms on the table, interlacing her fingers. She observed that several of the board mirrored her actions while others sat back in their chairs with their arms folded. A split of fifty-fifty. She would have to be careful not to alienate anyone.

'Okay, I'll answer my question for you. From what I gather, not only have your employees refused the job, but you can't find anyone anywhere who is interested. Is that right so far?'

A few glum nods around the table.

'But Carol Downey found me lurking in London, and since I am unemployed, I jumped at the chance to fly here for an interview.' She paused for effect. 'You were so desperate to get me here, you paid for me to fly business class.'

A few nervous giggles. Sam relaxed. This was in the bag if she played her cards right, but just for once, she wanted success her way.

'It's simple. I need a job and you have one. Why don't you explain the problem and we can work from there? If I think I can fix the issue, I'll visit the project for a recce. How does that sound?'

Silence reigned. Had she gone too far with the confident act? If they only guessed how difficult she found it to blag her way into a job. But she was desperate, and this made her braver than usual.

Dirk looked to the Chairman for permission. Morné Van Rooyen nodded his head and ran his fingers over his red moustache.

'We have a project in the northeast corner of Lumbono, a mixed greenfields and brownfields exploration.'

'Isn't that in the Gatava triangle?' said Sam.

'It's about thirty kilometres northwest of there,' said Dirk.

'Next door then,' said Sam.

'As the crow flies,' said Dirk. 'Masaibu's a great project with fantastic geological potential, but it's our problem child.'

14

He looked around at the rest of the board, but no one made eye contact with him.

'In what way?' said Sam.

'Serious management issues have arisen and we've found it impossible to discover the source of the problem. We've pumped money in with no sign of improvement.'

'Who is running the project now?' asked Sam.

'That's the issue. No one will live on site at Masaibu. All former project managers have run it from here.'

He swallowed. Sam struggled to stop her eyebrows flying up.

'Did any of them speak French?' she said.

'I don't know. I don't think so. Why do you ask?'

'This doesn't sound like a project you can run remotely, or through a translator. My spoken French is good so I can communicate with people without an intermediary. I'd insist on living on site at Masaibu if you want me to run the exploration.'

'You haven't been there yet,' said Dirk, raising an eyebrow.

'When do I go?' said Sam.

Dirk laughed. Morné stood up and gestured at the door.

'We need to discuss this among ourselves, Sam. Do you mind leaving the room? Miriam will make you a nice cup of coffee.'

Chapter 3

After Sam left the room, there was a joint exhalation of breath as the men relaxed. Several of them lit cigarettes and sucked with gusto.

'Well, gentlemen. What do you think?' said Morné.

'I don't understand why you are even considering letting a woman run an exploration camp in Lumbono,' said Paul Hogan, one of the more senior members of the board, his plump pink cheeks wobbling with indignation. 'You can't send a woman there. It's dangerous.'

'No more dangerous than sending a man. Anyway, we have people out there already without experiencing problems,' said Dirk.

'Wouldn't have happened in my day. I won't agree to it,' said Hogan, shaking his head.

'Are you going instead then?' said Morné. 'Because nobody else is offering.'

Hogan harrumphed and folded his arms.

'She seems like a capable young woman,' said Dirk. 'She worked in Simbako with no issues, on a diamond project in an area which was gutted by the civil war. My old pal, Harrison Simmonds, ex CEO of Redstone, told me that her dedication and work ethic are extraordinary. She had no problems working with local people.'

'He probably slept with her.'

There was an audible gasp around the table as Devin Ryan spat the comment into the conversation.

'Steady on there, Devin. There's no call for that,' said the chairman, his hand flying to his moustache for comfort.

'I don't imagine he did,' said Dirk, unfazed by the venom in his colleague's comment. 'He is ex British army and as straight as they come. He's not the sort to consort with his employees. Anyway, why don't we deal with the facts? She has a first-rate resume with a master's degree in geology. She has previous African experience, and she speaks French, so she should find the source of the trouble without too much fuss. Doesn't she sound like the perfect person for this position?'

'She's not a person, she's a woman,' said Devin. 'That spells trouble in my book.'

'We all know your opinion of women,' said Dirk, 'but company policy's left you behind in that aspect. We're not allowed to discriminate against a candidate because of their sex. You'll have to move with the times.'

'What financial experience does she have?' said Devin. 'The budget for this project is ten million dollars. How do we know she can manage a budget of that size?'

There was silence for a minute.

'That's a good question, Devin. We don't. But she has all the other prerequisites and we've no other candidates,' said Morné.

'I can supervise her spending if the board agrees.' Dirk had stood up and was waving his hands around in his habitual manner.

'There'll have to be a cap,' said Morné. 'She can spend small amounts without having to ask permission for every damn thing.'

'What about five thousand dollars?' said Dirk.

'What about one thousand?' said Paul, looking to Devin for support.

'I'd agree to that,' said Devin, 'But I've never seen a woman do a job like this before. I can't imagine that she's capable.'

'She says she is,' said Dirk, 'and I agree. How will we ever know what women can do if we don't give them a chance? Anyway, isn't a failing project the perfect place for an experiment? If she can't recover it, there's no harm done, and she takes the blame, and if she succeeds, it's a win-win for us.'

'You have a point,' said Morné. 'Okay gentlemen, can we agree to try her? Say, a one-year rolling contract?'

'Six months,' said Devin.

'Hear, hear,' said Paul.

'Okay, six months.'

Morné's exasperation showed on his impassive face. 'A show of hands please.'

Sam perched on the edge of a chair in the reception, tapping her foot.

'How did it go in there?' said Miriam, who appeared carrying a tray of coffee which she offered to Sam.

'Oh, um, not bad,' said Sam, fiddling with her necklace.

She accepted a cup on autopilot and swigged a large gulp. It was strong enough to trot a mouse across the top and she had to prevent herself from spitting it back out. She longed for some milk but was too polite to ask.

'Compared to what? You're brave, going into the lions' den like that. They're a difficult proposition,' said Miriam, putting the tray on a small hall table.

'It's lucky I had no warning of what was planned or I might have wimped out.'

'You don't fool me. I know a backbone of steel when I see it. Did any of them question your suitability for the job as a female?'

'There were two directors with their arms folded who didn't engage, even with my best jokes. I was so nervous I don't remember being introduced. They seemed to think women belonged in the kitchen, barefoot and pregnant.'

'What did they look like?'

'One was plump with pink cheeks and a bald head, and the other was younger, with lots of hair and a sharp face.' *He had the face of a rodent, and the other man resembled a serving of blancmange, all pink and wobbly.*

'Devin Ryan is the sharp-faced man and Paul Hogan is the plumper one. Be careful. They can be dangerous apart, but if you unite them, I don't fancy your chances.'

Sam was about to ask for more details when the intercom buzzed. Miriam picked it up and listened. She replaced it and smiled.

'It looks like you were a hit with the boys. Dirk Goosen wants to see you in his office.'

Sam felt her chest tighten. She played for time.

'May I go to the bathroom first? I've had a lot of coffee,' she said.

Miriam laughed and pointed.

'It's across the hall over there. I'll wait for you and then take you to his den.'

The toilet was small, with two cubicles separated with plywood covered in graffiti scrawled in blue and black ballpoint on the thin paint. Sam read some of it while she sat on the toilet composing

19

herself for the next meeting. D. is a complete bastard. Watch out for D. and his wandering hands. She couldn't make out the lettering. *Could that be Devin Ryan? Would he be that unprofessional?*

A large cockroach lumbered across the floor, staggering left and right as if drunk. As she watched it, the massive insect keeled over beside her foot and remained on its back wiggling its feet in the air. She tried to poke it upright, but it was hopeless so she pushed it into a corner with her toe. What a dump. *Was the men's bathroom like this?*

Washing her hands in the cracked basin, she dried them on a scrap of toilet paper. She gave herself a quick once-over in the mirror. Her mousy hair, cut for the interview into a severe bob and destined to spend the next six months in a bun, sat on her shoulders like a curtain of shot silk. It framed her brown face with its sprinkle of freckles and her bright green eyes which gazed back at her without judgement. *Come on, Sam. You've got this.*

'Sorry, Miriam. I got distracted,' she said, coming out to find her sitting on a chair in the corridor.

'That's okay. It's nice to take the weight off. Did you do any reading in there?'

'Um, I noticed a few scribbles on the wall.'

'Graffiti never lies,' said Miriam, avoiding Sam's inquiring glance. 'Come on. Dirk's a busy man.'

Dirk sat behind a big mahogany desk littered with files and photo frames and dirty coffee cups. His head rested in his hands as he read a document with studied concentration, raising an eyebrow from time to time. His thick hair sat on top of his craggy features which were wrinkled by years of chain smoking.

When the two women came in, he sucked in his stomach which had expanded since he had given up cigarettes.

'Sam, sit down. Do you want a cup of coffee or something?' said Dirk.

'Just some water, please,' said Sam who was still high on caffeine from the last cup.

'Thanks, Miriam.'

Dirk waited until Miriam had shut the door before speaking.

'Tough audience?' he said.

Sam smiled. 'I'm here all week,' she said.

'You're quite a girl,' said Dirk. 'Are there any more like you at home?'

'I have a sister,' said Sam.

'I think one will be enough.'

The telephone rang and Dirk picked it up.

'Morné? Yes, just a minute.'

He gestured at Sam to stay where she was and took the receiver out of the room. She examined Dirk's sanctum. Large pieces of hardwood furniture gave it a masculine air, accentuated by the oil paintings of elephants and photographs of men standing in front of large pieces of machinery that lined the walls.

Good job he hadn't asked her more questions about her sister, Hannah, now living with Sam's ex-boyfriend, Simon. It was hard to remain neutral on the subject even though the initial pain had waned. The galling thing was how content they both were, something she had never managed to achieve with the cheating bastard. Maybe it was fate. Anyway, it was all over now, and they had baby Jack, the balm that had healed the open wound between the sisters.

Sam had consoled herself with the hope that her latest flame, Fergus, would choose to commit to her instead. His work also involved extensive travel to remote sites making it difficult to schedule any quality time together. But that was not the only reason they seldom got together, and reluctant to

21

force a decision from him, she bided her time and stayed single.

Dirk returned and dropped heavily into his chair. His jaw was clenched but the news was good.

'Sorry, about that. Where were we?' said Dirk. 'Oh yes, that was Morné Van Rooyen. The board are offering you a six-month rolling contract as general manager of the project. Does that suit you?'

How had Van Rooyen persuaded the board? He must have the passing vote. Their obvious resistance to her appointment made her uneasy but she would be insulated from their interference in Lumbono. They might even change their mind about women running projects if she did a good job. How often would she get a chance like this?

'That sounds perfect. When do I start?' she said.

'Can you start on the first of the month? That makes it easier for our accounting department. You need to give them your details,' said Dirk.

'Um, how much will Consaf pay me?' said Sam, blushing.

Dirk slapped his hand to his forehead. 'I forgot to ask. They'll know in accounts. If it's not satisfactory, come back and tell me.'

'Will I get any training?' said Sam.

'Not as such. I'll be supervising you, so you can call or email me any time you've a problem. The senior guys out there should be of help with any company protocols you don't find in the on-site documentation.'

Sam felt the buck being passed, but she'd just have to wing it. Anyway, the less bureaucracy the better as far as she was concerned. *How hard could it be?*

'What rotation will I be on?' she asked.

'Most of our managers on remote sites work ten weeks in and then take three weeks out.'

'Do we have travel days?' said Sam.

'We pay them out, you pay them in.'

Miriam reappeared as if by magic and beckoned her outside. Sam hesitated, but Dirk was already reading the document again and didn't see her wavering, or didn't want to. Anyway, it was a sign she would have free rein at the project. His attitude shouted hands-off management. She got the hint.

She followed Miriam out into her office, her head swimming with the speed of developments.

'Can you use email?' said Miriam.

'I haven't tried. Is it difficult?' said Sam, hoping it wasn't.

'No, it's simple. We use a company called CompuServe. I presume you can use a word processor?'

'Yes, I learnt to use WordStar in London,' said Sam.

'We use Lotus Notes but it's almost the same thing.'

'Can you show me?'

'Sure, come with me to the tech department and we'll get you set up before you go to HR.'

Paul Hogan and Devin Ryan met in the pub down the street from Consaf, a faux old-world mock-up that shouted dated from every corner. They made themselves comfortable in a walled booth, facing each other across a battered oak table. Both ordered large sirloin steaks which almost covered their plates in succulent meat. Hogan trowelled the food into his mouth, his head bent low and his serviette tucked into his shirt.

Ryan observed him without comment, his lip curled. He pushed back his own plate with its half-eaten contents. Hogan glanced up from his trough and eyed the plate with something approaching lust. Ryan signalled to the waiter to remove it and Hogan's face fell. Ryan, who had done it on purpose so as not to have to watch Hogan plough his way through another plate of food, gloated at the small victory. *Disgusting old man. How does his wife stand him?*

He waited for Hogan to clean the plate with a piece of bread, stuffing it into his mouth. The waiter removed his plate, revulsion on his face replaced by servile attention.

'Dessert anyone?'

'We're on a diet,' said Ryan, before Hogan, who had turned to the waiter like a begging dog, could answer. 'Can you bring us a pot of filter coffee?'

The waiter shrugged in faux empathy at Hogan and glided off into the shadows at the back of the restaurant.

'I'm not on a diet,' said Hogan.

'You should be,' said Ryan. 'What do you want, anyway? Couldn't we have talked in the office?'

'Not about this. You should know how dangerous it is. There are PC spies everywhere.'

'You're being paranoid.'

'I resent Morné forcing the vote. No good can come of it,' said Hogan.

'She doesn't stand a chance. I don't know what you're worried about,' Ryan retorted.

'Hormones.'

'Hormones? For God's sake, Paul. They're not poisonous. Anyway, no woman can survive out there. Look what happened to the last three managers.'

'I blame Dirk. I can't understand why Morné agreed to it.'

'They're as thick as thieves. Best not to reason why. Let's have a coffee.'

A phone rang in the office of Charlie Okito, country manager of Lumbono. 'Charlie? It's me.'

Urbane, handsome, deadly, Charlie Okito occupied the position of country manager in Lumbono and he reigned supreme in the Consaf office in the capital city, Goro. He had little time for sympathy as he was taking his new secretary to lunch in an hour, and she didn't know it yet, but she was the main course.

'To what do I owe the pleasure of this call?'

'We've got trouble.'

'Hang on a minute.'

He put the receiver down, lit a cigarette and put his feet up on the desk, taking a couple of puffs and exhaling before he picked it up again.

'Come, come. My dear chap, it can't be that bad.'

'They've chosen a new manager for the project at Masaibu.'

'Big deal. Will he be based in Johannesburg?'

'It's a woman. And she's insisting on living in camp.'

Charlie Okito choked on his cigarette.

'They're sending a woman?' he said, taking his feet off his desk. 'A woman? Are they mad or desperate?'

His sinister laugh echoed down the telephone line but it didn't side-track the speaker.

'Both. But she's no pushover, Charlie. She has bigger balls than any of the board.'

'Ha! That remains to be seen. She's just made my job much easier.'

'So, our plans won't be affected?'

25

'Of course not. If she resides at Masaibu, even better. She doesn't stand a chance. I'll deal with it.'

'Okay. I'll leave it with you. Bye then.'

He sounded doubtful. Charlie Okito replaced the receiver. It was not true that the idea of a woman running Masaibu hadn't fazed him. Women were dangerous. He shook his head and smoothed his tight curls onto his regal skull. He adjusted his tackle, shook out his trousers and smacked his lips. *Thinking of women, where was that secretary?*

Chapter 4

The four-seater aeroplane sat on the tarmac in the intense heat. Its wings shimmered in the sunlight and a man sprayed water at the fuselage with studied concentration. Sam waited in the shade of the wing of a large aircraft parked beside it, her cheap sunglasses fighting to dull the glare that bounced off the concrete.

The man turned to face her. He had a large head with a straggly beard, which balanced on a skeletal frame.

'Sam? I'm Mad Mark, your pilot.'

How to make your clients feel relaxed, lesson one, failed. He struck her as the kind of scary nutter she would avoid by crossing a road or exiting a bus. But there was no next bus. She painted on a smile.

'Hello. Nice to meet you.'

He approached her and stuck out a bony hand with nails chewed to the quick. Sam took it without enthusiasm.

'Let's go then. Time's a wasting,' he said, jerking his head towards the plane.

Sam dragged her massive suitcase nearer the hold. Mad Mark raised an eyebrow and shook his head.

'We can't take that,' he said. 'This plane has a weight limit.'

'There's just me and the suitcase,' said Sam. 'Isn't your plane a four-seater?'

'We have another passenger.'

'Someone from Consaf? They didn't tell me about that.'

Mad Mark frowned and peered at the ground.

'He's not from Consaf.'

'So, how come he's on the charter?' said Sam.

Mad Mark scratched his head and his eyes flicked from side to side.

'I've got to make a living,' he said. 'If I don't bring the odd local official back and forwards, they won't let me land in Lumbono.'

'I need to bring my suitcase,' said Sam, arms folded, jaw set. 'And how heavy is he? We should be all right with just the three of us and a suitcase?'

'He's bringing his niece.'

'His niece? Are you serious? I don't mind you bringing a local official if that makes life easier, but this is ridiculous. I insist you take my bag instead. If not, I'll call head office and ask them to choose.'

'Head office? You can't.'

'I don't want to interfere with your business, but I must bring my luggage. I'm not leaving it behind,' said Sam.

Mad Mark's shoulders slumped. 'Wait here,' he said. He marched off stamping on the tarmac with his large feet and disappeared into a nearby hangar, leaving Sam standing in the blazing sunshine with her suitcase.

Five minutes later, he emerged with a short dapper black man who was wearing a suit and carrying a briefcase. The man inspected Sam with the air of a connoisseur. Whatever he was looking for, she passed the test. He held out his hand.

'Victor Samba, enchanté,' he said. If his niece being left behind had annoyed him, he betrayed no emotion. Sam took his hand and squeezed it.

28

'Également. Je m'appelle Sam Harris,' she said.

'You speak French? Great,' he said, in guttural French. 'Let's go then.'

'I'm sorry about your niece,' said Sam. 'I can't survive without my luggage.'

'Don't worry,' said Victor. 'I have more nieces.' And he winked.

They took off from the main runway.

'How long is our flight?' said Sam.

'Two hours, all being well. There's a newspaper in the pocket in front of you if you want to read it,' said Mark.

She didn't but reached over and removed it out of politeness. The front-page shouted porn. Naked women posing with petrol pumps, vegetables, each other, adorned each article. A glance at the headlines gave her all the information she needed about their content. Sam almost dropped it in shock and folded it shut shoving it back into the seat pocket. Victor didn't appear to have noticed.

Had the pilot done it on purpose? She examined his thin arms on the controls and watched him to see if he glanced back at her. Mad Mark was oblivious, humming and nodding his big head like one of those novelty dogs her aunt Lottie kept on the dashboard of her ancient Morris Traveller. There wasn't a cloud in the sky and he didn't seem as erratic as his name. Perhaps these scandalous rags were the norm.

Sam relaxed and marvelled at the view. The flight path took them over a black lake with choppy waters buffeting the small boats littering the surface. Sam gazed out of the window at the scenery, but her mind soon wandered to Fergus, her favourite daydream. She'd had a fleeting but passionate relationship with him in Simbako, but he had bailed out just when things started to get real between them.

He had called her when she got back to London but only to put their relationship 'on hold'. It was unfinished business as far as she was concerned. Given his history, she had been expecting the outcome, but it didn't stop her feeling miserable. She remained convinced their relationship had legs, and she planned to try and get through his defences again one day.

'You're the new manager of Masaibu project?' said Victor, cutting through her daydream.

'Yes, that's right,' said Sam.

'Will you be staying long?' he said, giving her a frank stare.

Sam hesitated.

'It's just that the other managers only visited for short periods,' said Victor.

'Oh no,' she said. 'I plan to live on site.'

It was Victor's turn to appear confused. A shadow of concern blanketed his face.

'Are you sure that's a good idea?' he said.

'There's only one way to find out,' said Sam, her jaunty tone covering her own unease about his reaction.

'It's a brave decision. Consaf is not popular in the town for various reasons.'

'Aren't they the major employer in the district?' said Sam

'Yes, but there's resentment brewing, both from people who have jobs with the company and those who don't.'

'Do you live in town?'

'I'm the mayor,' said Victor

Bugger. I shouldn't have insisted on bringing my suitcase. She turned to face him.

'You should've told me earlier,' she said, blushing, and flashed an annoyed look at Mark, who flew on oblivious.

'I thought you knew,' said Victor.

'I do now,' she said. 'It's an honour to meet you, sir. Your advice will be key to my understanding of the Masaibu project's problems. I hope we'll have the chance to meet again to discuss them.'

'Masaibu is a problem,' said Victor.

'Oh, I'm sorry to hear that.'

Sam struggled to find something suitable to say. Victor laughed, creasing over in his seat, his stomach straining against the seatbelt.

'Masaibu is the Swahili word for problem.'

He patted her hand and smiled. *In empathy or sympathy? Problem project.* Her apprehension increased as they came in to land, bumping and skidding on the crude runway lined by long grass and manioc plants. She appeared to have found an ally, but only time would tell.

It took her over an hour to emerge from the tiny airport building. The mayor walked straight through, shaking hands with the officials and waving back at Sam. Disappointed he had not smoothed her passage through the aggressive customs and immigration procedures, she sulked in a chair. Her visa and work permit were scrutinised, photocopied, faxed and reviewed for ages while she sat in the sweltering waiting room.

Next, they subjected her to a surreal interrogation.

'You live in Hill Street, London? I've never heard of it, and my brother lives in Sheffield.'

Mad Mark was no help either. He had disappeared into town on an unexplained errand with a sack of goods he extracted from the bowels of the plane. He grunted as he heaved it onto his back. No wonder he didn't want to take her bag. The aircraft must have been overloaded.

Having cleared immigration, Sam tried to head for the exit, but three plump women in uniforms with the buttons straining against the tight material,

31

barred her way. They observed her like cats around a mouse, sneering as if she was something they had found stuck to the sole of their high heels. They opened her suitcase to inspect its contents. They removed her clothes one by one with disdainful expressions that suggested they had expected better. One woman poked at Sam's sponge bag with a long, manicured nail, painted a lurid red.

'What's in here?' she said.

'Toothpaste, shampoo, soap, moisturiser,' said Sam, pulling on the zip and handing it to her.

'Where is your makeup? We need to inspect the lipstick.'

'Um, I don't wear makeup,' said Sam, wishing she did.

'How is that possible? Are you not a woman?' said another of the women, looking at her breasts.

'I don't wear makeup at work,' said Sam. 'I work with lots of men. I try not to distract them.'

'Look,' said the other, holding up one of Sam's bras.

'Is it new?' said the first woman.

'I didn't bring any new clothes with me,' said Sam.

'Will you travel home often?' said the second woman.

'Every ten weeks for a break,' said Sam, desperate to get out of their grasp before they took her underwear as tax. 'I could bring lipstick for you next time if you like.'

The three women underwent a total change of attitude, their grumpy expressions replaced by beaming smiles. They nodded at each other and folded and replaced all the clothes they had removed from the bag, forcing the zip closed again.

'You may go now, but you will bring us lipstick next time. Six lipsticks.'

'What colours would you like?' said Sam.

'Any colours,' said the fattest agent, pointing to the door.

An ancient jeep with brand new company stickers was parked outside the arrivals building. A young man leaned against the bonnet smoking a hand-rolled cigarette. As she approached, he threw it down and stamped on it, standing formally beside the vehicle.

'You are Mama Sam?' he said.

'Yes, that's me,' she said. *Mama?* She let that ride.

'Shikamo Mama. I'm Ezekiel.'

He grabbed her suitcase and placed it into the back of the jeep. The doors rattled as he slammed them shut, grunting with exertion. Sam opened the front door of the jeep. Junk of various descriptions lay spread over the seat. Empty cigarette packets jostled with scrunched up pieces of paper bearing long, redundant lists of errands. Rotting banana peels filled the car with their pungent smell.

Ezekiel opened his door as she was about to wipe the seat clean for sitting on.

'Aren't you going to go in the back? All the managers sit in the back,' he said.

'I don't like sitting in the back seat,' said Sam. 'The front seat has more legroom and seatbelts.'

'But I'm a good driver. Are you worried about my driving?'

'I'm worried about everyone's driving.'

Ezekiel sniffed and cleared the rubbish from the seat into an old plastic bag which had holes in it. He dropped it on the ground where it split open, spilling its content on the grass.

'Please don't leave that there,' said Sam. 'We'll throw it in a rubbish bin in camp.'

Ezekiel sighed and collected the rubbish into a second less ancient bag, which he threw into the back seat. They got in and Ezekiel started the car. He activated the air conditioning and put up windows covered in the black film used by politicians. It was lifting at the edges and it tempted Sam to pull it off.

'Why do you have this on the windows?' she said.

'It's so that local people cannot tell who is in the car with me. Some managers are not popular.'

This alarming comment only reinforced Sam's misgivings about the project. *Had she bitten off more than she could chew?* Her bravado had evaporated since she had been home to pack her field gear and books, not helped by people's reactions on hearing about her new job.

'Isn't Lumbono lawless? There were reports on the news about illegal mining and local conflicts, women being raped.'

Her family were used to Sam's remote job locations and had their usual pragmatic reactions.

'Have you renewed all your jabs?' her father said.

'Don't forget tea bags,' her mother said.

'Don't stay out there too long, I need a babysitter,' said Hannah.

Sam found their lack of interest comforting. How bad could it be?

As they drove through town, down what seemed to be the main shopping street, Sam inspected the battered buildings, with their half-built second storey and tin roofs. Children with bare feet scampered between piles of vegetables and plastic utensils, splashing in puddles of pig and dog urine. Women wrapped in traditional wax print materials staggered by, burdened by whole branches of bananas or sacks of rice balanced on their heads, and babies strapped to their backs.

Groups of men sat in the doorways of the scruffy shops, smoking and playing cards. Some of them had bright yellow boots on, and others were wearing rain gear with the Masaibu Project logo.

'Do those men work for Consaf?' said Sam.

'No, they are shopkeepers,' said Ezekiel.

Why were they wearing company-issue clothing? There was plenty of time to find out more. A dark shape appeared in the windscreen and there was a loud thud as it hit the glass making a dirty mark. Sam threw her hands up in fright.

'What was that?' she said. Her heart thundered in her chest making her feel sick. What on earth possessed her to take this job? It would be a nightmare.

'Someone threw a manioc root at the car.'

'Should we stop?'

'No, Mama Sam, that would not be a good idea.'

As they approached the outskirts of the town, Ezekiel headed for a metal gate which had wooden booths on either side. One had a sticker of a man over the entrance door and the other of a woman. Smartly dressed security guards at the gate raised the barrier for the car to enter.

Ezekiel stopped the car and tapped his fingers on the steering wheel, avoiding Sam's inquiring glance. One of the guards knocked on the window and indicated the booth to her.

'What is the protocol?' said Sam.

'You must register any valuables when you arrive,' said Ezekiel.

'I have none,' said Sam.

'You must show them your suitcase.'

For the second time that afternoon, she tolerated the probing of her belongings by a woman who was putting things aside in a disconcerting manner. Sam filled out a form with the information about her CD player and digital camera, and she signed and dated the piece of paper the woman thrust at her.

The guard then zipped up Sam's suitcase without replacing the items she had put to one side. She indicated that Sam should go.

35

'I can't go yet,' said Sam. 'You've not put my things into my bag.'

'I'm keeping them,' said the woman, hands on hips. Confidence radiated from her smug face.

'No, you aren't. Do you know who I am?' said Sam. *I can't believe I said that.*

'No, and I don't care.'

'I'm the new manager of Masaibu.'

The woman appeared uncertain and made a grab for Sam's clothes. Sam put her hand on the pile, daring her to wrestle for them.

'You're a woman. It's not possible to be boss. The clothes are mine now,' said the guard.

'Would you prefer to keep your job?' said Sam.

The tiniest smidgen of doubt crept on to the woman's face and she grimaced. Ezekiel knocked on the door of the booth.

'Mama Sam, are you ready?'

The guard crumpled. 'Mama Sam?' She slumped on a chair and wept crocodile tears. Sam was unmoved. She unzipped her bag and put her clothes back inside. She pulled the suitcase through the door and gave it to Ezekiel.

'Let's go,' she said.

Behind her, the woman's keening rose louder.

'What did you say to her?' said Ezekiel.

'Nothing. She's having a bad day. Does this search happen to everyone?'

'Yes, Mama Sam. People get searched on their way out, but.'

'But what?'

'You need to speak to the security manager. I don't want to get into trouble.'

Chapter 5

The car pulled up in front of a large wooden office building at one end of a grass rectangle with a gravel road running around it. Sam examined the scene for clues of overspend. Shabby prefabricated bungalows with tar roofs occupied the left hand and bottom end of the rectangle. Two larger wooden structures sat on the right-hand side of it, one of which had a faded sign above the door reading Canteen. The other looked unused. Greying curtains hung in the windows which were opaque with dust. *Wherever the money was going, it wasn't on building maintenance.*

The office building had a semi-circular wooden patio in the front with chairs and tables in the shade of a lean-to. One table was occupied by two muscle-bound men in blue-grey uniforms with dark glasses. Neither of them moved when Sam got down from the jeep, but cold eyes assessed her as she mounted the steps to the patio.

Suddenly, both men stood up, rigid limbed. Arrogance, or something like it, emanated from the taller, bulkier man. He thrust out his hand.

'Hans Kerber, head of security,' he said in accented French. *Franco Austrian with a whiff of lederhosen.*

He had a bone-crushing handshake. Sam tried not to wince. His strange, small head balanced on a long neck, like a forceps delivery gone wrong. Every whisker had been scraped off his face, leaving it raw. He had the cold, grey eyes of a wolf in winter. *Dangerous.*

His sidekick shook Sam's hand with a forthright manner. He had a gentle, broken air, but a grip like concrete and ligaments standing out on whiplash forearms. He resembled Tintin with his blond quiff and small blue eyes twinkling at her.

'Jacques Armour at your service,' he said.

Sam smiled.

'Yes, I know, Armour, soldier, funny no?' he said.

'Which outfit?' said Sam

'We served in the French Foreign Legion together,' said Hans. 'We are brothers in arms.'

Jacques nodded and turned to her again, his manner open in contrast to Hans who crossed his arms.

'And you, Miss Harris? What's your background?'

'Please call me Sam. I'm a geologist. I manage exploration projects on remote sites. Consaf sent me to troubleshoot this project. I'll need you to brief me on the goings-on here.'

'Have you had experience of working in Africa?' said Jacques.

'Yes, I managed a project in Simbako, and several other short contracts here and there.'

Hans snorted.

'I've never worked with a woman before,' he said. 'I'm not sure how this will work.'

'Pretend I'm a man,' said Sam. 'That works for most people.'

Hans examined her with a practised eye.

'That will be difficult,' he said.

'I'm sure we'll manage,' said Jacques, and he kicked Hans under the table. Hans grinned, unfazed by his own frankness. *Cards on the table then. At least she didn't have to guess.*

'I'd like a cup of tea,' said Sam. 'How do I organise that?'

'We don't have tea, only coffee,' said Hans.

'Coffee will do until I rescue tea from my suitcase.'

'Let's go to the canteen,' said Jacques.

Mr Problem and Mr Solution. Good to know.

'Before we do,' said Hans, 'it might be an idea to orientate yourself. The prefabs on the left side of the square are senior accommodation where you will live. At the end is the clinic and sickbay, and on the right are the canteen and community buildings. It's simple to find your way around.'

Sam didn't comment. His manner suggested that he didn't expect her to leave the confines of the square. *What sort of managers had Masaibu had before? Did they never leave the office building?*

The coffee was disgusting, old, cheap, instant. *Surely, they could afford decent coffee? And why didn't they have tea?* In her experience, remote camps ran on coffee, tea and cigarettes. Despite the money being thrown at the place, the most basic requirements were missing.

'What makes you think you can fix this project? You're not the first to try,' said Hans. 'The rest returned home with their tails between their legs.'

Jacques coughed, but Hans ignored him.

'We don't have time to carry you. This district is vulnerable to gangs of brigands made up of ex-rebel forces. Security is a full-time job.'

Sam held her breath and counted to ten, refusing to be drawn. She fixed him with a glare.

'I'll get on with my job if you do yours,' she said. 'If I need your help, I'll ask for it.'

Hans smirked and sat on his chair; his legs splayed apart showing a tear in the crotch of his trousers. *He didn't know when to stop. It would be a battle.*

39

Just as Sam teetered on the brink of capitulating and admitting her exhaustion, a worker came running up and whispered in Hans' ear. He got up without formalities and headed across the square.

'Anything important?' said Sam.

'Just firefighting,' said Jacques. 'There's always another problem to solve around here.'

'Can you show me my room, please?'

'Of course, it's directly opposite.'

He held the door of the canteen open for her and she couldn't help noticing the blonde hairs on his brown arms as the sunlight fell on them. They walked across the grass to the prefab in the searing heat. It had recently been cut and green blades stuck to her shoes.

'You must be tired. What time did you get up?' said Jacques.

'Oh, I didn't sleep. I flew overnight from London to Uganda,' said Sam.

'You should ignore Hans. He spits out random poisonous phrases like a demented machine gun but he's not a bad man. If you ever need him, he'll put his life on the line to save you.'

'Are you in the habit of sweeping up after his tirades?'

'He doesn't have an off button. I try to send him signals, but he doesn't always respond.'

'Is he always like this?'

'He lost his beloved wife in a plane crash a few years ago. The vicious comments are his way of coping. He has never grieved her.'

Chastened, Sam followed Jacques into the prefab's sitting room. It had a hard-looking sofa and some dingy curtains and smelt of mildew. A kitchenette to the right of the entrance contained a rusty fridge and a stained sink. Jacques pushed open the door to the bedroom. A large double bed almost filled the room. Above it, a fan wheezed into life as Sam tried the switches. An old and useless mosquito net hung over the bed.

The place hadn't been tidied since the last occupant left. There were cigarette butts on the floor. At least the bed appeared to have clean sheets even if there was an odd lump in the middle. Jacques grunted and put his arm up to stop her entering.

'Wait,' he said, leaning forward and grasping the corner of the sheet which he whipped off the bed like a waiter with a tablecloth. There was a huge black snake on the bed. It seemed bewildered for a second, long enough for Jacques to take out a pistol and shoot it. It wormed around for a while and then lay still.

Sam's ears rang with the retort of the gunfire. Her jaw had dropped to her chest in fright. She wasn't sure whether to be shocked or grateful. Snakes did not frighten her, but having one in her bed was another matter. A pool of blood seeped into the sheet and onto the mattress.

'That was a mamba,' said Jacques. 'A nasty welcoming present.'

'Are you sure it was deliberate? Couldn't it have found its way in here on its own?'

She had no doubt about its purpose, but for her own peace of mind she had to pretend otherwise.

'I suppose it's possible.' But he shook his head. 'Your presence in camp will upset a lot of apple carts. Hans and I know about most of the goings-on, but our hands are tied as we are contractors and not part of management. We try to control the worst of it but we need someone to take charge. It's a big job.'

'But you can help me figure this out?' said Sam. 'The problems are labyrinthine. I can't do it alone.'

'Yes, but not today. Come to the office with me and I'll introduce you to the staff while someone cleans this mess.'

41

'Um, can you get them to clean more than the mess on the bed, please? I don't want to get off on the wrong foot with the cleaning staff, but this place is filthy. They even left a snake lying around.'

Jacques laughed.

'I'll tell them.'

Hans burst into the prefab, sweating, his gun in his hand.

'I heard a gunshot. What the hell is going on?'

'Oh, I had an unwelcome visitor, but he's dealt with,' said Sam, gesticulating at the snake.

'I thought you meant Jacques,' he said. 'Is this how you deal with all unwelcome visitors in your bed? Fuck. I'll keep it in mind.'

And he beamed at her. A lovely smile that almost erased Sam's misgivings about him.

'Can you take Sam to the office, please? I'll stay here and make sure the cleaning ladies do a thorough job. The place is disgusting,' said Jacques.

'It's okay, I'll do it and make sure none of her stuff disappears. You take her,' said Hans.

'Okay, let's go,' said Jacques.

'Is it possible to find me a comfy chair, please?' said Sam. 'I do a lot of reading.'

Hans reacted as if she had asked for a unicorn.

'That's not in my job description but I'll see what I can arrange,' he said and rolled his eyes to Jacques. Sam pretended not to notice.

After a quick trip to the bathroom, she made her way to the office. Someone had jammed the front door open with a piece of cardboard to encourage airflow through the building which was elongated down a passage leading from the entrance. The offices on either side of the front door were both occupied.

The office on the right hand of the entrance had a nameplate that read Security. It was open and Sam could see Jacques at his desk talking to one of the

42

security guards. When he saw her, he mouthed 'one minute' and winked.

Sam examined the door on the other side of the passageway. It was closed but she could hear noise from inside. Someone had stuck a piece of paper over the original nameplate. It read HR Manager, Philippe Mutombo in scrawled script. Sam slipped her finger under the paper and lifted it up to reveal the original inscription - General Manager.

She jumped as Jacques emerged from his office and reached past her to knock on the door.

'Entre.'

They entered the office to find a young black man sitting behind a huge desk, heavy-framed glasses perched on his nose, his slight frame dwarfed by the massive mahogany structure. He scrutinised her from behind his computer, his face a picture of irritation. Sam glanced around the room, admiring the windows on two walls giving her a view of the square and all the goings-on. This was perfect for her purposes and would be her office, but she was loath to say anything yet.

'Yes?' A tone that implied he was being interrupted and didn't like it.

'Hi, Philippe. I'd like to introduce you to Sam Harris, the new General Manager.'

'Nice to meet you,' said Sam, keeping her distance from the undisguised resentment seeping out of this individual seething behind HER desk.

'I don't have time for introductions today. Can't you see I'm busy?' said Philippe.

Wow, that attitude has to go, but I need to check something first.

'We can do this later,' she said. 'I didn't mean to disturb you.'

A look of triumph flashed over Philippe's sharp features. He rooted around in his desk drawer and fished out a booklet which he handed to Sam.

43

'What's this for?' she said.

'It's a visitor's booklet. You might need it.'

He smirked. Sam stiffened and Jacques pulled her arm.

'Let's go, Sam. We can come back.'

Sam followed him out into the corridor. She gritted her teeth and stuffed the booklet into her shoulder bag.

'There's good stuff in there,' said Jacques. 'Give it a read. You won't regret it.'

'Who does he think he is?' said Sam. 'Jumped up little shit.'

'He's teacher's pet. Protected by Charlie Okito, the general manager of Lumbono.'

'Where does Okito hang out?'

'In the Goro office. He's a powerful individual, not to be crossed if you want to succeed here in Masaibu.'

'I think he was on speakerphone during my interview in head office. He didn't encourage the board to approve my appointment. I'll be careful. Can we see the office I'll be using?' said Sam.

Jacques took her up the corridor to another room that had an identical piece of paper stuck over its nameplate. Someone had written General Manager on it in blue ink. The legend HR Manager was hidden underneath it. Sam pulled the piece of paper off the door and crumpled it up.

'We won't need this,' she said, pushing it open. There was nothing wrong with the room, besides being a little gloomier than the other. It was the same size, but the desk was not as glamorous. That gave her an idea.

'I forgot to tell Philippe something,' she said. 'Can we go back and see him?'

Jacques shrugged. Sam was steaming, but she affected nonchalance. *I have to do something or Philippe will walk all over me. He must think he has*

44

*the support to act like that with senior management.
That act of pique has just lost him his corner office.
He'll soon see who's in charge.*

They headed back up the corridor passing the offices of the Maintenance and Union Managers. Sam knocked on Philippe's door and entered without waiting. Jacques followed her with a bemused expression.

'Philippe, I know you're busy, so I won't keep you. I had a look at the other office but it's not the right one for me. It must be distracting for you trying to work in this office, what with all the windows. I need to see what's going on outside so I'd like you to swap back to the HR office. Now.'

Philippe's eyes opened so wide that his eyeballs almost fell out and bounced across the desk. His mouth moved, but no sound came out.

'We must get you moved straight away. Can you organise it, please?' she said before he recovered. She had put down a marker. *The look on Philippe's face was worth any consequence. No time like the present to leave a large boot print.*

'You can keep the desk,' she said, and walked out, resisting the urge to laugh as she left. They headed outside where Jacques offered her a cigarette which she refused.

'That was impressive,' he said. 'I thought you were going to cave in but you were just warming up. You'd have done well in the Legion.'

'I doubt it. I've been meek all my life, accepting what I got, being polite, waiting my turn, but I had an epiphany. The meek don't inherit the earth; they get shafted. This project will be my proving ground.'

'You? Meek? Hard to believe, but if it's true, that was an excellent start.'

'She said what?' Hans doubled up with laughter. Tears ran down his cheeks. 'I can't believe it. What did Philippe do?'

'His mouth opened but nothing came out,' said Jacques.

'I bet he was straight on the telephone to his minder,' said Hans.

'Doubtless. We need to be on our guard against repercussions.'

'I can't believe the snake didn't faze her. Most people would have got back into the jeep to the airport. It seems as if she's here to stay.'

'She's a woman on a mission, but how much can we tell her?' said Jacques.

The smile disappeared from Hans's face. He blew out his cheeks.

'We're between a rock and a hard place here. Our boss wouldn't take kindly to us upsetting the apple cart. Consaf are a big client.'

'Let's play it by ear. We can tell her on a need to know basis.'

'Okay, but don't get too soft. The way you gawked at her was not business-like,' said Hans.

'That was admiration. How many women do you know who'd take on this job?'

'None. She's no pushover.'

'Anyway, you can't talk,' said Jacques, poking him in the shoulder.

'I don't know what you mean,' said Hans.

'Where's your reclining chair gone?'

The smell of mildew had lifted from Sam's cabin. Someone had replaced the uncomfortable armchair with a tatty leather recliner. *Where had they come up with that?* She couldn't resist sitting in it for a moment breathing in its masculine odour with covert enjoyment. *This place was no picnic but Hans and Jacques would protect her if she kept them on her side. Philippe would look for revenge. She'd have to keep an eye on him.*

She transferred her tea bags and chocolate supplies from her suitcase into the kitchen. The fridge contained a lone carton of UHT milk. She put the chocolate at the back, wrapped in a plastic bag to prevent easy identification. In her experience, cleaners liked chocolate.

There was a ten-gallon plastic drum of water with a tap at the bottom on the now clean countertop. She ferreted around in the cupboards and produced a saucepan and a mug. She lit one of the gas rings and put water on to boil.

While the water was heating, Sam whipped the sheet off her bed again, but this time it was empty. Gingerly, she checked the mattress for bumps but they had changed it. The foam bounced back under her hand. A new mattress. At least that meant no bedbugs. She didn't mind reptiles, as she'd already slept with a few, but there was real intent behind her unpleasant visitor. *Who was behind it? Someone who didn't want her on site.*

It was disturbing, but it had also piqued her interest. Sam loved a riddle. A frisson of excitement rose up her back. The water was boiling, and she went back into the kitchen to make tea.

'Boss, it's me,'

'Philippe? What's new at Masaibu? Have you any good news for me?' said Charlie Okito.

'Ms Harris arrived today.'

'I know she arrived, but has she left yet?' said Okito

'No, sir, she's still here.'

'Did she like the present?'

'One of the security guys shot it.'

'Is she leaving tomorrow?'

'I don't think so. She asked me to move out of my office so she can have it.' Philippe's voice quavered with self-pity.

'You wimp! I suppose you agreed?'

'She's the general manager. What was I supposed to do?'

'Jesus, it's bad enough that you are pussy whipped at home, without capitulating to this new woman,' said Okito.

'She's no pushover, boss,' said Philippe, but it was not possible to guess to whom he was referring.

'Never mind, just make things as difficult as possible for her. She'll never cope with it all,' said Okito

'Okay boss. I'll get on it.'

'And report back as often as you can. Keep her in the dark, or we must use stronger measures.'

Charlie Okito replaced the receiver. This wasn't going to be as easy as he had imagined. *En garde, Miss Harris*.

Chapter 6

L oud voices woke Sam from her slumbers. She had been too tired to retrieve her mosquito net from her bag and had used the old one as a stopgap. It was worse than useless. She had wound herself in her sheet to keep out the mosquitos that invaded through the holes in the material, and she struggled to get free.

Swinging her legs over the edge of the bed, she shook out her shoes before putting them on to shuffle to the bathroom, a habit borne of experience. All sorts of insects and reptiles liked to snuggle in the toe of a sweaty shoe or boot, and some of them had ways of retaliating if you squashed them.

The mirror was so small she could only see one part of her head at a time. She tied her hair back in a bun and gave her face a quick once-over. Creased from sleep, it was nevertheless glowing after her shower. She smiled at her reflection. The challenge of the new job had animated her features making her look younger.

It was frustrating having a tiny mirror, but it wasn't as if she had anyone to impress, not yet anyway. She put on her khaki trousers and shirt and tied her work boots with new laces. Then she pulled a curtain to one side and peeped out onto the square. Hans was drilling the local security men with something approaching fanaticism. They carried a truncheon-like stick each but no weapon. *Perhaps they didn't drill with them.*

Breakfast was basic in the extreme. The cooks hadn't pushed the boat out for the new manager. Two cold, greasy fried eggs sat on a bed of lukewarm rice in front of her. The ketchup resembled toxic waste such was its bright red colour. Sam didn't risk it. At least she had commandeered a small metal teapot full of boiling water into which she had dropped her tea bag.

Sam could not function without tea. She guarded her supplies and always hid the majority in her room locked in her suitcase. It was odd that no-one had ever noticed how much she relied on a brew. The easiest way to destroy her would have been to take her tea bags hostage and threaten to destroy them. *They were all so obsessed with their attachment to coffee; it had never occurred to them you could feel the same way about tea.*

Hans came in and sat at her table with a huge plate of evil looking sausages and some fried bread. He sniffed his coffee with an air of suspicion.

'Sometimes I think they use ersatz coffee in this place. Haven't we got money for proper stuff?' he said.

'I imagine so. The budget is huge and we spend it all. I can check if you want me to.'

Hans grunted. He took a large swig of the coffee.

'Did you sleep okay?' he said.

'I did, thank you. I never have problems sleeping. Oh, thank you for the chair. You saved my life.'

Hans sniffed. 'Jacques did also, with the mamba, so we are even, no?'

The strong competition between the two men fascinated Sam, but she changed the subject.

'Um, this morning you were training the security guards. I wondered where their guns are?'

'The government do not allow us guns on the project, only sticks.'

'But you and Jacques have guns.'

'We work for a private security agency so we have permits.'

'But what happens if someone attacks us? I understood there was still rebel activity in the area.'

'The local police are supposed to protect us as we pay their salaries, but I wouldn't hold your breath. We have emergency evacuation plans in place in case of an attack. I'll tell you about them later in a formal briefing.'

'Is there any informal management get together in the mornings?'

Hans raised an eyebrow. 'No. Everyone gets on with their job after breakfast,' he said.

'I'd like to meet them all today. Could you round everyone up for nine o'clock, please? I know it's not your job but if you help me today, I should be able to cope from then on.'

'No problem.'

The putrid smell of the sausages drove Sam from the table. She gulped down the dregs of her tea and stood up.

'Bon appétit. See you at nine,' she said.

After she had brushed her teeth, Sam walked to the office building, where there was a hive of activity. They were swapping the contents of the offices as she had requested. Loath to interfere or give Philippe an excuse for backtracking, she left to investigate life outside the main square. She noticed an obese young man wobbling down the path towards the office from the far end of it. He tried to avoid her inquiring glance, but she reached out in greeting.

'Bonjour, I'm Sam Harris. Who are you?'

'I'm Bruno Kabila.' He stared at his feet with determination.

'Which department are you from?'

'I'm the deputy head of Maintenance.' For a moment he seemed to inflate, but his shoulders slumped as quickly as they had risen.

'Can you help me, please? I'm the new General Manager here and I'd like a tour of the site.'

His gaze rose to her face as if examining it for subterfuge. Finding none, he smiled, a shy smile that crept across his features like a dog expecting a kick.

'Yes, Mama Sam, I'd be honoured.'

Sam examined him. *Did the puppy fat represent a protective shield, or just an inability to avoid the biscuit tin?*

'Lead on.'

Bruno headed back down the road and passed through the gap in the left-hand corner between the prefab accommodation and the Clinic. There was a large open area behind the square screened off by a fence. It fell away and broadened into a plateau covered with basic buildings built from breeze blocks with sloping corrugated roofs.

'The maintenance office and buildings are on the left. The geology office, core shed and prep-lab are on the right,' said Bruno, pointing them out. 'That building at the end is the logistics office and stock room for spares. The heavy machinery park is beyond the maintenance office, and there are some extra storerooms for tyres and caterpillar tracks.'

Workers scurried back and forth between the buildings. Some of them wore company-issue overalls and boots, others did not.

'Why doesn't everyone have a uniform on?' said Sam. 'Is there a shortage?'

Bruno froze and fiddled with the zip on his overalls.

'They sell them,' he said, avoiding her eyes.

'Sell them? To whom?' But then she remembered all the men in Masaibu sitting outside the shops.

'The company issues them to all workers, including the ones on a short contract. Those guys sell them in town to make more money.'

'How long are the contracts?' said Sam.

'Three months. It's something to do with the labour laws.'

Bruno's expression turned to alarm as Sam scribbled a note in her workbook.

'Please don't tell anyone I told you,' he said.

'Okay, I promise, as long as you tell me everything you know.'

Trapped like a rabbit in the headlights, Bruno nodded.

'Let's get on with the tour,' said Sam.

The maintenance building ran the length of the works area. They had divided it into sectors for washing, maintenance and repair of vehicles. The office was halfway down the building, its grubby windows obscured by a covering of grease and dirt. A man sat on the steps smoking a cigarette with the air of an addict. When he noticed Bruno, he clenched his jaw in fury.

'You stupid fat bastard! What are you doing here? I told you to take the worksheets to Philippe.'

Bruno cowered behind Sam, his blubber wobbling in fright.

'It's not his fault. I asked him to help me,' she said.

'And who the fuck are you?' said the man.

'I'm Sam Harris, the new General Manager.'

The man dropped his attitude with his cigarette and scrambled to his feet, wiping his hand on his filthy overalls.

'Jesus, I'm sorry. Not a great start, eh? I'm Frik Els, the maintenance manager. Welcome to Masaibu.'

'Thanks, Frik. Let's start again, shall we? I was hoping to get a feel for the place and Bruno walked by, so I collared him.'

'No, that's okay. Sorry lad,' said Frik, patting Bruno on the shoulder. But then he muttered to Sam under his breath. 'Don't let him fool you. These blacks are good lads but they're all the same: bone idle.'

He said black with a strong accent so it came out as 'bliks'. Sam didn't comment. Bruno gave no sign he had heard. He shrugged and grunted. Sam was not ready to investigate this relationship yet, but she noted the antagonism, the sorry state of the garages and the sullen air of the mechanics, who were all black. *A toxic mix of racism and resentment.*

This was prime territory, but Sam had learned a few things over the course of her career. *Never try to solve a problem if you don't know the root cause. Why was everyone so resentful that blame had turned to racism?*

'What's your biggest problem?' she said to Frik. 'If I had a magic wand, where would you like me to wave it?'

Frik inspected her as if to gauge whether she was joking. Her calm expression seemed to reassure him. He beckoned her to follow and set off to the far end of the building. Bruno shuffled behind them. Not close enough to converse, but in hearing range.

They rounded the corner into a yard with a concrete floor.

'Voilà,' said Frik.

Chapter 7

The rectangular meeting table was full. Several people who could not fit around it sat on chairs lined up against the wall. The air was thick with cigarette smoke and rebellious mutters. Sam made them wait for a full five minutes before entering.

Philippe sat in the chair at the head of the table intended for Sam. He had left a chair at the other end for her, squashed beside another holding a man she did not recognise.

She didn't sit down. She walked past the people seated beside the wall and parked herself behind Philippe.

'Good morning, everyone. For those who haven't met me yet, I am Sam Harris, the new General Manager. Philippe, can you do the introductions, please, clockwise from where I'm standing? When you've finished, can you move to the other chair? I'd like to sit here so I can see everyone.'

A frisson went around the group. Philippe had the grace to look embarrassed. He vacated the seat and introduced the other managers.

'On your left is Frik Els, maintenance manager. His deputy, Bruno Kabila, is behind him. Then there's Hans Kerber, the security manager, and Jacques Armour, his second in command. Beside him is Ngoma Itoua, the union manager, Alain

Folle, the geology manager, Dr Frederick Ntuli, the health and safety manager, and Moussa Dueme, the supplies manager. Joe Haba, the community relations manager is absent.'

'Probably having relations in the community,' said Hans, sniggering.

Several people snorted. Sam walked around the table shaking hands and sat at the top.

'I'm sorry to drag you away from your work. From now on, we'll hold the meeting at seven thirty on Mondays, Wednesdays and Fridays. That should give you time to issue instructions and do your toolbox talks before the meeting.'

Dr Ntuli's hand shot up.

'Yes?' said Sam.

'What is a toolbox?' he said.

This is awkward. The health and safety manager doesn't know what a toolbox talk is.

'You probably call it something else,' she said smiling. 'The morning safety briefing.'

Dr Ntuli didn't reply. He sank back in his chair. From people's expressions, there was a general lack of comprehension surrounding this concept. *It's worse than I imagined. I need a strategy.*

'The purpose of this meeting is to update other departments about the projects being carried out and for requesting technical help from them. Any detailed discussions will take place with me after the meeting. Understood?'

Heads nodded.

'Okay then. Five minutes each only, please. Frik, will you go first?'

'Hi, Dirk,'

'Sam. Good to hear from you. I presume you are calling from Masaibu?'

'Yes, I got here okay. Everything is as expected, well not exactly...'

'Let's hear it.'

'I took a walk around the works yard this morning with Frik Els, the maintenance manager.'

'I know Frik. Old school.'

If you mean a racist misogynist.

'Yes, that's him. Well, he took me to the machinery park. It's not good news, I'm afraid.'

'How so?'

'All of the heavy machinery is out of order except for one small bulldozer and they're only keeping that going by cannibalizing the other one. Both excavators need a new set of tracks and the grader needs new tyres.'

There was a long silence, and Sam was about to redial, presuming the line had dropped.

'Dirk? Are you still there?' she said.

'I see.' She could hear him lighting a cigarette.

'Frik says he ordered the spares for the machinery six months ago, but no one has replied or queried the list.'

Another long pause broken by the sound of a chair scraping the floor.

'Those spares are expensive. I'm not sure if head office authorised them. The project was sponging up money, and the board stopped all purchases,' said Dirk

'I can understand that, but I'm here now and I'll make sure the spares don't go missing. Can you please expedite the order?' said Sam.

'Okay, but I'll need you to send it again. I'm not sure where it ended up.'

'I'll fax it to you today. Is this item in the budget?'

'No, I'll get permission for the expense and we'll top up later. Send in the order.'

'Okay, I'll fax it to you later.'

Sam put the phone down and switched on her word processor. She waited for ten minutes while the computer attempted to connect to the internet. *That bloody dialling tone would drive her scatty.* Then she composed an email to Dirk detailing their conversation and sent it to him.

She made a paper copy to keep in a file in case the computer got damaged. Not being an expert, she was suspicious of floppy discs. She had also taken a photograph of the machinery up on blocks, intending to keep a visual log of progress.

After emailing Dirk, Sam dropped by to see Philippe in his new office. The sullen expression on his face told her all she needed to know about his reaction to having his office usurped. She was not anticipating his co-operation, but she had to establish a line of communication if she was to send red herrings to whoever was masterminding the losses.

A winning smile on her face, she sat in a chair facing him. He did not return it.

'I hope your office is better suited to your needs. It was good of you to be so efficient in moving here. I see you kept the desk.'

Philippe sounded like he was swallowing a plum. He sniffed.

'Yes.'

'I need your help with something. Can you spare me half an hour?'

The look he gave her suggested he would rather eat slugs.

'I suppose so.'

'You're the expert around here, and I will need to tell you all my secrets if we are to succeed with Masaibu.'

As if.

58

Philippe perked up. He smoothed his hands over his bald head and sat forward in his chair with his chest puffed out. His lips peeled away from his teeth, which were a startling yellow colour.

'I'm listening,' he said.

Vanity, thy name is man. Hooked.

'I need you to explain the composition of the workforce. Can we start with the contract workers from the local town?'

'We use two hundred men as labourers for unskilled work like grass cutting, digging ditches and platforms for drilling, and carrying goods from one place to another.'

'Why are they on short contracts? Don't we need unskilled labour all the time?'

'We signed an agreement with the mayor to share the labouring jobs among the local populations. We rotate new people into the job every three months.'

'That's great. Whose idea was that?'

'Mine.' A smug expression sat on his face like that of a toad with a bluebottle in its mouth.

Sam smiled. 'Some workers don't have overalls or safety boots. Do we have a problem with supplies?'

Philippe's eyes widened and he shifted in his chair.

'Everyone gets an overall and boots when they start here. Perhaps they have lost them.'

'They must have lost them in town then, because half of the male population are wearing them.'

'Perhaps.' Philippe fiddled with the buttons on his shirt.

'Isn't it compulsory to wear high-visibility uniforms and safety boots on site?'

'You would have to check with Dr Ntuli.'

'Oh, I don't need to. It's in the list of regulations in the visitor booklet you gave me yesterday.'

Take that! She raised her eyebrows in inquiry. Philippe shrugged but his eyes were blazing with fury.

'But what can we do? People lose things,' he said.

Unless they lost a container full of uniforms on the way to Masaibu town, she doubted the veracity of his excuse but she let it slip. There was an easy place to get this information.

'How often do we pay the local workers?' she said.

'We pay them in cash on Saturday afternoons before they go home.'

'Who pays them?'

'I do.'

He shifted in his seat again and wiped his hands on his legs.

Sam knitted her eyebrows together in fake confusion.

'Um, so what happens to the overalls and boots at the weekend?'

'They wear them home.'

Sam pretended to write something in her A5 spiral notebook. She did not require rocket science to figure out this money-making scheme. *Did Philippe take a cut from the sales of the gear or from the salaries? Or both?* There wasn't much she could do about paying the wages in cash as it was unlikely any of the labourers had bank accounts. But she could put a spanner in the works.

'Two hundred men. How much is that in cash?'

'About ten thousand dollars,' said Philippe, who was scratching at his face.

'Do you use security?'

'I don't understand.'

'Security for the cash.'

'I don't need—'

'Let me get this straight. You have ten thousand dollars in your office every Saturday morning.

Isn't that asking for trouble? Aren't there rebels operating in this area?'

'We've done it this way for years without any problems.'

'Hans tells me rebel activity has increased in the last few months. It can't be a secret that we have that much cash on site.'

'Yes, but—' Philippe's face registered panic.

'We can't allow that to continue. I'd hate anything to happen to you. It is my responsibility to keep you safe,' said Sam.

'It's not necessary.'

'Oh, but I insist. I'll talk to Hans about providing cover.'

Without waiting for a reply, she frowned once more at her fake notes, gathered them up and left. She was giggling with glee inside. *Gotcha.*

The sun blazed down on the dusty trees and bone-dry ground of the hilltop where the camp was situated. Several scrawny chickens pecked at the surface, their beaks bouncing off the hard earth. A skeletal cat stalked them without enthusiasm, her belly so stretched by repeated litters of kittens it almost touched the soil.

Sam headed straight to the logistics office. She had a fair idea of who was cooking the books on the supply side. There was only one person with access to the uniform orders and distribution.

Moussa Dueme, the logistics manager, was picking his nose with practised enthusiasm and inspecting the results on the end of his finger as Sam put her head around the door. He jumped, wiping his digit on his trousers and putting his hand to his chest as if staving off an attack of palpitations.

'Mama Sam. Welcome,' he said, breaking out into a spontaneous sweat.

Perhaps Philippe wasn't the only one making hay in Masaibu. This man appeared to be having a heart attack. Must be small fry, or he would be better at dissimulating.

Sam had learned over the years that thinking too well of people often allowed them to be better than they otherwise would be.

'I hope you're not too busy, Mr Dueme.' *Picking your nose.*

'Please call me Moussa. No, I always have time for you.'

'Excellent, because I need your help. I want to set up a uniform collection scheme.'

Moussa frowned and screwed up his face.

'A what? I'm sorry, I don't know what you mean.'

'I understand the casual labourers take their uniforms and boots home every weekend?' said Sam.

'Yes.'

'Are the overalls or the boots numbered?'

'No. Why would we do that?'

'We need a system for tracking them so they don't end up for sale in town. I'd like you to collect the uniforms on Saturdays, store the boots and send the overalls to the laundry. If you number the items, you can record them under the name of the worker who signs them out, and use the same number to ensure they return the items at the weekend.'

'I suppose so.' A look of dread had crept across Moussa's features.

'You can give them two tokens, a red one for the boots, and a blue one for the overalls with that number on them to take to HR.'

'What if they don't present the tokens to HR?'

'Anyone who doesn't have a token will have to pay for a new overall or set of boots from their pay. Or both.'

'What if they steal someone else's tokens?'

'You will provide HR with a copy of the stock sheets so that no one can present a token which doesn't correspond to the items you issued to him.'

'They won't like it.'

'They won't have a choice. Please don't issue any more company clothing or footwear without first numbering them and registering them under the name of the person who receives it. You'll need to explain about the tokens and inform them of the amount that will be debited.'

Sam waited. Moussa Dueme swallowed, his Adam's apple bobbing up and down in agitation.

'But what if they damage the clothes at work?' he said.

'They can swap them with you here at the stores and you can put the same number in the new article.'

Moussa was not beaten.

'I don't have enough storage here.'

'I'll talk to the carpenters. Do we have suitable timber for the shelving?' said Sam.

Moussa brightened up.

'No, but if you sign a purchase order, I will buy some.'

'Why don't we go together? You can show me the town.'

Gloom descended once more.

'Yes, Mama Sam.'

Hans' eyes widened and he supported his chin on his hands. He inspected Sam as if he had never seen her before.

'So, can you do it?' said Sam.

'Provide security in Philippe's office on a Saturday? You're the general manager, you only have to ask me.'

'I'm asking,' said Sam, sticking her chin out.

'You're poking a bear with a short stick.'

'I'm doing it on purpose. And I intend to keep going.'

'Do you want my advice?' said Hans.

'Shoot.'

'Do things one at a time. Build the shelves, buy the tokens, set up the stock room in time for the next intake of workers. Don't make your next move until this beds in.'

Sam was about to argue, but she could see the sense in what Hans had said.

'Anyway, aren't you on a contract? Why not get paid for a little longer?' said Hans, winking, and Sam smirked back. *Touché.*

Chapter 8

The first weeks at Masaibu went by in a blur as Sam got to grips with the writhing anaconda that was the exploration project. Every time she pinned down one problem, another emerged, sliding out of her grip and trying to escape.

Most of the managers had come onside with her plans, or were pretending to, but Ngoma Itoua, the Union Manager, did not engage with her. She tried to bring him into the group discussions at morning meetings but he folded his arms and refused to contribute.

This was not necessarily sinister. As far as she could make out, he didn't seem to communicate much with anyone. She looked for signs he collaborated with Philippe but they never sat beside each other in the canteen or out on the porch. When she offered to meet him once a week to talk about workers' issues, he claimed to be too busy. So, she left him to himself hoping he would come around at some stage.

Apart from her failure to bring Itoua onside, one of the most pressing matters was the parlous state of community relations. The memory of the manioc hitting the windscreen on her arrival in town still haunted Sam. There was one way to get to the root of the problem, so to speak, and that was by starting at the top. She arranged to meet Victor Samba, the mayor of Masaibu, who had shared her flight to Masaibu.

With Joseph Haba, the community manager, still in hiding, due to his varied and illicit relations in town, one of which had resulted in a pregnancy, she asked Hans to accompany her to Samba's house one evening. They set out from camp in another of the ancient jeeps, rattling and shaking on the bumpy road. All the jeeps belonging to the project had seen better days and most of them needed scrapping. Sam was still trying to figure out where the money had been spent in a project where the fleet of both heavy and light machinery was prehistoric.

'Where does the mayor live?' she said.

'On a hill overlooking the town. It's cooler there,' said Hans, gesticulating at a green slope rising behind the houses.

They drove through town, enduring the usual catcalls and rude gestures. Sam did her best impression of the Queen, smiling and waving as if she was on a royal tour, to be met with blank faces and turned backs. The road out of town folded back on itself like puff pastry, the greenery increasing with altitude and walking distance from axes. Banana trees lined the route with their bright flowers like rows of birds' beaks, dangling yellow and red below their green Mohican crowns. Pigs snuffled in the dry ditches munching on the rotting fruits which had been dislodged from the stems.

A child-like figure stepped out in front of the car. They were going at a crawl due to the state of the road, so Hans halted the vehicle without hitting him. But it wasn't a child. It was a minuscule man. He wore rags and had bare feet. A basket full of grass hung from a strap of woven palm leaves which dug into his forehead. His wizened face turned towards

66

the car. Eyes wide with terror, he spun around and ran from the road back into the bush where he disappeared, leaving Sam with her mouth open.

'Was that a pygmy?' she said. 'I didn't know they lived around here.'

'There's a tribe of them living at the edge of the forest to the west of town,' said Hans.

'Why did he run like that? Hasn't he seen a car before?' said Sam, trying to spot him in the bushes.

'Oh, they've seen plenty. That's why he ran away.'

'I don't understand.'

'During the civil war, the rebels used to catch the pygmies and eat them.'

Sam's breath caught in her throat.

'Eat them? I don't believe you.'

'They considered them to be a species of monkey.'

Sam glanced at Hans to see if he was joking but his eyes were fixed on the road, jaw set like concrete, and no smile creased his Teutonic features.

Before Sam could get her head around this horrific image, they arrived at the mayor's house, a two-storey affair which had been dug into the hill and rose above the citrus trees in the garden. The light was fading and the noise of a generator broke through the wave of sound created by frogs and crickets. Moths were flocking to the light bulbs strung along the first-floor balcony. Mosquito netting wrapped around it was festooned with their corpses.

Victor Samba was waiting on the balcony. His wife, Mbala, a pretty woman with lively eyes, showed Sam and Hans up the stairs.

'So, you're still here,' said Victor, shaking Sam's hand.

'You'll need a large crowbar to remove her,' said Hans.

'I like Masaibu,' said Sam. 'Why would I leave?'

'She's a cheap date,' said Hans, and Victor roared with laughter.

'Cheaper than my nieces anyway,' said Victor.

Sam turned around to see if his wife had heard the comment, but she had melted back into the house. They relaxed on the balcony, Hans swinging in the hammock making rare interjections but letting Sam chat to Victor uninterrupted.

'How can I help you, Sam?' said Victor.

'You told me on the flight that despite being the town's major employer, Consaf were almost universally unpopular. Could you please tell me why? Are there specific things we could improve?'

'Everything.'

'Can we start at the beginning? How did things get this bad?' said Sam

'Well, for a start, you're the only manager of Masaibu to visit me in the last five years.'

Sam studied him to see if he was joking but his gaze was steady. Hans grunted in assent from the hammock.

'I can't believe it,' she said.

'Also, the community relations manager, Joseph Haba, spends his time bed hopping instead of working. We used to have a stakeholder meeting between representatives of the project and the community leaders once a month to talk about mutual issues but we haven't held one for eighteen months,' said Victor.

'That's terrible.'

'There's a Catholic NGO causing trouble too. They have persuaded people Consaf will throw them out of their houses to build the mine,' added Hans.

'But we haven't finished exploration yet. That decision is years away. We don't even know if we have a deposit big enough to exploit,' said Sam.

'Ah, well that's another issue. And then there's the local labour who want a turn working a rotation at the mine,' said Victor.

'I'm dealing with that already,' said Sam.

The mayor fiddled with a placemat and avoided her eyes. She didn't pursue it. *Could he be taking a cut too?* She changed the subject.

'We saw a pygmy on the way here. Do they take part in the community meetings?' she said.

'No. They don't come into town unless they have to,' said Victor.

'Has someone approached them?'

'I don't know. I doubt it. They're shy people. They live off the forest and have traditions and culture all their own,' said Victor.

'I'd like to meet them. Do you think that would be possible?'

'They'll run away if you go to their village. But if you go alone, they might come back if you wait. Don't bring any security people with you.'

Sam considered this for a moment.

'But how do we communicate. Does your wife speak their language?'

'Only pygmies speak that dialect, but they also speak Swahili so she could translate for you.'

'May I bring her with me?' said Sam.

'I don't tell her what to do. You need to ask her if she is willing to help,' said Victor.

Mbala emerged from the shadows as if on cue.

'I will come,' she said. 'Meet me at the gates of the community hall on Saturday morning.'

'At what time?' said Sam

Mbala seemed confused. 'Saturday morning,' she repeated.

'That'll be fine,' said Sam, giving up. 'Thank you. Can we organise a meeting of the committee for next week?'

'I don't see why not. Is Wednesday okay?' said Victor, energised by new hope.

'Wednesday is good,' said Hans.

Sam nodded even though she felt under siege. *There was so much to do. Hans had been right. One thing at a time.*

'Why do you want to meet the pygmies?' said Hans on their way home.

'Oh, just curious,' said Sam.

She was being economical with the truth. Sam loved a hard-luck story. The plight of the pygmies had piqued her interest, and she was determined to integrate them into the social plan for Masaibu, somehow.

***

Sam searched her brain for the word in French but it would not come to her. She was desperate for jam to put on her toast to cover up the taste of the cheap margarine that they served in the canteen. The kitchen staff were busy serving breakfast and clearing the tables so she made her way behind the counter and searched for the storeroom making her way down a filthy passageway with random grains crunching under her feet.

The door of the pantry was ajar, a rusty lock hanging from the latch. She pushed it open and peered in to see dirty shelves half filled with flyblown pineapples and overripe bananas. Bags of dried haricot and fava beans sat on the bottom shelf. Some of their contents had spilt out and mixed with faeces that could have been from rats or mice. Sacks of rice and sugar sat in the corner with plastic bag dispensers beside them, like a local store. *Were they selling the rice or just stealing it?* Concealing it under their skirts would be easy.

She opened the decrepit freezer and found only anorexic chickens and dried salted fish. The smell made her retch. No wonder she had diarrhoea for days. It was surprising they hadn't killed someone with food poisoning. *And where was the kitchen?*

There was a door opposite the storeroom and she pushed through it expecting to find herself surrounded by the usual paraphernalia of ovens and counters and fridges. Instead, the door led to a concrete floor covered with a roof where there were women cooking on open fires in large pots and skillets.

The women were wearing dirty clothes and there was no sink, only one cold faucet which opened onto the floor. One of the women was washing the plates with a stained rag and piling them on the floor to dry. A tall woman sat on a stool eating bacon from a plate filled with fried eggs, sausages and bacon. She shovelled it into her mouth as if afraid someone would take it away. When she noticed Sam standing aghast in the middle of the floor, she pushed the plate towards her. Sam shook her head.

'You are Mama Sam?' said the woman. She ate with her mouth open showing Sam the contents.

'Yes, that's me. What is your name?'

'Mama Sonia. I am in charge of the kitchens.'

A million questions flooded Sam's head but none of them seemed appropriate.

'I am looking for something to spread on my toast.'

'It has run out. I can order you jam from Uganda or we can buy wild honey in town.'

'Let's do both,' said Sam. 'How do you coordinate the orders?'

'I send a list to Moussa Dueme and he sources the food for us.'

'Where does it come from?'

'The Masaibu area produces manioc, chickens, beef and fruit, pineapples and plantains. They import other products on sale in the local shops from Uganda and sell them at inflated prices so it is more economical to order them from Entebbe.'

From what she had seen in the storeroom, Sam couldn't remember anything other than local products, but she didn't want anyone to spit in her food so she said, 'Okay, thank you, Mama Sonia.'

The woman pulled the plate back towards her and picked up a whole fried egg which she shoved into her cavernous mouth. Sam fought to avoid retching and left the way she had come in. She found it hard to believe anyone in head office in Johannesburg was aware of the state of the kitchen. They were breaking every health and safety rule in the book.

In her experience, a clean and well-equipped kitchen was essential in any remote site where the staff lived far from home comforts. No wonder morale had slumped if this was typical of their monthly consumption.

She returned to the canteen to finish her tea and toast. Bruno, the deputy head of maintenance, had sat down at her table, away from the other managers, and was eating his food with his arm around his plate as if protecting it. When she sat down, he jumped up.

'So sorry, Mama Sam. I had no idea you were already sitting here.'

'That's okay, Bruno. Sit down. I'm just finishing.'

He sat at the end of the crude bench opposite her and ate without looking up.

'Can we do anything to fix the kitchen?' she said.

'What do you mean?' he said.

'Have you seen it?'

His face told her he had. His eyes flickered around in their sockets like flies in a jar.

'Um, well, I could help.'

He blurted it out as if he was embarrassed.

'Oh, I think it needs more than a coat of paint,' said Sam, amused.

'No, I mean, I could draw it.'

'Draw what? I'm not following you.'

'I'm an architect, qualified, honestly. If you want, I could design a floor plan for the kitchen. Would we install equipment like ovens and so on?'

'You are?' Sam tried not to look too astonished. 'Yes, that would be amazing. How soon—'

'Right away. I was, I have...' Bruno stuttered to a halt.

'You have what?'

'I've already been working on it. I can bring it to you in a couple of days if I work on it in the evenings.'

'Why can't you do it during the day?' said Sam.

'Frik doesn't like me wasting my time.'

He shrugged and stabbed his fork into his bacon.

'Okay. You do that. Bring it when you are ready. All right?' said Sam.

'Yes. Thank you.'

He was quivering with emotion. *You learn something new every day.* Sam finished her tea and went to the office.

73

Chapter 9

After tolerating the staff meeting, with its usual mix of firefighting and complaints, she followed Moussa Dueme to his office. The enthusiasm he displayed for the new system of distributing uniforms to the local labourers had surprised her. His organisational skills had turned out to be excellent. The next intake of workers would all get numbered uniforms, stopping the old, corrupt scheme in its tracks.

Moussa had not yet advised the workforce about the new system. Sam chatted to a couple of them who were hanging around waiting for lunch one day, hoping to gauge their reaction to it.

'How much do you guys get paid?'

'Eighty dollars a month after tax.'

'The government taxes you?'

They glanced at each other and laughed at her.

'The only government here is the law of the jungle,' said one.

'What do you mean?' said Sam, who had a fair idea.

'The strong take from the weak in Masaibu.'

'How do you imagine men get chosen to work here?' said the other. 'If you refuse to pay the tax, you don't get picked. It makes a big difference to get well-paid work.'

'Who gets the tax?'

'Him.' He threw a thumb towards the office building.

'He shares it with the mayor,' said the other.

'But he turns a blind eye when people sell their uniforms to recuperate the difference. Ow!'

His companion had kicked him hard.

'So, everyone's happy?' said Sam.

They both nodded, embarrassed now. This was just what she needed to hear. If she stopped them selling the uniforms, but they got their entire pay packet, the only loser was Philippe. Even the project would profit. *Win-win.*

Moussa had the air of a man who was just waiting for her to leave so he could pick his nose again. He was not an evil man, but he was incapable of resisting pressure, making him a prime conduit for procurement fraud in the project.

It made it easier for Sam, who planned on pinning him down again and getting answers. He shifted in his seat and avoided her eyes.

'I need your help again,' she said.

Sweat appeared on his brow. She could almost read his mind. *Not the toughest nut to crack.*

'Can you show me the latest procurement list for the kitchens, please?' said Sam.

'I'm not sure where it is.'

His eyes darted around the room.

'I'm sure you can find it,' said Sam, crossing her arms and sitting back. She could see a file on his desk that had Uganda written on the cover. Moussa faffed around for a minute, opening and closing drawers. Her patience broke.

'I can see a file on your desk that looks promising,' she said.

He touched it with the tip of his finger as if it might bite him. She tried to keep a stern expression on her face. It was like dealing with a ten-year-old who had been caught taking a tenner from a wallet. The temptation to smile was intense.

'Oh,' he said, but did not open it.

Sam resisted the urge to grab it.

'Can you show me?' she said.

He shrugged, defeat on his face, and took a receipt from the folder which he handed to her but did not release. She jerked it out of his grasp. Scanning the order, she struggled to keep her features neutral. The company had paid for steak and pork, fresh fruit and salad, coffee and tea, tinned fruit and vegetables, but none of these had been evident in the barren, filthy, storeroom.

Sam made Moussa wait before she commented, making a note of the company and phone number before handing it back.

'I don't remember eating any of these things in the canteen,' she said.

Moussa's eyes bulged.

'They're finished. We have ordered more.'

'When will they arrive?' said Sam.

'Mama Sonia and I will collect them tomorrow.'

Sam stared into his eyes and he broke into a sweat and gulped. *He was so transparent.*

'Great, I can't wait.' She smiled. 'How are the shelves going?'

All the tension disappeared from Moussa's body and she sympathised.

'They are ready.'

'That's great news. Good work Moussa. I wish everyone was as hardworking as you.'

He had the grace to blush.

'Thank you, Mama Sam.'

'Will you have the uniforms numbered for the new intake of labourers next week?'

'They are already on the shelves with the boots and tokens.'

'Well done. You didn't let me down. I'm easy to work for...' she said, pausing and letting a fly buzz through the office. 'Most of the time.'

A nervous grin creased his features, and she left before it had faded and headed over to the geology office.

Alain Folle, the geology manager, was fast becoming a favourite with Sam due to his enthusiasm and proactive manner. Their friendship had started on the wrong foot as he tended to overreact when things didn't go his way. He had made an order of plastic moulded core boxes which caught her eye, and she had joshed him about it.

'That's made a hole in your budget, Alain. Why don't you stick to the wooden ones? We can get local artisans to make them. Where's your community spirit?'

Alain's reaction was not the one she expected.

'Those local guys are thieves. They make the boxes out of uncured wood that splinters and twists as it dries, throwing the core on the ground. Do you have any idea what a metre of core costs?'

His eyes were bulging out of his skull in frustration.

'I do,' said Sam.

'They rot in this climate, wooden core boxes. They turn to mush. It wastes hundreds of thousands of dollars spent on drilling because the core falls out and gets mixed up.'

He paused for breath, panting with exertion.

'You're right,' said Sam, trying to soothe his passion. 'I wasn't refusing your request. I was testing your rationale.'

'You think I'm stupid because I am black.'

Sam flinched.

'Where did that come from? You have added two and two together and made ten. I questioned you on the order because head office have tasked me with reducing expenditure on site. I don't care what colour you are as long as you save money.'

He flushed. Whether in regret about what he had said, or that he said it out loud, Sam couldn't tell.

'Alain, I only care if you are onside or not. Your colour is irrelevant.'

'What do you know about discrimination? You're white.'

Sam raised her eyebrows but she stayed calm.

'I may be white, but I'm a woman in mining. I get treated like a leper at a wedding. At least black guys get to be waiters.'

She smiled right into his eyes and his pupils relaxed.

'I never considered that,' he said. 'We're not so different.'

'We should be concentrating on our similarities, not our differences. I need to know I can count on you. Geology is the lifeblood of the project, which puts you in charge of the most important department in Masaibu. We need mutual trust so I can back you up. If I question your actions, it's so I can defend them in front of the board.'

She put her hand on his shoulder and shook it gently.

'Trust is earned.'

But he relaxed under her hand on his shoulder.

'Let's work on it then.'

His bad moods only lasted a couple of minutes, after which he seemed to forget all about it. But Sam was wary of upsetting him from then on and concentrated on geology.

As they got to know each other better, her daily visits to the geology department became the best part of the day. It was the only time she could relax knowing that she was safe from the constant stress engendered by most of management lying through their teeth to protect their interests. She tried to arrive after he had finished distributing the daily tasks so they could discuss the geology without interruptions. Their shared passion for a job well done bound them together against the rest.

It was not necessary to visit the department every day. To a certain extent, the geology took care of itself. She could not influence the results, nor was there any advantage in trying. Consaf was one of the few major mining companies doing its own exploration. She was enjoying work for a company that didn't need to get good results to raise money. Her only responsibility was to carry out well-executed exploration programmes. No one accused her of being shit if she didn't find gold where there was none.

'How's life in the real world?' she said.

'Good. We got the drill rig moved yesterday so we can drill again this morning,' said Alain

'That's excellent. Have you got the map of the proposed drill sites here?'

He sighed.

'No, I forgot it in my cabin.'

'Can we fetch it? We can spread it over a table in the canteen and have a nasty coffee.'

'Sure.'

Sam had not entered any of the other prefabs in her row and was not prepared for the shabby interior of Alain's dwelling. Bare wires hung from the ceiling and the fridge door had detached and leant against the counter. There was a single log stool pulled up to the old Formica table where the map was lying open.

'Sorry about the lack of facilities,' said Alain.

'How long has it been like this?'

'Months. I don't think head office cares how we live as long as they get their results.'

'Are all the prefabs like this?'

'Most.'

Sam didn't comment. Consaf boasted in their publicity about the good treatment of their staff and modern facilities in their camps. No one had bothered to check on the welfare of the people who worked at Masaibu. It had taken her a few weeks to discover the extent of the deterioration in standards there. Managers on flying visits hadn't flagged up the issues which had become obvious to her.

Dirk had given her a box of leaflets which contained the mission statement of the company where it listed ten principles that employees had to follow. The first principle was equality. The company expects staff members to treat everyone equally no matter their race, religion or gender. She was supposed to hand them out to the people at Masaibu, but the hypocrisy of it stuck in her craw. *If you treat people like shit, they behave like it.*

No wonder people on site were so disaffected they were stealing from the project. Management were raiding their salaries, feeding them terrible food and making them sleep in rat-infested, dilapidated housing. It was natural to fight back. If she wanted to turn the project around, she needed to start from the bottom, not the top. The leaflets would stay in her office until she was no longer embarrassed to hand them out.

She headed for the office after coffee, her head full of the things she needed to do. A long list, but not a difficult one to accomplish. Hans had been right. She needed to do things in sections so she could judge the results of one change without it being influenced by another.

She was so caught up in her thoughts that she almost stepped on a rhinoceros beetle, which was lying on its back, legs flailing, in a small indentation in the path. Reaching down she flipped it upright with her finger and directed it back onto the grass, where there were several other beetles blundering around. One of the local workers watched her and shouted out, 'Mama Sam, you can't save them all. They come out to breed at this time of year.'

'I can try,' she said, beaming.

With Mama Sonia in Uganda, Sam took advantage of her absence to give the kitchen a spring clean. When the staff had finished washing up after breakfast, she organised them into three groups. One she sent to empty the storeroom and clear out the freezers, before scrubbing the shelves and the floors with bleach. A second group were delegated to clean the back kitchen and the third to disinfect the canteen area.

There was no enthusiasm for the task in the beginning. Some resentful glances were directed at Sam, who decided to muck in to gain support. Once the boss was engaged, the atmosphere improved measurably as the women joshed her about her cleaning skills. They made strange clicking noises of approval to each other.

Frik provided a plumber to fix the hot water boiler and soon the sinks were full of hot soapy water as the women warmed to their task. When the job was finished, one of them produced a plastic bottle full of large bright green grasshoppers, which

81

they threw live into a pan of hot oil before Sam could protest. They fried them to golden brown and then scooped the insects out and placed them on some paper napkins spread over a plate to drain the fat.

The women ate them enthusiastically and offered one to Sam. She knew it was a pivotal moment but she dreaded it. She grasped one by the abdomen but was at a loss for what to do next. One woman saw her hesitating and laughed. She took the grasshopper from Sam and removed the hind legs making a face at them and shaking her finger. *Who knew? The back legs are nasty.*

The woman handed back the grasshopper with a nod. Sam was now the focus of attention in the room. There was no way out. She put the insect in her mouth and forced herself to bite down on it. To her relief, it tasted like a prawn but without any trace of sea. She nodded enthusiastically.

'Good,' she said. 'Thank you.'

But she didn't take another, making gestures of typing and she left them gobbling the fried goodies.

'Hi, Dirk. It's me.'

'Sam! I was just getting concerned. You need to call me more often.'

'Sorry. There's nothing major happening. I spend most of my days firefighting.'

'How's it going? Any news on your progress?' said Dirk.

'I feel like I'm getting somewhere. A lot of the discontent in camp stems from the terrible food and the state of the senior accommodation on site.'

'Visitors said good things about the food.'

'I suspect the cooks change the menu when they have visitors from head office. And also...' Sam hesitated.

'Also, what?'

'Well, it seems the food we order is taking a detour organised by the head of catering here in camp.'

'Can't you fire her?' said Dirk.

'The employment law really doesn't cater for firing, only for extracting money from employers. I am going to implement my own solution.'

'Is it legal?'

Sam guffawed. 'Of course.'

'Okay, get on with it. By the way, what's wrong with the accommodation? Those prefabs aren't that old.'

'They are structurally sound as far as I can tell. I'd like to spruce them up and give people satellite television to watch. Working twelve-hour days for thirteen days out of fourteen is tough going when there are no facilities. We don't even have a volleyball court.'

'How much would it cost?' Dirk's voice had stiffened.

'No more than thirty thousand dollars, including new fridges and televisions for the prefabs. I'd like to rewire them too. The electrician here hasn't got the training to wire the houses to the correct safety standards. Could you lend me someone from the other project in Lumbono to train up our guys?'

'I can arrange that. Have you made any progress with the safety training?'

She hesitated.

'Not yet. It's delicate.' *If only he knew.*

'It will be more delicate if someone gets injured. Get on it straight away,' said Dirk.

'Does any of the other projects run a training programme? I suspect our health and safety officer is a plant. He didn't know what a toolbox talk was.'

'They have organised an intensive course at Ntezi project next week for anyone who needs a refresher. I suggest you send him to that.'

'That's brilliant. I'll see Dr Ntuli tomorrow and send him there.'

Sam punched the air.

'Send me the bill for the accommodation upgrades. I'll push it through,' said Dirk.

'Oh, and I need to buy safety gear.'

'What sort of safety gear?'

'Oh, you know, boots and helmets and so on,' said Sam.

'I'll let you into a secret. Safety gear is the one exception where budgeting is concerned. No one will criticise you for buying safety equipment, no matter what it costs. My advice is to buy now and apologise later.'

'Thanks, Dirk. I will.'

'Anything else to report?'

'I haven't spotted anything major down here, you know. Small tweaks should fix most of it.'

Dirk let out a big sigh of relief. Sam imagined he had been expecting worse news.

'I found a few great beetles too,' she said.

'I don't need beetle news.'

'Not even amazing ones?'

'No beetles. Have a nice weekend.'

Chapter 10

D r Ntuli's face fell when Sam entered his office. His pince-nez glasses were cloudy with oily residue and so tight that they had raised a red ridge where they struggled to grab enough nose to stay on. His bushy eyebrows were going grey, matching his close-cut hair. He frowned and shuffled a pile of papers with the air of a man who was far too busy to chat.

'I'm not ready yet,' he said.

He couldn't meet her eyes and Sam could feel his panic through her pores. *Who was he related to that had got him this plumb job in charge of a department for which he didn't seem to be qualified? Was he even a doctor?*

'That's okay,' she said, in her most soothing tone of voice. 'We can review your progress together. Where did you study?'

To her chagrin, Dr Ntuli started to cry. The anticipation of his turn to face the terrible Mama Sam had been too much for him. She let him weep for a good couple of minutes, handing him a tissue and waiting for calm.

Finally, he sniffed loudly and looked up at her.

'I studied in the capital,' he said.

'Did you work in a hospital there?' said Sam.

He froze in horror but she waited.

'I'm a doctor of philosophy,' he said, cringing.

'Do you have any training in health and safety?'

'Not-as-such.' The blood drained from his face in anticipation.

'You poor man,' said Sam. 'How dreadful for you.' She was not pretending. His demeanour had touched her empathetic side. *Poor bastard, no wonder he's terrified.* 'We must do something straight away.'

'My rotation is over next week.'

'That's perfect.'

A look of horror crossed his face.

'I have a family,' he said.

A wave of sympathy hit Sam. *He had imagined she would fire him.*

'I was thinking of sending you for some training. How would you like to spend a couple of weeks in Ntezi project? Dirk Goosen told me that they are holding a course there and you could tag along.'

'Really?'

'You can't carry on like this. Can anyone fill in for you while you are away?'

'No-one on site is qualified.'

'Okay, I'll sort it out and don't worry. The course is intensive and may be totally new to you, so you will have to put all your effort into it. Someone at Ntezi should give you a large supply of leaflets and materials to help you get started.'

Dr Ntuli scrutinised her face. Whatever he read there seemed to placate him.

'You could fire me and get someone more qualified,' he said.

'Why would I want to do that? You have lots of important experience gained in this project. Who would be better suited than you to change the regime without upsetting anyone?'

Dr Ntuli beamed.

'I am well liked,' he said.

'That's a great start.'

Mbala Samba, the mayor's wife, stood outside the gates of the community hall in the shade of a large umbrella attached to a stall selling roasted sweet corn stalks. Sam and Jacques, who had settled on ten o'clock as a happy medium, drove up beside her and she got into the back of the car.

Several people pointed and hissed at the vehicle but there was also frank interest in the contents of the car. Sam was due to attend the first community meeting soon and word had got around.

'Good morning, Mama Mbala,' said Sam.

'Good morning, Mama Sam,' she said, ignoring Jacques who had not merited more than a sharp nod of her head.

'I trust you are well.'

'I am well, but my sister will have to visit the hospital soon to have a baby.'

'Congratulations,' said Jacques.

But Mbala only gave another stiff nod of her head. It was unusual for local women to have babies in hospital but Sam was unaware of the significance and made no comment, feeling out of her depth with Mbala's reaction.

They drove out of town along dry, uneven roads which got narrower and bumpier the further away they got. After about twenty minutes, Jacques pulled into the side of the road beside a path leading into the scrub.

'The village is a kilometre away. Just follow the path. I can't come any further or your visit will be a waste of time. The pygmies are afraid of soldiers,' said Jacques.

'I would be too,' said Sam.

'You must not speak until I tell you. Keep your gaze on the ground until they ask you a question,' said Mbala whose tone was business-like.

Sam got out of the car with Mbala and they headed towards the village. It seemed to Sam that it was further than a single kilometre, but it could have been due to the heat and the fact she was unfamiliar with the path. As they neared the village, she could feel her heart rate increasing with anticipation but they arrived to an empty clearing.

The houses were so small that Sam checked around for Candid Camera. They were about shoulder height on her with round bases, no windows, and wattle and daub walls with palm leaf roofs. Smoke was pouring out at the top of one house. It appeared to be on fire but there were no flames.

Mbala held her hand up to stop Sam from asking questions. She indicated a tiny bench under a large mango tree and they both sat in the shade, which was almost as stifling as the open clearing. Sweat ran down Sam's back and her legs were stiff from squatting on the minuscule bench. There was a putrid smell in the air as if a rotting body lay in the undergrowth.

They waited ten minutes before the first person emerged from the bush, an ancient woman almost bent double with age, with the air of a sacrifice. She examined the women with something approaching dread.

'Shikamo Mama,' said Mbala, keeping her eyes on the ground.

Sam did the same, but she remembered not to speak. The old woman did a double take.

'Marahaba,' she said, looking surprised.

There was a rustling from the bushes. A small group of women pushed their way out of their hiding place. They came over to Sam and Mbala. One of them approached Mbala and inclined her head. Mbala did the same so that their foreheads touched, almost falling off the bench in her effort to complete the gesture.

'My name is Habimana Benga. We are from the Mbuti tribe,' said the woman. 'What do you want here?'

Mbala nodded at Sam who came forward.

'This is Mama Sam. She is the new boss of Consaf's Masaibu project up there on the hill above town.'

'Shikamo Mama Habimana,' said Sam.

'Marahaba.'

'I am honoured that you welcome us to your village. Consaf consider the Mbuti to be an important part of the community,' said Sam

Sam waited while Habimana translated this for the rest of the women. She hadn't anticipated the scornful expressions that followed. One woman spat on the ground. She ploughed on.

'We are starting the stakeholder meetings again in Masaibu town hall and we would like you to send a representative.'

'Us?' said Habimana. 'Are you serious?'

Sam stammered under her stare.

'Um, completely. I understand that it is far for you to come, but we can send a car to pick you up if you're willing. And to return you to your village.'

'What about the others at the meeting? They don't respect us and they'll mistreat us.'

'No, it won't be like that. I promise. The meetings are democratic. No one will be allowed to insult you. The Mbuti have a strong tradition in preservation of the forest and deserve their say about what happens in the area,' said Sam.

'We will discuss this tonight around the fire. If we agree, my husband, Ota, will attend the meeting.'

'It is on Monday afternoon,' said Sam.

'How many days from now?' said Habimana.

'Two days. Not tomorrow. The next day.'

'Send the car. If we agree, Ota will wait on the road at the end of the path.'

Jacques was sound asleep, his car seat tipped so far back that Sam didn't spot him until she peered into the window. She knocked hard on the glass intending to give him a fright. He sat up in one quick gesture, a gun in his hand which pointed at Sam. She jumped backwards in fright and ended up on her back in the ditch.

Mbala laughed, the first sign of her true character, and stood there giggling as Sam tried to stand up. Jacques stood at her side in an instant. Smiling at her predicament, he offered her his hand. She took it with bad grace.

'Jesus, you gave me a fright,' said Sam.

'And me? How were the pygmies? Did you speak to them?' said Jacques.

'We invited them to the stakeholder meeting on Monday,' said Sam.

'Will they come?' he said.

'I don't think so,' said Mbala, serious again. 'They are afraid.'

They sat in the car for a minute, each absorbed in their own thoughts, listening to the chirping, clicking and buzzing from the forest. Just when Jacques leaned forward to switch on the ignition, there was a trumpeting sound from deep within the trees.

'Did you hear that?' said Sam.

'Elephants,' said Mbala.

'Elephants? In the forest?' said Sam. 'I thought they lived on the savannah.'

'They are a sub-species of elephant, smaller than usual, with pink tusks.'

Sam laughed.

'Now, you're pulling my leg. It's not funny,' she said.

'It's true,' said Mbala.

'The pink tusks are straighter than usual, and harder. They're of immense value to poachers, so they are a protected species. The rangers who guard them are paid for by Consaf,' said Jacques.

'I'll need to see them as part of my verification,' said Sam, eyes shining with excitement.

'Okay. I'll take you,' said Jacques.

'When?' said Sam.

Jacques laughed at her impatience.

'We'll drop Mbala back at her house, and then we can come back if you like?'

Why had she agreed to this wild goose chase through the jungle? Thick mud crept up over the top of her boots and her face was bright red with exertion. Ahead of her, Jacques glided over the surface as if he had a mini-hovercraft. It was so galling. Sam sighed and pulled her boot free of a sticky patch that threatened to swallow it.

They followed the trail for almost an hour, Sam's patience wearing thinner than a favourite T-shirt. *Why had she forced Jacques to show her the herd?* Maybe it was because he resembled Tintin, despite being an ex-officer in the French Foreign Legion, his thinning blond hair framing his ridiculously youthful face. *Could someone who looked like a choirboy kill in cold blood?*

They reached a clearing that contained a pool of shallow water. Millions of small insects danced in the last rays of sunlight, which filtered through the trees onto the water. Small bats swooped among them filling their mouths with crunchy prey. Sam crouched behind a tree and peered through the approaching gloom of the African dusk.

After twenty minutes, her knees ached with the effort. She needed to stand up and shake out her legs.

'I can't see anything,' she said, her voice betraying the exhaustion threatening to overcome her anticipation.

'Shush,' said Jacques. 'Not long now. Ah, here they come.'

How did he know? He must have radar. Then a slight judder ran up her legs and into her back caused by massive footfall on the bush floor. The faint sound of leaves being brushed aside by large bodies. She shut her eyes and tried to work out which direction it was coming from.

Her hand slipped on the smooth bark of the tree trunk and snapped off a small twig. The sound reverberated around the clearing like a gunshot just when a massive shape glided from the shadows out onto the grass. The elephant lifted its trunk in the air to check for danger but the wind was carrying their scent away into the trees. It turned to face her, huge ears flapping in warning, its pink tusks catching the light. It was like Barbie's version of an elephant but the tusks were sharp.

'Don't move a muscle,' said Jacques in a hoarse voice.

He pulled her upright and pinned her to the trunk of a tree, keeping her out of sight of the elephant. She could feel his breath on her neck, the warmth

92

of his body pressed against her. They breathed in harmony as they watched. Her temperature rose with excitement, but he did not show any reaction to being in such close contact with her. It was thrilling and confusing at the same time.

The bushes across the water parted and a small elephant emerged shaking its head and gambolling in the grass, followed by another larger animal with shorter tusks. They played together under the supervision of the adult elephant, the smaller one weaving in and out of its massive legs, entrancing Sam who forgot about her embarrassment and gazed in wonder.

'Do you believe me now?' said Jacques.

***

Sam lay in bed that night, her whole being tingling with excitement. It was patently absurd to imagine Jacques having any other reason for what he did than the obvious one of removing her from the elephant's line of sight. But he was slow to move away when the elephants left, and she couldn't help wondering if she was the only one who felt excited. *Maybe this was a one-off. Maybe.*

Chapter 11

They held the stakeholder meeting in the community hall in Masaibu. Representatives of thirty different groups who lived in the Masaibu area turned up despite Sam's misgivings. Even the ex-rebel leader, Joseph Kaba, swept in, his Kalashnikov slung over his shoulder. He placed himself opposite Sam, who sat between the mayor, Victor Samba, and an empty seat they had designated for Ota Benga, should he turn up. The chair had been raised by putting it on a bed of bricks but Sam was uncertain how Ota could reach it.

'Welcome, everybody,' said the mayor. 'This is Mama Sam. She is the general manager of the Masaibu project and she'll listen to your requests for help with your projects or issues. Please do not interrupt when someone else is speaking. You'll get your turn. Understood?'

A general murmur of assent rippled around the hall.

'Okay, I'll decide who speaks. If I point at you, you must name your group before you start,' said the mayor.

He pointed to a man Sam recognised as a shopkeeper from the main street and the meeting got underway.

The first hour was uneventful. Sam wrote every comment into a spiral-bound pad she had allocated for the purpose. The inputs from the local people consisted of a list of complaints about their share of the pie, Consaf's obtuse attitude and life in general. The shopkeepers complained about the lack of local purchasing, the artisanal miners about their working conditions, a doctor about the hospital, lorry drivers about the state of the local roads and the ex-rebels about a lack of jobs.

'You might need a bigger notebook,' said the mayor, elbowing Sam in the arm and smiling in a conspiratorial manner.

She winked at him and kept writing.

The door to the hall opened, and Ota Benga entered to a chorus of gasps and sniggers. Diminutive in stature, he almost disappeared from view as he walked behind the chair backs, dressed in rags with a spear strapped to his back. Sam stood up and beckoned to him. He walked towards her through the astonished comments that had accompanied his entrance. She offered him her hand in greeting.

He inclined his head to her in the gesture she had seen at their village. She went down on one knee to give them equal stature and did the same. Their foreheads touched. His skin was warm and slightly sticky. He raised his eyes to hers and was gazing into her soul. She tried not to blink and returned the look for as long as she could.

Whatever he had seen in her appeared to please him. He leaned his spear against the chair beside her and sprang up onto the seat with surprising agility. Settling himself with legs crossed, he peered out into the room.

'Who ordered the hors-d'oeuvre?' said Joseph Kaba, his hand on his gun.

Sam went rigid with fury, but the mayor put his hand on her arm and shook his head.

'Live to fight another day,' he whispered, and then said out loud. 'Honestly Joseph, this is a public forum. Please keep your insults to yourself. Thank you. Okay, where were we? Yes? Mama Lena?'

Ota did not react to the insult, staring straight ahead. Neither did he speak at the meeting but listened to the proceedings, rubbing his chin between his thumb and index finger, pulling at the straggly hairs which populated it. When the session was over, he shook Sam's hand and turned to leave. Jacques was waiting to drive him home.

'Will you come again?' said Sam, to his retreating back.

'I will,' said Ota.

After the meeting, a tall, bald white man approached Sam and introduced himself.

'Jean Delacroix. I run the local office of the Wildlife Conservation Organisation, the WCO. They call us wackos.'

He managed to be handsome in a gangly way. She smiled.

'I'm so glad you came. I need your advice,' she said.

'You do? Can I call the Pope? I don't think a mining company has ever asked for my help. I may have to declare a miracle.'

Sam laughed.

'Oh dear, and I hoped being a woman was my only failing,' she said. 'Could you come and see me at my office tomorrow? I want to get started straight away.'

'Wow! Um, okay, I'll see what I can do. Shall we say midday? Why don't we have lunch? There's a half-decent restaurant on the main square.'

'What's it called?'

'Le Bistrot du Parc.'

'I'll see you there at midday.'

Sam was careful not to make an obvious effort on her appearance for lunch the next day. So careful that a small child in the street asked her if she was a nun, causing Jacques to crouch over in hilarity. Sam shrugged at him, opening her hands in question.

'It's your clothes,' he said, tears running down his cheeks. 'The nuns wear something almost identical. He's hoping you have sweets to give him, or a holy medal.'

'I'm trying to blend in,' she said, hurt.

'You're camouflaged,' said Jacques. 'If you go into the jungle, you'll be lost forever.'

Sam reviewed her uniform of khaki shirt and trousers, and Doc Marten boots and sighed. She had never affected glamour, and being a geologist made it easy for her to hide behind utility clothing. She was an attractive woman and aware of it, just not capable of taking advantage of her looks without feeling stupid or awkward.

'Safety first,' she said.

'Are you sure you don't want me to come with you?' said Jacques. Was he flirting?

'Yes,' she said. 'Quite sure.'

'Enjoy your lunch. Radio me if you need a lift back,' he said.

The Bistrot du Parc stuck out like a sore thumb in Masaibu. It had a chic air that would have been more at home in Nice than central Africa. Large picture windows flooded the place with light. Blue and white checked paper tablecloths covered the tables matched by the tiled floor.

Was she hallucinating? She squeezed her eyes shut and when she opened them again, Jean was standing in front of her, stooping to avoid imaginary obstacles in the atrium. He swept his hand over the remnants of his hair drawing it over the top of his shiny head.

'You're here. Excellent! Shall we sit down?' said Jean.

They sat at a table for two in the corner of the dining hall. Tropical plants in tubs surrounded them, making them almost invisible to anyone coming into the restaurant.

'Great table,' she said. 'I feel like I'm eating in the forest.'

They ordered steak frites with green beans. Sam was salivating at the idea of tasty food. The canteen in camp only served stews, rice and fried food. She had been living on fried eggs and rice. *Where on earth did they source their ingredients?* She needed to speak to the owner.

'So, how can I help Consaf?' said Jean, leaning towards her and putting his elbows on the table.

Did he think this was a date? Sam put on her business voice and shifted away from him.

'What do you know about the group of pygmies that live outside the elephant reserve? Their leader, Ota Benga, came to the community meeting.'

'I know they're a pain in the arse,' said Jean, frowning.

'What do you mean?'

'Our forest rangers spend most of their time trying to keep them out of the reserve instead of looking for poachers.'

'What are they doing in there? They can't be hunting elephants with spears,' said Sam.

'Believe it or not, they've been known to kill the odd one, but that's not the problem. Their main prey is blue duiker, an antelope. They'll travel many miles to raid bee colonies for honey. But neither of those is available outside the reserve anymore.'

'So where are they supposed to hunt?' said Sam.

'That's just it. The government doesn't want them to hunt. It considers them to be a stone age tribe who should send their children to school and farm the land like the other people around here,' said Jean.

'Is that why your rangers chase them out of the forest?'

'They are your rangers too. Consaf pays for them through the community budget. We need a licence to operate here. It's hard enough keeping the townsfolk happy as it is. We have to compromise. Anyway, there are too few rangers to protect the elephants and control the pygmies at the same time.' Jean shrugged.

Their food arrived and there was silence while they ate. Sam gobbled her food with her usual enthusiasm and had to wait while Jean picked his way through his food, pushing the fat to one side and only eating the perfect chips. No wonder he was so thin.

'Are you married?' said Jean, looking up from his dissections.

'No, I'm too busy. Are you?'

Annoyance crossed his face for an instant but he recovered.

'Yes, kind of.'

'How can you be kind of married?' said Sam, rolling her eyes.

'Oh, you know, she doesn't understand me.'

Sam couldn't help it. She spluttered and coughed, trying to damp down her guffaw of laughter. *That old chestnut.* She hadn't believed men said that but there it was, dangling in the air between them.

Jean couldn't look her in the face. He had not been expecting this reaction. Sam guessed that like most French men, he expected her knickers to fall off at the possibility of sex with a married man.

'Well, you're a complex person,' she said.

'Yes, I am,' said Jean, grateful for the out. 'I was hoping we could reach some sort of understanding, you know, what with you being alone here.'

'We already have one,' said Sam. 'You are married, that I understand.'

'I didn't mean to insult you. I find you attractive. You can't fault me for trying.'

Sam had the urge to punch him but the self-indulgence of it stopped her. *Just because I am single doesn't mean I'm desperate.*

'I'm sorry, but I have to go back to the office. I have meetings,' she said.

She didn't, but encouraging him was the last thing on her mind. She had to get out of there.

Sam stood up to go, giving her an unobstructed view of the entrance. Joseph Kaba, the ex-leader of the local rebel group, who had insulted Ota Benga, the pygmy, at the community meeting, had just arrived with a Chinese man in a shiny suit. They were roaring with laughter and slapping each other on the back as if checking for weapons. The waiter showed them to a table.

There was something shifty about the way Kaba cased the restaurant. Sam ducked to avoid detection.

'Is there a back door?' she said.

'I presume there's one through the kitchens,' said Jean.

'Let's ask the waiter if we can go that way,' said Sam.

'What reason will I give him?'

'Tell him you don't want to be seen with me, in case it ruins your environmental credentials.'

'Hilarious. Okay, I'll think of something.'

Minutes later, they shuffled through the kitchens avoiding plates and pots and chefs in a hurry and walked out through the corridor at the back, passing the people washing plates in the sinks. A large woman was giving orders, a woman Sam recognised. Some pieces of the puzzle started to fall into place. She pushed Jean in the back to hurry him along.

'Get out quick,' she said.

'Okay, I'm going. What's the big rush? Is someone following us?'

'No, it's not that. I couldn't figure out where this restaurant sources its food, and now I know.'

Hans rubbed his forehead with his left hand while tapping a cigarette on the ashtray with his right.

'That's a serious allegation.'

'Come on. You guys are security. Don't tell me you had no idea what was happening. In fact, don't tell me you don't know everything that's going on. I'm not stupid, you know. You have an obvious conflict of interests, but I wish you could give me a clue now and then to speed things up,' said Sam.

'Fair enough. We know a lot more than we've told you. I promise not to lie if you ask me a straight question.'

'Who owns Bistrot du Parc?' said Sam.

'Mama Sonia,' said Hans.

'Where does she source the supplies for it?'

'Uganda.'

'She buys the food in Entebbe?'

'Not exactly.'

'What exactly?'

'Moussa Dembe orders the food as part of the Consaf rations and then drives it back from Uganda to Mama Sonia's storeroom at the edge of town. They swop it for local goods that they buy in town for a quarter of the price. That's why meals are so monotonous here.'

'Why don't you do anything? Aren't you supposed to be security?'

'Security has a remit to protect the camp from attack. We are not the police.'

'But I can ask you to supervise stuff, right?'

Hans beamed like a child being told he could open his Christmas presents.

'Yes, you can. A written order from you is all it would take.'

Sam tried not to be smug.

Chapter 12

Sam dialled the number she had copied down in Moussa Dueme's office. It had taken far longer than she expected to call it, but better late than never. Now she had found out about Moussa and Mama Sonia, and the missing food, she could solve this without anyone having to get fired or hauled over the coals. She would deal with it her way and then enjoy the result. *Who me?*

'Hello? Is that Stoddard's? I'd like to speak to your orders department, please.'

'Certainly, Madam, who shall I say is calling?'

'It's Sam Harris. I'm calling from Masaibu Project in Lumbono on behalf of Consaf.'

'May I ask in what capacity?'

'I'm the new general manager.'

'One moment, please.'

The line went quiet and then an old man answered the phone, his voice quavering.

'Hello? Miss Harris? This is Rahul Singh. How can I help you?'

'I was hoping to speak to Bill Stoddard.'

'That is me. I bought the business about twenty-five years ago but I didn't change the name. The brand was part of the deal.'

'Rahul, nice to talk to you. I have a problem with transport on site here at Masaibu. Several of our trucks are out of commission and we won't be able to continue picking up the orders from you. Do you provide, or can you organise, a delivery service to Lumbono?'

'As it happens, I can. I deliver to several NGOs in your area. It would be easy, and cheap, you'll be glad to hear, to add you to the route. It will probably be cheaper than collecting it yourselves.'

'That's fantastic. Is there any reason we aren't on your route already?'

'Oh, I offered, but your Mr Dueme said he preferred to collect.'

'I see. Okay, how do we organise this?'

'You'll have to follow the normal protocol to pick up the food this week but we can arrange our first delivery to your project next time you need one. Seeing as we already have a long relationship with Consaf, I'll send the contract with the driver for you to sign. How does that suit you?'

'Perfect. Thank you. Do you sell safety equipment, uniforms or training materials?'

'My neighbour sells everything in that line. Do you want brochures? I could send a box for you to distribute to your managers. I'm sure we can come to some agreement on transportation of any purchases you might make.'

'Um, can you lay your hands on a comfortable chair? An old leather recliner would be perfect.'

'I believe the junk shop down the road can help with that. Leave it with me. We'll bring you something and you can send us the cash by return with the contract.'

'Excellent. That's settled then. I'll tell Mr Dueme.'

Sam hung up, but she did not have time to reflect on her triumph. There was a timid knock on the door of her office.

'Come in,' she said.

Bruno's plump body insinuated itself into the room. Big damp sweat patches marked the armpits of his overalls. He approached her as if she might bite him and thrust a piece of paper onto her desk.

'Here it is,' he said.

'Here is what?' said Sam, her irritation showing.

He cowered. *Damn. She had snapped at him in her impatience. She was no better than the others.* Bruno had a miserable time at work. He was always being bullied and pushed around because he was an easy target, being both fat and shy.

'The kitchen,' he muttered. 'I made you a kitchen.'

'Oh lord, I forgot. I'm so sorry, Bruno. I didn't mean to be rude. I was just distracted. Please sit down while I review it.'

He sank into the smallest chair, almost falling off in his determination to make himself insignificant.

Sam unfolded the crinkled piece of paper and gasped in amazement. She recognised its quality at a glance. The clean lines and precision of the drawing struck her as perfect. She hadn't been expecting anything too wonderful, having only agreed for him to draw it to be kind.

'This is wonderful. I love it,' she said.

Bruno flushed and squirmed in his chair.

'Can you cost it for me? Or is that—'

'No, I can do it. I can.'

Bruno held on to the arms of the chair, his knuckles white.

'Okay then. This is great. No one told me we had an architect on site. How come Frik doesn't know about your qualifications?'

'He doesn't speak French. And...'

'And what?' said Sam.

'He never asked me.'

'How soon can you get it done?'

105

'How much?' said Dirk.

'Twenty thousand should cover it,' said Sam.

'I'm hurt. You only call me when you want money,' said Dirk, whose voice betrayed no sign of emotion.

'At least I ring you. Anyway, I found a great new beetle today. I've never seen one like this before. It's got weird circles on—'

'Yeah, yeah, yeah. Beetles, blah, blah, blah. Have you done any work?'

'I've been talking to the Wildlife Conservation bloke.'

'Jesus, do you want them to close us down? Don't go anywhere near him.'

'Don't be silly. He's helping us with the elephants. I think the pygmies will guard them with the rangers.'

'What? Are you running a wildlife park now? Don't tell me.' He sighed. 'Any improvements? Beside the ones I'm paying for?'

'I'm making some great progress but I want concrete results before I report to you, just in case. Is that okay?'

'Do I have any choice? By the way, I got you your machine parts. They should be delivered from Uganda sometime next week.'

'Brilliant! I can't wait to tell Frik. He may even smile.'

'I doubt it. You have to pay him first. Okay, get on with it. Don't let me die wondering.'

'Bye, Dirk.'

Dirk put down the phone.

'Miriam!'

'Yes, sir?'

'That girl's gonna kill me.'

She laughed.

'Shall I get you some coffee?'

Dirk nodded and swung himself around in his chair to face the window. So far so good. Tinkering around the edges of the main problem without getting to the nub. It was what he had expected from a woman with her experience. *No need to worry.*

When Moussa Dueme and Mama Sonia pulled into the yard behind Le Bistrot du Parc, Hans was leaning against the door frame smoking a Gitanes and blowing smoke circles into the still air. Only the tip of his cigarette glowed in the dark night and it was a few seconds before they spotted him.

'Good evening, Mama Sonia, Monsieur Dueme. What brings you here this evening?' he said.

'I have every right to come to my own restaurant. What are you doing here?' said Mama Sonia. 'You are trespassing.'

'Sam asked me to make sure the food got to the canteen without any problems.'

'This is not the canteen,' said Moussa Dueme. 'You have no jurisdiction here.'

'That is correct. But I'm not here to interfere with Mama Sonia's business. I'll just wait until you are finished and go with you to site.'

'We don't need you to supervise us. We are perfectly safe. You can go,' said Mama Sonia, pointing to the gate.

'Oh, I'm not looking after you.' Hans took a piece of paper out of his pocket and pretended to read the phrase even though it was almost pitch black in the

yard except for the dim headlights of the pickup.
'I'm ensuring the integrity of the cargo.'

'How dare you.' Mama Sonia spluttered but the
words got stuck in her throat. She took a couple of
deep breaths with her back to him, her immense
bosom heaving with distress.

Hans waited. After less than a minute, her
panic disappeared and was replaced by her old
confidence. She moved towards Hans, her walk
insinuating.

'Come now, Colonel, surely we can reach some
sort of arrangement.'

His eyebrows flew up and he laughed, a cruel
sound.

'You couldn't pay me enough. Get back in the car,
madame, and you, Dueme, go with my driver. I'll
drive the pickup.'

***

Sam was sitting on the steps of the canteen with
Dr Ntuli and Bruno when Hans arrived in the
pickup. He gave her a thumbs up signal. Beside
him, Mama Sonia's face emanated thunder and
suppressed fury. Moussa was nowhere to be seen.
He had probably sneaked home rather than face the
inquisition bound to result from their abortive trip
to the restaurant.

Sam stood up and descended the steps with a
welcoming grin on her face. Hans got out and
shook her hand. Mama Sonia slid off her seat and
planted her feet on the ground in the manner of a
sumo wrestler. Every aspect of her body language
indicated she was spoiling for a fight.

'Ah, Mama Sonia, I hope you had a good trip to
Uganda. It's been a long day for you. You must be

108

tired,' said Sam, with as much sincerity as she could muster.

Mama Sonia did not reply. She stomped indoors pushing Dr Ntuli aside and heading for the storerooms. Cries of outrage indicated she had noticed the invasion of her kingdom.

'Who's been in here? I did not authorise this,' she said, returning and blocking the door to Bruno who was carrying a box of supplies.

'I did,' said Sam. 'I know how busy you are, so I organised a thorough clean of the kitchens and storerooms while you were away. The women did a great job, don't you think?'

Mama Sonia stayed in the doorway.

'I need you to move, please,' said Bruno, sweating. 'This box is heavy.'

Defeated, Mama Sonia moved aside and slumped on a bench in the canteen watching the boxes pass.

It took about twenty minutes to unload the pickup and take the meat from the ice boxes and store it in the freezer.

'You'll be glad to hear that I've obtained money from Consaf to refurbish it and put in a brand-new modern kitchen for you,' said Sam. 'No more cooking on fires or washing plates with cold water.'

'The women do not know how to use modern equipment. It is dangerous. I'll complain to Ngoma Itoua, the union manager, about this. He will stop you.'

'I doubt it,' said Sam. 'It's a health and safety matter. Dr Ntuli is one hundred per cent behind the move.'

Dr Ntuli nodded and smiled.

'Okay,' said Hans. 'Everybody out. I need to lock up.'

He produced some shiny new locks from his pocket and put them on the freezers and storeroom

109

doors. Mama Sonia's jaw dropped but then she recovered and held out her hand.

'Give me the keys,' she said. 'Now.'

'I'm afraid it's a security matter,' said Sam. 'There have been several thefts from the stores and until we figure out who is responsible, security will lock them every night and open them for you in the morning.'

'But...'

Mama Sonia trailed off. She fixed Sam with a glare and crashed down the stairs threatening to smash them.

'Wait 'til she finds out about the deliveries,' said Hans.

'Sonia-geddon, I expect,' said Sam.

Chapter 13

Sam observed the casual labourers filing in and out of Philippe's office. Their faces were etched in surprise and glee. Several of them stopped to recount the bills before stowing them away. *Oh, to be a fly on the wall and see Philippe's face as he had to pay out the full amount on each slip.*

When the last worker had left patting his pocket, Jacques strode out with a spring in his step. Sam liked the way he walked. He was hard to ignore. Being the only professional woman on site was hard, but it had its compensations. She loved being surrounded by burly, grumpy men, most of whom she could wrap around her finger just by looking at them from under her eyelashes like a certain princess.

'How did it go?' she said.

'Fine. Everybody got paid in full.'

'And Philippe?'

'Have you got any tissues?'

She guffawed.

'I think it would be better if I stayed away,' she said.

The presence of Jacques during the payments to the labourers had stymied Philippe, who ground his teeth with frustration. That bloody woman! He couldn't figure out how she did it. She appeared to be a pushover, but she had a core of steel.

He had hoped she would try to fire people and come up against the Lumbono labour laws. They were so biased in favour of the worker that no company had ever won a case in the labour court. Instead, she was like a strict head teacher who went around locking doors to rooms she didn't want the children to be in, herding them down the corridor to the classroom and handing out gold stars for good behaviour.

She had his hitherto ally, Moussa Dueme, in the palm of her hand. He practically offered her his belly for scratching. *How do you fight that?* He brought his fist crashing down on the desk and reached for the phone. He dialled with some trepidation, but he was desperate.

'Hello, boss, it's me.'

'Jesus, Philippe! How many times have I told you not to call me at home?'

Charlie Okito's voice, incandescent with rage.

'She's a problem, boss. I don't know how long it will take, but I think your time is up.'

'You do, do you?' An exquisite sarcasm invaded Okito's tone. 'Don't you dare say that, scum. It's your job to bring her down. Do I have to replace you?'

'No.'

'Are you sure? Because I can get you fired tomorrow.'

'It's not that, boss. I was hoping you could give me some advice.'

'Do I have to do everything myself? What colour is she? What colour are you? Compile a dossier of her racist acts and send them to head office. You know how sensitive they are about diversity. The government is pressing hard for black takeovers of mining projects.'

'But she isn't racist, she—'

'I don't give a fuck. Make something up, you idiot. Send me some incidents and I'll see if I can get attention directed at the racist in charge of Masaibu.'

Sam glanced up as Frik and Bruno entered her office.

'Good morning, gentlemen. Sit down please.'

The two men sat on the chairs facing her desk. Bruno, eager, perched on the front of his. Frik, sullen with arms folded, leaned against the chair back. A contrast in attitudes she hoped to change.

'Great, okay let's get started. You'll be glad to hear that head office has re-ordered the parts for the heavy machinery, and they should be here in a week,' said Sam.

'You beauty! How did you wangle that?' said Frik.

'I told them it was essential and put my foot down,' said Sam. 'Which one is the most urgent?'

'The bulldozer is vital.'

'Can you move it into the garage and get it prepped for maintenance?'

'We'll get on it straight away.'

Frik let out a sigh of contentment and rubbed his hands together.

113

'Bruno, I've got permission to build the kitchen you designed.'

'What kitchen?' said Frik, glaring at Bruno, who shrank away.

'Bruno's an architect. I asked him to design one for me to tack on to the back of the canteen. The present arrangement is dangerous and unhygienic. It has to go,' said Sam.

'You're an architect?' Frik's manner underwent a sea-change. He turned to Bruno with frank interest. 'Why didn't you tell me? I have loads of projects just waiting for someone to design and cost them. Oh, my word. I didn't see that coming.'

Bruno squirmed. He couldn't look at Frik or Sam. His cheeks were pink with pleasure. The volte face in attitude fascinated Sam. Frik was a simple man, hardworking and gruff. Someone who took things at face value. His whole demeanour changed as he engaged with the plan.

'What do you think?' said Sam. 'Can you schedule it?'

'Absolutely,' said Frik. He slapped Bruno's leg hard. 'Have you got the funds?' he said.

'Yes, you can start straight away,' said Sam.

'We must move the present canteen and kitchens next door to the communal building. It has an identical layout so it shouldn't be difficult,' said Frik.

'If it's identical, why don't we adapt the communal building instead? That way we don't have disruptions,' said Sam.

'We could lay the piping and drainage on the back patio and cement the lot in place. Do you have the layout plan, Bruno?'

'Yes, sir. I calculated the voltages and the metres of wire and pipe too.'

'Will we need a bigger generator?' said Sam, hoping the answer was negative.

'No. We have massive overcapacity on site in anticipation of a project expansion that did not materialise,' said Frik.

'Okay, can you get the new sparky to deal with that, please? How's he working out?' said Sam.

'Fantastic. I forgot to thank you. The lads are learning a huge amount from him,' said Frik.

'That's great news. And just for good measure, I got us some cash for maintenance on the site accommodation. Can you please start on Alain's quarters first as he is on leave? I'd like that finished as soon as possible. Could you make a list of the fixtures and fittings you'll need and get Moussa to order them from Uganda, please? I think most rooms will need fridges and televisions,' said Sam.

'Televisions?' said Frik.

'Yes, I'm ordering satellite television so we can watch the sport on our day off. Is that okay?'

'Brilliant.'

Frik stood up.

'Hang on. We're not finished yet.'

Frik sat down again, but this time mirroring Bruno's attentive state.

'Health and safety programmes have almost shrunk to nothing on site.'

Frik went to interrupt, but Sam put her hand up to stop him.

'Dr Ntuli has been lax on this matter, but it is no excuse to stop doing safety training.'

'Where's the Dr? If he is a doctor,' said Frik.

Sam ignored the slur.

'I sent him to do an intensive refresher course in the Ntezi project. He should be back next week, full of new ideas. Please be tolerant if he is overenthusiastic at first. But meanwhile, I want you to restart the daily toolbox talks.'

Frik and Bruno regarded each other in embarrassment.

'Safety talks. In the morning. Daily...' Sam trailed off but recovered. 'Okay. A toolbox talk is a short talk about an aspect of safety that affects your working environment. So, for example, tomorrow you could talk about having a clean floor area, tidying away trip hazards like pipes or wiring. The next day, hygiene, washing your hands after going to the bathroom and before eating. We can write out a list of topics.'

'No, that won't be necessary. We've got this covered, haven't we, Bruno?'

'Yes, sir, Mr Els.'

Bruno beamed, a smile that lit the office.

Chapter 14

The next day, Sam and Hans took a drive around town to monitor the sites that bought artisanal gold. They were illegal, but the amounts sold to them were pitiful and Sam was loath to get them shut down just to prove a point.

On their way back to site, they drove past the hospital. Sam spotted Mbala Samba, the mayor's wife sitting on a concrete bollard weeping her heart out.

'Stop. It's Mbala,' said Sam.

'We shouldn't get involved,' said Hans. 'It will only bring trouble.'

'We are involved. Stop the car.'

He pulled into the side of the road so Sam could get out. She went up to Mbala and crouched down beside her. Hans stood behind her, impotent in the face of such pain.

'Mbala. It's me. Sam. What's wrong?'

Mbala raised her head and sighed. Tears coursed down her cheeks and dripped onto the pavement.

'My sister. She died.'

'Oh no. I'm so sorry. How awful. What happened? Wasn't she having a baby?' said Sam.

'She was. They cut her open to take it out because it was stuck. She contracted an infection after the operation and died this morning.'

'And the baby?' said Hans.

'Also, dead.'

Mbala wailed in sorrow. Sam tried to comfort her, but the bollard made it awkward. Hans stepped forward and picked Mbala up in one movement. He put her into the front seat of the car, locking the seatbelt over her damp chest.

They drove her home to the house on the hill. Hans carried her inside following Victor Samba who shrank from sorrow at the news, his head sinking into his shoulders with grief.

'Can you wait for me?' said Victor. 'We need to discuss the hospital. This can't go on.'

Sam sat on the steps listening to the dry chirping of the crickets. The air was full of dust and smelt like rotten leaves. Hans leaned against the car smoking a cigarette. His face betrayed the struggle he was having to control his emotions. Then she remembered.

'Jacques told me you lost your wife a few years ago,' said Sam. 'I'm sorry.'

Hans whirled around as if she had fired a gun at him, his eyes wide. He appeared thunderstruck as if caught doing something forbidden.

'It was an accident,' he said. 'A plane crash.'

'You must miss her.'

He stared at her as if looking for a trap in her words. Finding none, he sighed. A sad sound.

'I do. Every day.'

He turned away. Sam searched for something to say, but was saved by the appearance of Victor Samba, who had tear tracks on his cheeks.

'I'm so sorry about your wife's sister. You must be devastated,' said Sam.

'We're stunned, but not surprised. If you go to that hospital, you're likely to come out in a coffin,' said Victor.

'But don't Consaf pay a monthly supplement to improve it as part of the community programme?' said Sam.

'Unfortunately, the money is absorbed with no visible results,' said Victor, unable to look her in the eye.

'Can you take me to see it?' said Sam.

'I wouldn't recommend it. You might pick up a disease,' said Hans.

'It can't be that bad,' said Sam.

'It's worse,' said Hans. 'Like the gates of hell.'

'Don't exaggerate. Anyway, I need to go,' said Sam.

'We can visit tomorrow,' said Victor.

'Do we need permission?'

'As the mayor of Masaibu, I'm entitled to do an inspection whenever I feel like it,' said Victor. 'Can you meet me at the gates mid-morning?'

'I'll be there. Please let me know if we can help with Mbala.'

Victor shrugged and returned indoors.

Sam and Hans drove back to the camp in silence. The air was thick with unspoken words. Hans smoked with quiet desperation like a man who needed to be alone to cry. Sam did not want to intrude on his thoughts. Her own fought for supremacy inside her head.

How could this happen? The mayor appeared weighed down by guilt or remorse. *Did he absorb the money meant for the hospital? Or was he just powerless when confronted by his wife's grief?* She didn't know whether to feel sorry or furious.

Sam needed to be alone to digest the morning's events but to her chagrin, she could see Jean Delacroix waiting in her office, his back to the window. He had draped himself on the visitor's chair, limbs too long for comfort.

When Sam entered, he jumped up, dropping a book on the floor. Sam bent over to pick it up,

119

almost knocking heads with him. She wasn't in the mood for a visit, social or otherwise but she composed her features.

'Good afternoon, Jean. What can we do for WCO today?'

'I bear good tidings...' He hesitated, as he caught the strain on her face. 'And from your expression, you could do with some. What's up?'

'The mayor's sister-in-law died in childbirth at the hospital,' said Sam. 'The baby died too. Victor and his wife are in mourning.'

'That's awful, if predictable. Why did she go there? It's a death sentence.'

'I don't understand. What's wrong with the hospital?'

'You haven't been?'

'No, but I'm planning on a visit tomorrow morning,' said Sam.

'Prepare yourself for a nasty shock.'

'Is it that bad?'

'Worse,' said Jean, screwing up his face in disgust.

'Why are you here?' said Sam, desperate for him to leave.

'The extra rangers. I had a chat with head office, and they are one hundred per cent behind the idea. I don't know why we didn't think of it before, but we'll need help with the funding.'

'The stakeholders will have to agree to pay for them from the Consaf community fund. I'll get permission at the next meeting.'

'It won't be as easy as you expect. Nobody around here cares about wildlife, except to eat.'

'There's only one way to find out,' said Sam. 'I'm sorry but I'm not feeling social right now. The wind has been knocked out of my sails by the death of Mbala's sister.'

'No problem. I was in town anyway. I wanted to keep you posted.'

Jean pushed the small book across the table as he stood up to leave.

'You might like this,' he said.

She picked it up. The Beetles of West Africa. To her surprise, a beetle similar to the one she had found was on the cover. She had put it on the windowsill in her cabin. Before she could remark on it, he was leaving, holding the door open until she noticed him go.

'Let me know if you suggest any changes. I put our fax number at the bottom of the page of regulations,' said Jean.

'Okay, thanks for the book.'

Sam worked late on an email to Dirk, filling him in on the plans for the kitchen and her projected visit to the hospital. She was careful not to mention any wildlife, even though she was dying to tell him about the beetle book.

Finally, she shut down her computer and left her office intending to sit outside on the porch and stargaze for a few minutes to rest her eyes before going to bed. Not a single cloud interrupted her view of the sky which resembled a planetarium. She stood transfixed; her head tilted to the stars.

A cough told her she had company. Half hidden in the shadow, Hans lounged at a table with a bottle of whisky and a bowl of ice in front of him. It was only afterwards it occurred to Sam that there were two glasses on the table. She jumped.

'I didn't see you there,' she said.

'Will you join me for a sundowner?' said Hans.

'It's a bit late for that, but yes please,' said Sam, pulling up a chair.

'Ice? Well, ice and water. It doesn't last long in this heat.'

'Perfect, thanks,' said Sam.

He handed her a tall glass filled almost to the brim with whisky and icy water.

'It's only red label, I'm afraid,' said Hans.

'It's good. I didn't realise how much I needed a drink. It's a tough gig out here.'

Sam took the glass, cool in the heat, and relaxed. She leaned back against her chair, peering again at the blanket of stars hanging over Masaibu. They sat in the dark without speaking much for over an hour. Just drinking whisky and muttering about work. Every now and then Hans would bark out a laugh at something she said. It was nice.

She was thinking that it was time to go to bed when Hans fixed her with one of his wolf-like stares. It made her uncomfortable to be scrutinised so closely.

'What?' she said.

'You're beautiful,' he said.

'Don't be silly. That's the whisky talking,' said Sam, biting her lip.

'No, not beautiful outside. Beautiful inside. Brave and stubborn and intelligent.'

Sam couldn't decide if she was insulted or not. It was a strange sensation. This was how prey felt.

'Um, thank you. I think.' She stood up. 'I have to go now. I enjoyed our drink.'

Hans stood up too. He stretched out an arm and pulled her close to him. She looked into his eyes expecting to see lust and saw only sorrow.

'You are like her,' he said.

He did not try to kiss her and she drew away again.

'Goodnight, Hans,' she said and went down the stairs where she almost bumped into Jacques who was standing at the bottom. *How long had he been there?*

'Oops,' she said, and kept walking.

'You're some hypocrite,' said Jacques, as they walked to their prefabs.

'All's fair in love and war. You should know that,' said Hans.

'You don't even like her.'

Hans stopped and faced him.

'And you do? You're married.'

Hans turned away and sighed, a long sad sigh. 'She reminds me of Helga,' he said.

Jacques put his hand onto his friend's shoulder.

'I'm sorry. I should've known. Sam is like her. I can see that,' he said.

'I'm not trying to seduce her. I just get comfort from the way she is,' said Hans.

'Okay, let's call a truce. It would be better if neither of us gets too close. Just in case. If we have a crisis, we must be able to think clearly.'

'You're right. I let my guard down. It won't happen again.' Hans smiled.

'Brothers for life?'

'Of course.'

Chapter 15

The next morning, Hans and Jacques didn't sit with her at breakfast as usual. Instead they ate side by side with Frik and Bruno. Her breakfast lost its taste as she ate alone with her thoughts. It was hard not to feel resentful. *How is this my fault? It wasn't me who set up a whisky ambush.*

The truth of the matter was that she needed her security men to be friends and to depend one hundred per cent on each other. If that meant she became isolated, so be it. She picked at her food unwilling to think about the day ahead. *Could the hospital really be that bad?* She was about to find out.

Ezekiel dropped Sam at the hospital gates. The mayor waited for her with ill-concealed impatience. He had deep bags under his eyes and his handshake was feeble.

'How is Mbala?' said Sam.

'Sad, very sad. She sends you regards.' He wiped his eyes which had filled with spontaneous tears. 'Let's go. Don't touch anything.'

A porter in a filthy uniform opened the gate, and they entered a compound surrounded by a breeze block wall lined with wilting trees. A row of dustbins leaned against the wall. Bloody bandages dangled outside their lids attracting swarms of flies. The air smelt of sewage. Sam turned away from the gruesome site, her stomach heaving.

The hospital comprised a series of parallel bungalows in two rows on either side of a concrete path. The walls of the bungalows had iron stains crawling down to ground level from gutters hanging loose in their fittings. Large cracks crisscrossed the bare earth and plastic bags glided around in hot zephyrs of air.

They entered the first bungalow, which housed the staff room and reception. A metal reception desk, piled high with mildewed files, languished in the gloom. The porter pushed open the door to the staff room which had frosted glass panes, two of which were missing. It was full of people in blue or white housecoats smoking, drinking coffee and playing cards. No one noticed them when they entered, or if they did, they didn't care.

'Where is the administrator?' said the mayor, frowning at the scene.

A plump, self-satisfied man with a goatee stood up from the table still holding his cards.

'Good morning, Mr Mayor. What brings you here? Who's the lovely lady?' he said.

'My name is Sam Harris. I'm the General Manager of the Masaibu project. I'd like to see where you are spending our donation, please,' said Sam.

Her no-nonsense tone of voice cut through the room, silencing the occupants. The mayor rocked back on his heels as if he had discovered a cliff at his feet. When the administrator glanced to him for help, he shrugged and jutted his chin out at Sam.

'Of course, Mrs Harris,' said the administrator, recovering.

'It's Miss but you can call me Mama Sam.'

'This way please, Mama Sam.'

The administrator led the way out of the bungalow, his thighs slapping together in their polyester flannels. There was a large stain on the back of his housecoat the colour of vomit. Sam scanned the ground but spotted a discarded syringe, instead making her feel sicker.

'Let's start at the malaria ward,' said the administrator.

He opened the door to hell. It was worse than Sam could ever have imagined. The overpowering smell of sweat and urine brought bile to her mouth. The floor was sticky with bodily fluids and there were stains of blood and vomit on the walls. Sam had to peel her feet off the floor to walk across the filthy linoleum. She struggled to keep her breakfast down. Lucky she hadn't finished it.

'Sweet Jesus,' she said. Her head swam with horror. She looked to the mayor for his reaction but he stared into space as if he was trying to be somewhere else.

Basic metal beds lined the ward, many of them without mattresses. Those that did had thin sponge pads poking out of ripped, stained covers. None of the beds had linen or pillows. Their occupants were lying or sitting on the thin mattresses and bare metal supports. Most of the beds had two or more occupants, skinny women wrapped in sweat-soaked material, with babies at their flat breasts. A thin wailing broke the silence.

When the visitors entered, the women surveyed them as if hoping for a doctor or a relative among them to bring succour. One woman pushed herself to a standing position and tottered over to them. She tugged at Sam's sleeve.

'Matibabu,' she said. 'Tafadhali nipe dawa.'

Sam shrunk from her touch.

'What's she saying?' Sam asked the mayor.

'She's begging you for treatment, medicine.'

'But where are the nurses and doctors?' she said.

'In the staff room,' said the mayor.

126

'Why aren't they—'

But the administrator had set off again leading them through a couple of wards of similar horror before Sam had had enough. But there was one place they hadn't visited, and she needed to know the whole truth.

'I'd like to see the surgery, please,' she said.

'Okay,' said the administrator whose smug expression was still plastered onto his face.

Sam vomited onto the ground outside the surgery. She couldn't believe what she had just seen. The decrepit operating table, the filthy floor splattered in blood, the plastic bags thrown against the wall with their ghastly contents, made worse by seeing the rusty instruments they were using to operate. *No wonder the patients died.* She coughed up more bile.

The men stood apart from her, embarrassed by her attack of weakness, not wishing to acknowledge it. General managers didn't do that. It was better to pretend they hadn't seen her.

Their reticence gave her time to damp down the incoherent fury threatening to escape her. *Those bastards. How could they sit there playing cards like everything was fine? How many people had they murdered with their casual attitude?* She struggled to regain her composure. She wasn't the only one. The mayor was red-eyed and speechless, shaking his head like a madman. They had to leave but she wasn't finished.

'How often do they clean the wards?' she said to the administrator.

127

'They can't clean. There is no water, and we finished the supplies of detergent and bleach,' he said, shrugging.

'What happened to the water?' said Sam.

'The pump packed up weeks ago. It's past repair,' said the administrator, avoiding her eyes.

'But what about the toilets? Where do people wash?' she said.

'People go behind the wards. We bury the faeces when we get time, or the dogs eat them.'

Sam put her face in her hands and took a deep breath. *Solutions, not problems. Come on, Sam. You can do this.*

'I will send you a replacement pump straight away,' she said. 'My maintenance supervisor will come down and install it this afternoon. He'll take the other one away to fix.'

The administrator shook his head.

'He can't do that,' he stuttered.

'Why not?'

'Someone sold it, stole it, I mean.'

It was even worse than she had imagined.

'Okay. Never mind, we'll cement it in place so no-one can steal this one. I'll investigate the detergent supply,' said Sam.

'We will need gloves. The cleaners will not do their jobs without gloves. I can't make them work if they are not safe,' said the administrator.

'We'll discuss this and get back to you,' said Sam, grabbing the mayor's arm and pushing him towards the gate. They stumbled towards the exit and out onto the street. Sam was still retching. Victor Samba was green and trembling. To Sam's amazement, he shook as sobs wracked his body.

'It's my fault,' he said. 'I killed her.'

'Killed who?' said Sam, but she knew.

'My wife's sister. I take a cut from the hospital money every month.'

128

Sam's mouth fell open. She looked at him in incomprehension.

'But why? Don't you earn enough as Mayor, Victor?'

'Ha! They haven't paid me in eighteen months. The Governor of the Province siphons off the funds. If it wasn't for Consaf, no-one would ever get paid. Even the police are subsidised by your company,' said Victor.

'So that's also happening in the hospital?' said Sam.

'Yes, no-one has been paid so they take the money for medicines and cleaning equipment sent by Consaf. They have families too. They've lost hope, and it's made them immune to the suffering of the patients.'

'How terrible. We must do something about it right away. Let me organise the water pump first, and then I'll come up and see you later, if that's okay.'

The mayor nodded, still sniffing, tear tracks marking his cheeks like slug trails. He shuffled off down the street towards his office in the municipal building. Ezekiel, who had been standing a discrete distance away, opened the car door for Sam.

'What is wrong, Mama Sam?'

'Many things. But we can fix them. Take me to the maintenance yard, please,' she said.

***

Sam found Frik having a cigarette in front of his office.

'Hello, Sam. You look rough. Would you like a cigarette?'

Sam was not keen on cigarettes ninety-nine per cent of the time, but this was different.

'Yes, please. Budge up.'

She sat beside Frik on the steps and he lit her cigarette. He let her smoke half before he spoke again.

'Tough day?'

'You've no idea.'

'Need help?' said Frik.

'The water pump at the hospital has gone AWOL. Do you have a spare here we can donate? A two-inch outlet should be sufficient. It's just for pumping water from a well.'

'You went? No wonder you are under the weather. That place is like a death camp.'

'I'm aware of that now, but we must try to improve conditions in there. We can go elsewhere but our staff and their families have no choice but to use it.'

'My lads won't go there,' said Frik. 'They are afraid.'

'I need your help,' said Sam. 'Can you do without your workforce on Saturday morning?'

'If you leave me the maintenance crews, sure. What's the plan?'

'We will clean the hospital,' said Sam.

'Are you mad? Every germ known to man is lurking in there.' Frik stared at her in horror.

'People are dying. I can't stand by and pretend it's not happening.'

'It's self-inflicted. We pay them to keep it clean, don't we?' He flicked his cigarette across the yard and then thought the better of it and picked it up again.

'It's complicated. Can you do the pump today?' said Sam.

'Yes, we have an old pump that should do the trick.'

'You'll need to cement it in. They stole the last one.'

'Don't worry. I wasn't born yesterday,' said Frik

'Thanks,' said Sam.

'You watch yourself. People don't like change.'

'Stoddard's? It's Sam Harris.'

'Sam, it's Rahul Singh. I was just thinking about you. We boxed your supplies ready to go this evening. Do you need anything else?'

'Yes, please. We plan to clean the local hospital from head to foot on Saturday so I need enough bleach and Jif to float a boat in. Also, can you send six hundred pairs of industrial strength rubber gloves, medium and large sizes?'

'That's some undertaking. Do you need mops and scrubbing brushes and so on?'

'Send me six dozen of each and lots of strong cloths. Anything you think necessary,' said Sam.

'You're not doing it yourself?' said Rahul.

'I can't ask anyone to do something I wouldn't. So, yes, I am.'

'I'll send some knee pads.'

'Thanks, Rahul.'

'You're a trooper.'

'Let's hope I can persuade my workforce to muck in and I'm not left cleaning on my own.'

It was with some trepidation that Sam knocked on the door of Ngoma Itoua, the union leader the next day. His face wore a sour expression during the morning meetings as if he had just bitten into a lemon. He did not contribute to the discussions except to object to every change that Sam proposed, no matter how favourable to the workforce. She had suggested they have a weekly meeting in her office, but he never turned up.

'Come in.'

Ngoma was sitting behind a desk with a word processor on it, typing with two fingers. He hit each key with the caution of a cat patting a snake.

'Good morning,' said Sam.

'If it is a good morning, which I doubt. What do you want?'

'Have you ever been to the hospital?'

Itoua's brow furrowed, and he frowned, his eyebrows almost meeting.

'As a patient?' he said.

'In any capacity,' said Sam.

'God, no, I'd never go there. I don't want to die. Why do you ask?'

'I visited yesterday because the mayor's sister-in-law died in childbirth.'

'You took in the state of it? Shocking, isn't it?' said Ngoma.

'It's horrific. We should do something.'

'We? Since when were we on the same side?' His lip curled.

'Look, labour relations in Masaibu aren't on the best footing, but I've asked you for a weekly meeting to improve them, and you've never come.'

'It's a waste of time,' he said, sneering.

'How do you know if we don't discuss it? I can't solve the issues if I don't know what they are.'

'What have you done for us?' said Itoua.

He folded his arms and glared at her.

'I stopped Philippe from taxing the casual staff.'

'That was you? Didn't security do that?'

'And who do you think gave security the order to police the payments?' said Sam.

'Oh.' Itoua pursed his lips and fiddled with a pencil. 'What did you want to do?'

'I'd like to speak to the workers about cleaning the hospital. Can you organise a meeting for tomorrow first thing please?'

'They won't go there. They are afraid.'

'It will be a free choice. I promise,' said Sam.

'Okay, tomorrow at eight outside the maintenance sheds.'

Ngoma turned his face back to the screen and the meeting was over.

Stoddard's lorry turned up at the gates of Masaibu camp at sundown. Hans put his head around the door of Sam's office. He was smiling.

'Did you forget to tell me something?' he said.

Sam raised an eyebrow in enquiry.

'There's a truck outside from Stoddard's. Anything to do with you?'

'Oh! Yes. Gosh, didn't I tell you?' said Sam.

Hans shook his head in disbelief.

'No, you didn't. I think the shit is about to hit the fan.'

'I wouldn't miss this for the world,' she said, standing up. 'Let's go then.'

Sam walked down to the main gates with Hans. The security woman who had tried to steal Sam's belongings when she first arrived poked around in the back of the truck with the air of a child in a toy store. Hans banged on the back door making her jump with fright.

'You shouldn't inspect the contents of the delivery truck,' said Hans. 'That is not your job. You should only search the outgoing traffic. Don't make me tell you again.'

The woman stuck out her bottom lip and got out of the truck, making herself small as if avoiding a blow. Hans slammed the doors shut and went to talk to the driver.

'Please, can you drive to the Canteen over there on the square?' he said. 'It's the green building with a tarred roof.'

He took his radio out of his holster. 'Frik, come in please, over.'

'What's up Hans? Over.'

'Can you send a team of men to the canteen to unload the food delivery, please? Four or five will do, straight away if you can. Over.'

'Roger. I've got people right here. I'll send them straight away. Over and out.'

By the time the truck had manoeuvred its way around the square and parked outside the canteen, five workers were standing outside waiting for instructions.

Hans positioned himself beside the truck and Sam waited indoors directing operations and wiping the shelving down to receive the fresh food. She moved all the local flyblown food to one shelf and stacked the tins on another. The fresh vegetables smelled wonderful, and she popped some fruit into her pocket for later. She packed the meat into the freezers with care, dedicating one for the old chickens and smoked fish, and the other for the fresh meat that had arrived.

Mama Sonia waddled into the canteen as they were about to leave, wheezing and puffing with effort. She leaned against the table fighting for breath before turning on Hans.

'What's going on?' she said, pushing her face inches from his. 'How dare you go over my head? Who authorised this?'

'Excuse me?' said Sam, who had been in the larder. 'This is the order you gave to Moussa Dueme. You authorised it.'

Mama Sonia did a double take. Her mouth opened and shut but no sound came out.

'Who brought the food here? I am supposed to go with Moussa Dueme to collect it,' she said

'The truck broke down. I asked Stoddard to deliver the order instead.'

'But this is irregular. I must go to Uganda and choose the food myself.'

'I've supervised the unloading, and it's of excellent quality,' said Sam. 'I intend to ask Rahul Singh to organise a delivery once a week on their run to Lumbono. You may write the list of provisions that you require and give it to Mr Dueme, and he will fax it to Stoddard's. Anyway,' she said in fake comradery, 'you're far too important and busy to waste two days a week shopping in Uganda.'

'But...'

'That's okay. Don't thank me. I'm always trying to make your life easier, Mama S,' said Sam with a wink, and before the startled woman could reply, she waltzed out of the canteen with Hans following. One worker hopped into the cab of the truck with Hans and they headed off to take the cleaning gear to the stores. Behind them, Mama Sonia punched the wall in frustration, her entire world crumbling.

'Arrogant bitch! You'll live to regret this,' she muttered and stomped off to Philippe's office.

Chapter 16

S ilence fell over the packed yard as Sam
mounted the steps to the maintenance office.
She turned to face the workers, a mixture of trade
and labourers. They were not accustomed to being
called for a meeting that didn't lead to a strike.
Ngoma Itoua, the union leader, stood beside her
leading to further speculation.

'What's he doing here?' said one.

'She's resigning,' said another.

'Who told you that?'

'Shh, she's about to speak.'

Sam took a deep breath. Public speaking was not
something at which she excelled but she needed
to do this in person. Her sincerity could not be in
doubt if she were to persuade them.

'Bonjour,' she said, her voice quaking despite
herself.

'Bonjour, Mama Sam,' they chorused back, the
goodwill tangible. She must harness it.

'This morning I have a dilemma for you, one with
which you can help me. But first, I need you to raise
your hand if you know someone who died in the
Masaibu hospital.'

One by one, the hands rose. A horrifying visual
proof of the carnage wreaked by the medical

institute. It rendered Sam speechless for a second. She gulped and bit her lip.

'Okay. So, almost everyone. That's terrible. I am so sorry. You may know the mayor lost his sister-in-law this week. I have spoken to him and we are acting to prevent more deaths.'

'What can you do?'

'They are murderers.'

'It is a black hole which swallows our people.'

'I agree. We must do something. I have a plan, but I need your help,' she said. 'We must clean the hospital ourselves.'

A roar went up from the crowd, disapproval, fear, fury and disbelief. When the hubbub had died down, one electrician stepped forward. He was a shop steward and a much-respected member of the workforce.

'You want us to go in there?' he said. 'We'll die too.'

'No one will die. We've fixed the water pump and bought cleaning supplies from Uganda. Everyone will have a pair of industrial rubber gloves,' said Sam.

'Is it compulsory?' shouted someone.

'No,' said Sam.

'Will you be cleaning too?' said another.

Sam bristled.

'Yes, I will disinfect the toilets,' she said. *Oh God, what have I said?*

'You? I don't believe it.'

'If I clean the toilets, will you help sterilise the rest of the hospital?'

'Yes, Mama Sam. I'll do it.'

'Me too.'

'We'll go on Saturday morning instead of working here. No one will have to enter if they don't want to, but remember, if we can disinfect the hospital, people will survive instead of dying. I can't promise we'll save everyone, but it'll make a big difference,' said Sam.

'They'll just let it get dirty again,' said the electrician.

'No. No, they won't,' said Sam. 'I'll organise an inspection of the premises to take place every month before we pay the supplement. If the hospital is not spotless, we won't pay. Consaf will provide the cleaning materials. What do you say?'

'Clean the hospital. Clean the hospital. We will clean the hospital,' chanted someone, and soon everyone joined him, their rich voices swelling and filling the courtyard with sound.

A lump threatened to block Sam's throat. *Let's see how proud you are when you have to clean the toilets.*

'Okay then, we'll meet at eight o'clock on Saturday morning at the gates of the hospital.'

Ngoma Itoua put his hand on her shoulder. 'Is it true, Mama Sam? Will you clean the toilets?'

'Yes, I keep my promises, even when I wish I hadn't made them.'

She raised a rueful face to him. He beamed.

'I too will clean the toilets. We'll do it together,' said Ngoma.

'Wow! Brilliant. Thank you. I'm blessed,' said Sam.

'No, we are. It's the first time I ever felt positive about the project.'

⁂

Victor Samba and his wife were sitting side by side on their balcony in the moonlight when Sam and Jacques drove up to the house. They were holding hands and Mbala had tears on her cheeks. The mayor stood up and came downstairs to greet them, ushering them up to sit on the wicker chairs which flanked the settee.

'Sorry about the lack of light,' he said. 'There's a power cut, and I forgot to buy diesel.'

'Everything's better by moonlight,' said Jacques. He touched Mbala's arm. 'I'm so sorry for your loss.'

She bowed her head but did not reply, the suffering etched on her face.

'What's up, Sam?' said the mayor. 'You said you had an idea.'

'Two,' said Sam. 'I hope you will like them, both of you.'

'Let's hear it,' said the mayor. 'We could do with good news.'

'The workforce of Masaibu has agreed to clean the hospital on Saturday instead of working at site. We bought a large stock of cleaning materials,' said Sam.

'What about the water supply?' said the mayor

'Maintenance installed a new water pump yesterday.'

'Are you going too, Sam?' said Mbala.

'I promised to clean the toilets in a moment of bravado. Ngoma Itoua, the union leader, has offered to join me.'

'Then I too will do it. It is a fitting penance for me. I am so desperate to atone for my part in the tragedy,' said the mayor. He paused. 'Will there be gloves?'

Sam laughed. 'Industrial strength,' she said, 'but that's not the only thing I wanted to discuss. What's the point cleaning the hospital if they revert to playing cards and drinking coffee instead of disinfecting the floors? We need to make sure they keep it spotless. Someone should supervise the purchase of the cleaning products and the daily routine of the hospital cleaners.'

'That's a great idea, but who would do this?' said the mayor.

'Well, that's the second part of the plan. Mbala would be perfect for the job,' said Sam. She glanced at him uncertain of the reaction. There was a long silence. *Had she gone too far?* The intention was to replace the mayor's lost income, but she had not considered the consequences of offering his wife paid work. *Would this break any cultural taboos? She should have checked.*

At last, Mbala spoke. 'I would love to honour my sister this way. She would've been so proud.' Her eyes filled with tears and she tugged at the sleeves of her dress.

'You'll work with Dr Ntuli, the head of health and safety at Masaibu. He's not a medical doctor, but he's a good man and he's just returned from intensive training courses at Ntezi. You can get good advice from him on the best way to proceed,' said Sam. 'You'll need to register with Philippe in Human Resources on Monday. He'll find out what salary grade corresponds to the position and make sure it's okay with you. Don't let him suggest any discounts.'

'What do you say, my husband?' said Mbala.

'I'm unable to speak. My pride is too great, wife. Your sister will rest in peace,' said the mayor.

They embraced and Victor kissed Mbala with great tenderness on her forehead. Sam experienced a wave of jealousy. *What must it be like to be loved like that? Why had Fergus given up on her?* She sighed.

'Are you okay?' said Jacques.

'Yes, just tired. Let's go home.'

Breakfast the next morning was a revelation: bacon, eggs, butter, milk and coffee, even yoghurt. Sam put more on her plate than she could eat. Mama Sonia had the look of a volcano pre-eruption. Metaphorical smoke came out of her ears while Sam scoffed the delicious food. Hans was ecstatic.

'Proper coffee. I can't believe it,' he said, smacking his lips and slurping.

'Mood improving,' said Jacques.

They had gotten over their huff and were sitting with her again. Sam glanced around the room. The faces of her management team had approval written across them. *An army marches on its stomach. Everyone knows that.* She wandered over to the table containing Frik and Bruno and several of the other staff who were in the habit of bullying the latter.

'Good morning, gentlemen. Please don't get up. I hope you are enjoying your breakfasts.'

Lots of nodding and grunts of agreement from men with their mouths full.

'Frik, I'd like a tour of the kitchen installation after the morning meeting if that's okay with you?'

'No problem.'

'Bruno, your technical drawings have been fantastic. Congratulations on doing such a good job. I need more men like you around here.'

Bruno almost choked on his food. He blushed so deeply that he turned purple. The other men at the table appraised him with surprise and a new appreciation.

'You designed the new kitchen?' said one.

'I don't believe it,' said another.

141

'He's an architect,' said Sam, 'and an excellent one.'

She left Bruno basking in the glow of her compliment. *That should do it. I hate bullies.*

As she had expected, the morning meeting was a bad-tempered affair. Philippe was out to get her.

'Mama Sonia has been to see me. She says you insulted her by ordering the supplies delivered to site. I consider you to have demoted her, which, under the labour law, is illegal and racist,' said Philippe quivering with resentment.

'Mama Sonia is not being demoted. She is too senior to waste her time driving around buying vegetables in Uganda. Dr Ntuli is implementing a health and safety regime to operate in the new kitchens. I need her to train the staff and make sure everyone understands how the new equipment works. They are not used to electrical ovens or rings, and without the proper training could have nasty accidents. Mama Sonia is responsible for the wellbeing of her staff and looking after health and safety should be a large part of her duties as manager of catering. I am making sure the staff who work under her can do so without fear of injury,' said Sam.

'The unions will not agree to this,' said Philippe. He turned to Ngoma Itoua, who had been listening with attention. 'You must stop this racist woman mistreating the local staff.'

Itoua raised an eyebrow and sat up straighter in his chair.

'Are you telling me that the safety of our junior staff is of no importance to you? Mama Sam is correct. The company has a comprehensive safety policy that has been ignored or minimised for years to save money. It's a great improvement. Why should it be necessary to go to Uganda for supplies when they can be delivered to the door? I can't agree with you. I've seen no evidence of racism, and I can assure you I'd be the first to act.'

Philippe wasn't finished. He refocused his attention on Sam, sweat beading on his lip.

'You didn't inform me that you've ordered the workforce to clean the hospital on Saturday instead of working. This is a blatant exploitation and I won't allow it.'

'I gave no such order. I asked for help and the workforce agreed.'

'As if they have any choice. I don't suppose we'll see you down there.'

'Actually...' said Sam.

'Sam and I have volunteered to clean the toilets,' said Itoua, before Sam defended herself. 'Are you coming?'

The stunned expression on Philippe's face reminded Sam of a haddock on the fish counter at the supermarket. His mouth gaped open, showing his bright yellow teeth and gold fillings. He recovered enough to blurt out 'no way'.

The faces around the table showed a mixture of emotions. Doubt, fear, rebellion and stubborn expressions radiated from her team.

'It isn't compulsory. Anyone who feels unable to join in with the clean-up may work as normal. However, your teams may expect you to set an example so you need to discuss it with them, please,' said Sam.

The managers left the meeting muttering, but Sam refused to be intimidated. By the time she finished, they would eat out of her hand. Too many years of easy choices had made them forget about their responsibility to their staff and the local community. If the project was to succeed, this had to change. And now she had an unlikely ally, Ngoma Itoua. *Who would have believed it?*

Frik knocked on her office door.

143

'You ready?'

'Yup, just give me a second,' said Sam.

Sam skimmed the email she was sending to Dirk updating him on the hospital saga and the kitchen palaver. She had left out the stuff about the elephants on the grounds he would categorise it as 'more beetle news'. She pressed send and skipped around the desk to join Frik.

The new kitchen was taking shape. The concrete floor was in, and they had erected the breeze block walls with large holes for window frames and extractor units. There were gaps in the roof intended for skylights. Wires and pipes emerged from the floor beside the walls, waiting to be connected to ovens and fridges.

'How long?' said Sam.

'About ten days. I'll need to shut the kitchen one lunchtime to facilitate the move from one building to another. It will take most of the day.'

'Okay, I'll see what I can arrange. Saturday is the best day for the move. Can you do it next week?

'We should be ready then,' said Frik.

'I'll speak to Ngoma Itoua about sending the casual workers home without lunch next week. That way we only need to feed our full-time staff at lunchtime. Let me know if you won't be ready in time.'

'Sure.'

'How about Alain's room? He's back tomorrow, you know,' said Sam.

'Tomorrow. Shit. I forgot. It's only half done. Can you put him somewhere else for the night? I should be ready the day after tomorrow,' said Frik.

'Okay, I'll ask the geologists if he can bunk with them for the night.'

'Sorry about that. We are at full stretch with the kitchen.'

'That reminds me. I must get Dr Ntuli on the job. Mama Sonia needs to train her staff before the kitchen opens.'

Frik shook his head in admiration.

'Good luck with that,' he said.

Chapter 17

At first light on Saturday morning, Sam climbed into an old pair of overalls and wellington boots she had borrowed from the stockroom. Feeling sick with anticipation, she shoved her hair into a tight bun under a bright cotton turban. She made herself a cup of tea and ate a banana in her room, afraid that any additional breakfast would soon decorate the floor of the toilets. *You have changed many revolting nappies. This is no different.*

Ezekiel drove Sam and Ngoma Itoua, the union manager, to the hospital and dropped them off. Someone ran up to shout abuse at Sam but Ngoma placed himself in front of her and he glared. Ezekiel leaned out of the window.

'I'm sorry, Mama Sam. I want to do this but I can't face it.'

'That's okay, Ezekiel. Come and help Moussa distribute the gloves and cleaning materials instead.'

'Ready?' said Ngoma.

'The gateway to hell,' said Sam.

They set up a trestle table outside the reception bungalow and piled it high with gloves and bleach and scrubbing brushes. Workers trickled in at first, but soon a stream of them queued up for their materials. At eight o'clock, with the vast majority

146

ready to go, Sam and Ngoma headed for the toilets, followed by the entire group. *Were they making sure she kept her end of the bargain?*

'Oh my God,' said Ngoma, as the stench of sewage reached him. They had not even opened the door yet. Sam tried not to breathe through her nose and grabbed the handle. The scene that awaited them was so disgusting she almost ran away but she remained rooted to the spot trying to assess the situation and fighting the instinct to flee.

'We should start at the far wall and work our way to the door,' she said. 'They have restored the water supply, so we could try flushing the toilets a few times first.'

But it soon became clear that the toilets were full of dry faeces and paper stuffed to the brim. If she flushed them, it would flood the floor making the situation worse. There was no escape from the smell that penetrated their pores and sat in their nostrils. *What have I done?*

Sam stumbled outside to get a plastic rubbish bag and a tire iron from the stunned audience and re-entered before she lost courage. She dug at the excrement and paper with the tire iron, she dislodged lumps of coagulated sewage and forced it into the bag. Ngoma stared at her efforts, aghast. *His turn next, poor man. He must regret their joint show of bravado.*

She made good progress before running outside to retch against the wall. Five hundred pairs of astonished eyes saw her wipe her mouth, take a few deep breaths and push her way back into the toilet.

'Mama Makubwa,' said one.

As if by magic the crowd broke up and groups of men headed for each unit, singing to give themselves the stomach for the job. They helped bewildered patients onto the grass where they sat shivering or lay flat in the dirt.

147

The mayor turned up and scrubbed the floor with the application of a repentant sinner. He stopped to vomit in one of the now flushable toilets. Sam was scrubbing the edges of another with a rag tied around her mouth and nose. Despite their revulsion, the three of them made good progress and soon all the toilets were unblocked and charged with bleach.

'Why don't we leave these to soak for a while and have a go at the operating theatre?' said the mayor.

'Oh God, I don't know if I can face it,' said Ngoma.

'That's okay,' said Sam. 'Get some fresh air and join us when you feel better.'

They walked across to the unit containing the surgery and pushed open the double doors. Sam had already seen the theatre, so she wasn't as shocked as the mayor who shouted obscenities and hit the door with his fist. When he had calmed down, he joined Sam in one corner and they scrubbed the floor with bleach, working their way through the blood stains and rat droppings on the floor. Sam picked up the rusty instruments and threw them into a cardboard box with the plastic bags of human remnants. She had been sick so often already that she could only manage a dry cough now.

Sam got back on her knees and scrubbed her heart out. The mayor blasphemed and shouted his way across the tiles. Suddenly, a bright light illuminated the theatre. A camera crew were filming them. One of the team shoved a microphone under the mayor's nose. Sam held her breath, but Victor Samba was a professional.

He staggered to his feet and explained what they were doing there and how it would help the town. Gesticulating at Sam, he told them that Consaf were responsible for the clean-up. She did not comment and continued to scrub grimly at the floor as if she could erase all the deaths.

By the time she stumbled out into the sunlight, they had returned most of the patients to their wards where extra beds had been installed. New mattresses and pillows lay on every bed covered in cheap nylon sheets with numbers corresponding to their unit written on them in indelible ink. Mosquito nets hung from the ceilings and tanks of clean water with taps sat at the end of each ward. It wasn't perfect, but it was a paradise compared to before.

The workers were sitting and standing outside the units smoking and talking in low voices. Sam reviewed their tired faces and read pride and horror in equal measure.

'Well, done lads. I'm proud of you. Let's go home,' she said.

Alain Folle, the Geology Manager, came back from leave full of enthusiasm for the Masaibu project. After passing through the main gate, he walked towards the accommodation hoping to leave his bag in the room. *Where was everyone?* Saturdays tended to be social with people crowding into site to write up reports and maintain equipment but the place was deserted.

Then Alain spotted Philippe sitting on the porch outside the office building with his feet up on a plastic chair. He greeted him with a wave.

'Hello. This place is like a graveyard. Where is everyone?' said Alain.

'That woman has taken them to clean the hospital. I can't understand why anyone would go with her to that disease-ridden pit,' said Philippe.

'Really? She's not that bad. I've found her to be straightforward.'

'She's a racist cow. How can you support her after what she's done to you?'

'I don't know what you mean.' Alain flushed.

'She's demoted you to the geologists' communal bedroom because she wants your room for a white manager.'

'I don't believe you.'

'Come with me then.'

The two men arrived at Alain's room to find it under full-scale refurbishment, the door blocked by a bench holding several pots of paint.

'See?' said Philippe.

A rising panic gripped Alain by the throat. He pushed past Philippe and strode to the communal room in the next prefab, shoving open the door. To his horror, he recognised his belongings protruding from the tops of cardboard boxes lined up beside a bed at the end of the row.

'She's fair, is she?' said Philippe, who couldn't keep the malicious enjoyment out of his voice. 'You should report her for racism. Imagine putting a manager in with the juniors.'

A red mist descended over Alain. *That hypocritical bitch!* He should have known it was all talk. She must have taken him for such an idiot, sucking up to her like an Uncle Tom. Philippe waited.

'Can we do it now?' said Alain.

'I have the forms in my office,' said Philippe.

Even though she stood under the shower until the water ran cold, and scrubbed herself until she was pink, Sam couldn't rid herself of the odour permeating her being. The filth had ingrained itself on her eyeballs. The injustice of it all stuck in her throat.

Bastards, they were all bastards. But who was at fault? Could you blame people who didn't receive their salaries? Or the people supposed to pay them? Perhaps they didn't get paid either unless they stole salaries belonging to the hospital staff. What a godforsaken country Lumbono was, a genuine hell on earth.

She stayed in her room all day on Sunday with a 'do not disturb' sign on her door, unable to face anyone or talk about what she had seen. Fear that she might rant about the injustices of the system in Lumbono and alienate her management prevented her from voicing her opinions. She mourned in private for all the people who had died in that hellhole.

By the time she emerged on Monday, cleaner and braver, she was starving. She walked over to the canteen holding a precious tea bag in her hand. The door swung open and everyone turned to face her as she entered. Embarrassed, she turned to go again, unable to put up with the scrutiny, but Hans jumped up and pulled out a chair.

'Bloody hell, Sam, you're a celebrity,' he said, and showed her a copy of the local newspaper. To her chagrin, there was a large photograph of her bottom on the front page taken from behind her as she scrubbed the floor.

'Not my best angle,' she said, blushing.

'We all watched you on the television. You're a great leader. Not like the others,' said Bruno and the other managers nodded and smiled.

'Okay, everyone, go to work. I want to eat breakfast in peace,' she said.

They filed out one by one, shaking her hand as they left. Only Jacques and Hans stayed behind, flanking her while she ate, like large grey bodyguards.

Chapter 18

When Alain blanked her at the management meeting, Sam's feelings were hurt. She had been looking forward to seeing him and having cosy chats about greenstone belts and high-grade vein mineralisation. Perhaps he was cross that she had stayed in her room all day on Sunday? Such thoughts soon evaporated as she dealt with the complications of running a project with limited resources.

'I need the bulldozer today,' said Alain.

'You said I could have it,' said Frik, making puppy eyes at her.

'Yes, I did but...' said Sam.

'But I need it more than you.' Alain did not look at Sam, avoiding her plea for compromise.

'It's my turn,' said Frik, as if that was the clincher.

Friends had often asked Sam what it was like to run an exploration project, her stock answer being that it was just like a kindergarten with bigger children. Today was no exception. She sighed in a way that suggested tethers were at their end.

'You can have it first because we need to move the drill there later today. Frik, it's not an emergency. Can you please wait until this afternoon?' she said.

'Okay.' But his face didn't agree.

Give me strength.

Sam blew out her cheeks in the manner of a Frenchman and stared down the managers.

'Any more issues that can't wait? No? Okay. Alain, can you wait here, please?'

The men filed out muttering as usual about the fairness or injustice of her decisions. Sam ignored them. Alain was digging his pen into the surface of the damaged veneer of the meeting table. Sam ignored the implied tantrum.

'Okay, let's go then,' she said.

'I'm busy.' His aggressive tone surprised Sam.

'I need you to come with me anyway.'

A surly expression fixed itself on his face and he followed her with bad grace. As they passed Philippe's office, Sam could see him smirking at her. *What now? He was a nasty piece of work.*

As they neared Alain's room, he stopped dead, confusion written on his face. Sam couldn't read his mood, but she noted his hesitation.

'Come on. I want to show you something,' she said.

He shuffled two steps behind her. She threw open the door of his prefab.

'Ta-dah!' she said and stood back.

He stood there looking at the ground, unable to witness her happy face.

'What's wrong? Don't you like it? I had them paint it in geological colours for you. Look, there are even cork boards for your maps.'

Alain put his hand over his mouth and shut his eyes.

'Oh my God. I'm so sorry. I...'

But he didn't elaborate. Instead, he stepped into the room and glanced around, his eyes wide. He walked over to the boards and fiddled with one of the coloured drawing pins.

'You did this for me?' he said.

'My best manager can't have a shitty cabin. I know which side my bread is buttered,' said Sam.

Alain couldn't speak. He took a deep breath.

'Thank you. I thought...'

'What? Oh, my goodness. Didn't anyone tell you? You can't have believed I put you in the junior room.'

Alain wavered. 'No, of course not. Um, I'm sorry, I've forgotten something important. Thank you so much.'

He ran back towards the office.

'It's too late. I already sent it,' said Philippe, picking his teeth with a paper clip.

'What?'

Alain's face fell.

'Yesterday, by fax.'

'You must tell them it's a mistake,' said Alain.

'I have no intention of doing any such thing. That woman is a menace and we have to get rid of her before she ruins our project.'

'I'll tell her you...' Alain blustered but trailed off.

'You'll tell her what? That you called her a racist and reported her to head office. She'll fire you,' said Philippe.

'But you can't do this.'

'I already did.'

Frik was in his usual spot, smoking a cigarette on the steps of his office.

155

'Did Alain like his room? He was in a funny mood this morning,' he said.

'I think so, thanks. He seemed to be in a panic. Perhaps he's just having a bad day. It's always crap getting back to work after a long break at home,' said Sam.

'That's true. How can I help you?'

'Just wanted to make sure that we are still on schedule to move kitchens on Saturday.'

'Yes, you can inform the ladies that Thunderbirds are go,' said Frik, looking smug.

'Excellent. I'm off to see Dr Ntuli then.' She paused. 'While we're on the subject, how are the toolbox talks going?'

'Much better than I expected. Dr Ntuli is a star, surprising me. The local lads have taken them to heart. Have you seen the workshop?'

She had not. Sam entered the gloomy space and waited for her eyes to adjust. She gasped in admiration. Rows of tools hung in size-sorted order along new parallel lines of hooks across the back wall. Jars of nails and screws jostled for space on the shelving with neat piles of manuals. The concrete floor had a new coating of thick red sealant that was pristine.

'Wow! Congratulations. You could eat your dinner off the floor in there,' she said.

'The lads are thrilled about the spare parts you ordered. They had become apathetic and listless because of their inability to keep the fleet running. It's changed the whole attitude around here,' said Frik.

'I can't believe the change. You must be proud.'

Frik took a long draft of his cigarette.

'You too,' he said.

Sam winked and set off for Dr Ntuli's office. She almost bumped into him coming out with a sheath of paper in his hand.

'I was just coming to see you,' he said. 'I've elaborated a protocol for the kitchens and I was wondering if you could review it before I started the training. Um, I translated it into English for you.'

'Great. I'll send it to the guys in head office for their approval. Thank you. I'm sure it's perfect. I'll read it now and get back to you with any comments. Frik is pleased with the results of your toolbox talks. You're a natural at this,' said Sam.

Dr Ntuli managed a shy smile.

'Thank you. I'm enjoying it much more than I imagined. I was afraid of being inadequate for the position.'

'On the contrary. Ah, and I need your help with something. Mbala Samba, the mayor's wife, will join us as hospital liaison, making sure it is kept spotless and doing inspections once a month. Can you do some research into the protocols for disinfection for me? You could take a trip to the capital to visit a modern hospital.'

'I'll speak with her first and we can make a plan,' said Dr Ntuli.

'Okay, I'll get back to you with comments later today.'

Sam walked back to the office building with a spring in her step. Ngoma Itoua relaxed in a chair drinking a cup of coffee with Jacques Armour on the porch.

'Good morning, gentlemen,' said Sam. 'Can I join you?'

'I've got to go,' said Jacques. 'But we can talk later if you like.'

It was disappointing. She liked Jacques, but he was always too busy to talk to her. Maybe it had something to do with the night she drank whisky with Hans. Nothing happened since but Jacques' behaviour suggested he was jealous or hurt. He was always so quick to leave whenever she turned up. It was awkward.

'Frik's men have almost finished the new kitchen,' she said to Ngoma. 'Dr Ntuli gave me a copy of the new safety protocols he is suggesting for Mama Sonia and the other women. I would like to do something for them to soften the blow of moving to a new regime.'

'Simple. Buy them uniforms,' said Ngoma.

'That might not go down well,' said Sam, thinking of her own revulsion when she had to wear a polyester uniform working for a burger joint during her student days. She hated it, and school uniforms, and anything that made her conform. Rebel without a cause.

'They'd be ecstatic. The men get overalls and boots and safety helmets but the women have to wear their own clothes. They have complained many times but no-one listens to them,' said Ngoma.

That was a revelation. Sam changed her mind in an instant.

'What a great suggestion. Uniforms are cheap and safer than the clothes they wear now which can dangle in the flames or trip them up. I'll let them choose their own from the catalogue that Rahul Singh of Stoddard's sent me,' she said.

'That'll gain you support for your changes. Everyone needs to feel like part of the team.'

'I'll get right on it. Ah, Frik wants to do the kitchen swap on Saturday but that will mean we can't feed the local workers like we usually do. Will you explain to them, please? I don't want to disappoint them but it's the only way to do this with minimum disruption.'

'After what you did with the hospital, you've a licence to do whatever you like around here,' said Ngoma.

158

'You did it too, remember. We are shit royalty in this project.'

Ngoma roared with laughter.

'And proud of it,' he said.

'Can you ask the kitchen staff to assemble in the boardroom after the morning meeting tomorrow, please? If you'd like to be there, you can, but I fear it might be too girly for you,' said Sam.

'Oh Lord no. I'll okay the results if the women are happy.'

When Sam sat down at her desk, she focused her attention on the protocol given to her by Dr Ntuli. Taking a deep breath, she read it through once in French making a couple of minor adjustments in the margin in pen. Then she turned her attention to the English version. The words swam in front of her eyes as her boredom threatened to overwhelm her.

Then she noticed it. The headline on the document was 'Chicken Inspection Protocol'. She stifled a giggle, but it erupted again, so she sat there snorting with mirth. The door opened and Jacques came in. He seemed perturbed to find her laughing, and peered behind the door as if checking for somebody hidden from him.

'What on earth are you laughing about? Has the job got to you?' said Jacques.

Sam tried to tell him but no words would come out. She passed the document to him. He read it with total concentration but his air of puzzlement only increased. Mystified, he shook his head and tried to hand the paper back to her.

'What?' he said.

'The heading,' said Sam, 'read the heading.'

He threw his eyes to heaven.

'For God's sake, what the...'

He stopped and his face creased into a smile. He fixed Sam with a look of merriment in his blue eyes. 'But this is very serious. We must organise the chicken inspection right away.'

'Yes, we must,' she got out, giggling. 'Um, how do you inspect a chicken?'

Jacques burst out laughing, matched in intensity by Sam. The more he laughed the more she joined in and vice versa. Tears ran down their cheeks.

'Do you get it to open its beak? Or measure its eggs?' said Jacques, struggling to get the words out.

'I don't know. I guess we'll have to wing it.'

'Eggs-actly.'

The puns flew back and forwards. Sam hadn't laughed since she had arrived at Masaibu. Her ribs hurt with effort and her cheeks ached by the time they stuttered to a halt.

'What did you want anyway?' said Sam as Jacques staggered out again.

'Oh, I got what I wanted,' he said, leaving her wondering.

When she had stopped giggling, she forced herself to write an email to Dirk detailing the death of Mbala's sister, the hospital clean-up, the progress of the corruption prevention programme and the heavy machinery rebuild. As an addendum, she attached a scan of the chicken protocol and added a bullet point to her email where she asked for someone to check it and querying how a chicken inspection should be carried out. She was still chuckling as she pressed send.

Chapter 19

There were shouts of glee the next day as the kitchen staff reviewed the brochures that Sam handed out in their meeting. Choosing the correct uniform was not a quick process. Mama Sonia would not agree to anything and sat slumped in her chair looking as if the sky had fallen on her head. Sam guessed that Ngoma had insisted on her attendance because every fibre of her being indicated that she would rather have been anywhere on earth.

None of Mama Sonia's workforce feigned solidarity with her. Hilarity reigned as they filled out the columns on the whiteboard, relating to colour, style number, skirt or trousers, type of hat and materials.

They made their choice and the noise level only increased as they measured each other with a piece of string. Sam held it against a metal tape and proclaimed the numbers. Mama Sonia sighed and complained in a loud voice when her measurements were taken but she couldn't deflate the general mood.

'Right you lot, back to work. I'll send the order to Uganda today and let you know when the uniforms are due. Moussa will store and distribute them and you will use the same uniforms every time as they have numbers that are assigned to you. Please pay attention to Dr Ntuli today. The safety seminars are for your security. The new ovens are different to the cooking fires you are used to,' said Sam, affecting a strictness she did not feel.

'Yes, Mama Sam.'

They all trooped out wiggling their large bottoms. Despite the poverty in Masaibu, Sam had not seen many skinny women working for the project. A large posterior was a mark of honour. No wonder hers had appeared in the newspaper photograph. They were probably all commenting about its pathetic size compared to the average.

Mama Sonia might plot revenge, but apart from spitting in her food, Sam wasn't sure how much power Sonia had to do anything against her. When Sam had tried to initiate a complaint against her, Philippe had baffled her with so much legalese, it was clear he was protecting her. They were in cahoots.

There was no time to dwell on the vagaries of her staff as she was due at the community hall to chair the stakeholder meeting. Ezekiel had the engine running when she emerged from the office building. Hans was sitting in the front seat. Sam was torn between telling him to sit in the back and just getting in and avoiding unnecessary polemic. She chose the pragmatic approach and spent the short trip hating the back of his Teutonic head.

The car emerged from the camp and headed down the hill to the community hall. There was a cow blocking the main street, and they had to stop while a small girl tried to pull it to one side. Several people came closer to the car, peering through the window and pointing at Sam. She braced herself for another round of rotten vegetables, but none came.

A loud knock at the window made her jump. Hans leapt out of the car in one movement, his hand on his baton but a man inserted himself between Hans and the car.

'We want to see Mama Sam,' he said.

'She is busy. The stakeholder meeting starts in ten minutes.'

Sam cocked her head to one side in askance and examined the delegation. They didn't look dangerous. She got out of the car.

'Mama Sam,' said one, 'can I shake your hand?'

Sam turned to Hans for reassurance. He nodded, his hand still on his baton. She took the man's hand and shook it with a warm smile. Soon local people had surrounded her shaking her hand and calling her name with enthusiasm. Hans tried to control them but ended up shaking hands too. He raised his eyebrows at her. It was a strange feeling to have such a change in attitude.

After a few minutes, Hans got bored and persuaded people to clear the road. Ezekiel gunned the engine and Sam got back into the car. They drove the rest of the way to the hall through streets filled with people who smiled and waved.

'I think they liked the photograph of my bottom,' said Sam.

'They like large objects,' said Hans.

Ezekiel snorted.

'Mama Sam is too thin. She needs to eat more,' he said.

'I think she needs to eat less,' said Hans.

'I'm behind you, guys,' said Sam.

The meeting was well attended with all the usual suspects. Sam dealt with various requests before holding up her hand for silence.

'I'd like to suggest something,' she said. 'There are too few rangers to protect the elephants in the sanctuary. I propose that we hire ten more people with cash from the environmental fund.'

'Elephants? You want to protect the elephants?' Joseph Kaba jumped up with his hands on his hips spluttering like a fat teapot. 'What about helping people first?'

'Protection of the elephants would provide employment for local people,' said Jean Delacroix, leaping to Sam's defence.

'Don't we already have rangers? How come they can't protect them?' said Kaba.

'Forest elephants are rare, ones with pink tusks even more so. They're found here in Eastern Lumbono and in Gabon. Their ivory is harder than usual, and more valuable due to the pink colour. It appears someone is encouraging the poachers to target the Masaibu forest reserve and the rangers cannot protect it. We've garnered intelligence the elephants are in imminent danger of attack,' said Jean.

'What's the point in saving the elephants? They don't do us any good,' said one of the stakeholders.

'Ah, but they could,' said Jean. 'We should promote the area to tourists. If they come, it would provide jobs in the hotel and catering industries. It is a long-term project that can continue even if Consaf leaves. The WCO want to develop the sanctuary and encourage tourists to stay in town and spend money.'

'Tourists? What kind of tourists would come to this godforsaken place?' said Kaba, eliciting laughter and complaint in equal measure.

'The sort that go to the Mountain Gorilla parks in Uganda, people with lots of money,' said Jean Delacroix.

'What about the road?' said the shopkeepers' representative. 'No one can visit if we don't upgrade the road.'

'We don't have the extra money this financial year,' said the accountant. 'Unless we cut other services.'

'I agree. Why should we help the elephants when we are struggling ourselves?' said a woman.

Ota Benga, the pygmy representative, was following the discussion, his face animated, but he didn't interject. He sat with his legs crossed in his now customary seat. Whether he was following the tone or the meaning of what was being spat across the hall, Sam couldn't tell. *What must he be thinking?*

The arguments went back and forth but the overall attitude remained. They held a vote after everyone had their say. The result was close, but they rejected the proposal. Sam tried to mitigate the loss by accepting it without protest. There must be a better way. The meeting broke up, and she made her goodbyes.

As she left the meeting, the Chinese man she had seen in the restaurant with Joseph Kaba, was hanging around outside. *What could he be discussing with the rebel leader?* Perhaps they were trying to buy gold from the artisanal miners, although this seemed unlikely. The gold was fine-grained and not suitable for primitive equipment that spat most of it back out with the waste material. That didn't stop the ex-rebels from strong-arming the artisanal miners into handing over part of their production, the Lumbono version of a protection racket, but it was small beer for the Chinese. *Why would they bother?*

Joseph Kaba shook Chu Lin's hand with vigour, pumping it up and down as if trying to extract money from his wallet.

'How was the meeting?' said Chu Lin. 'Any problems?'

'That woman, the new manager at Consaf, was trying to get extra rangers posted in the forest. We must act soon or it will become too dangerous for my men.'

'But are they ready for action?'

'Just give the word. However...' Kaba removed a grubby white handkerchief from his pocket and mopped his brow. 'I need you to up the price.'

'And why would I do that?' said Chu Lin, his face like thunder.

'You didn't tell me about ivory being a special grade. The green guy from the WCO told us it's harder and pinker than usual so the price should be too.'

'We had a deal. You're not the only group of disaffected ex-rebels around here, you know. I'm sure I could find someone willing to do it for the price we agreed.'

'And you think I'd allow another troop into my territory? It's not just the elephants who would die in that case,' said Kaba.

Chu Lin scrutinised him as if assessing the weight of the threat.

'You can have a ten per cent premium when you hand over the tusks,' he said.

'And what should we do with them after we remove them from the carcasses? They will be almost impossible to carry through the forest,' said Kaba.

'Make the road closer. Round the elephants up and push them to the edge of the jungle with your weapons. Kill them near enough to the road for easy transport and then pile the tusks there covered in palm leaves and scrub. One of your men can guide us to the site. Make sure they aren't visible from the road.'

'Theory is always easier than practice in these matters.'

'Do your best. I'm paying you enough,' said Chu Lin, and he started down the hill.

There was an email from Dirk waiting for her in the office. Sam rubbed her hands together in anticipation as she opened it and read. To her intense disappointment, Dirk had not joined in with the joke about chicken inspections. He made some requests for photographs, and some anodyne comments of general approval, but no jokes about chickens.

Even worse, he pointed out the spelling mistake, deadpan. Perhaps they didn't have as much in common as she had imagined. It was isolating. Thank goodness she was going home for a break soon. Masaibu was aptly named.

Chapter 20

The kitchen transfer went through without a hitch. The anticipation generated by the new utilities and the promise of the longed-for uniforms created a carnival atmosphere. Ngoma Itoua had pre-warned the local contract staff about the lack of lunch which they took in good humour but with much grumbling, despite fruit and bread rolls with meat fillings being distributed to most of the men.

'The new larder looks fantastic. Those stainless-steel shelves should be easy to keep clean,' said Sam.

'Yes, we're pleased with it,' said Frik. 'Aren't you due out on leave?'

'I'm going on leave in a couple of days. I hope the project holds together while I'm gone.'

'Jacques is going out too.'

Sam feigned disinterest.

'Oh? I didn't know.'

But she did, and it was hard to avoid the frisson she experienced when he was around. Not like Fergus, but at least she wasn't bored. Sam found the security men difficult to fathom. Hans appeared insulted when she gave him back his chair. Jacques avoided talking to her. No one tolerated them much except her. Some locals were hostile and spat on the floor after they had walked past. Sam had tried

168

asking Frik the reason for the hostility but he wasn't much help.

'The French Foreign Legion are scum but at least they are not Belgians.'

The reference went right over the top of Sam's head. *Belgians? The only Belgians I can remember are Hergé and Papa Smurf.*

'Belgians?' said Sam

'Jesus, Sam, don't you know anything about Lumbono?' said Frik.

'I always do research before I travel anywhere new, but this contract was such a rush that I didn't get the opportunity. I'll buy some books while I'm out on leave.'

'About one hundred years ago, Lumbono was the private fiefdom of a Belgian King. He used the population as slaves to gather rubber and hunt elephants. The Belgians treated the locals like animals, or worse.'

'What happened?' said Sam.

'During a revolution in the 1920s, the local population massacred most of the Belgians living here. The ones who survived returned to Europe. They did not educate Lumbono nationals as a matter of policy. Governing such a sprawling landmass covered in a jungle with few amenities like roads and hospitals was a mammoth undertaking.'

'Is that why the place is such a train wreck?'

'Yes. And why the Belgians are so unpopular. They are blamed for the mess, and rightly so.'

'But Hans and Jacques aren't Belgians...'

'Hans isn't. I'm not sure about Jacques. Anyway, the French Foreign Legion are no angels. It's been a haven for men with criminal records, shady business dealings and deserters because it strips their old identity from them when they join and they begin a new life with a clean sheet,' said Frik.

'So, we don't know who we are dealing with?' said Sam.

'People give them a wide berth, just in case.'

That explained the cool relationship between the security men and the locals, but it didn't account for their relationship with her. With time running short before her break, she called Dirk to warn him of her imminent departure.

'Hi, Dirk.'

'She lives. To what do I owe this great honour?' said Dirk.

'I'm going out on leave tomorrow,' said Sam.

'It can't be ten weeks already. You're having me on.'

'You can't begrudge me a couple of weeks out after the shift I've pulled. I'm only taking two weeks of the three that I'm allowed,' said Sam.

'I'm kidding. I think you should take the full allowance. You've worked seventy days straight.'

'I know, but I'm afraid to leave the project for longer. Against my better judgement, I've had to leave Philippe in charge of the project.'

'Isn't there anyone else?' said Dirk.

'It's tricky. He occupied the position of interim general manager before I arrived, self-appointed as far as I could make out, but it might seem racist if I asked Frik to do it instead. I'd like Ngoma Itoua, the union manager to do it, but he's out on leave in a week's time.'

'In that case, can you come back next week?'

'No.' She didn't leave room for negotiation in her tone.

'I was only kidding. Are you doing a handover with him?'

'Yes, and I have forbidden him from making any retrograde changes to the protocols we are now operating. I have told him to use Stoddard's delivery service, but I can't stop him sending Mama Sonia to Uganda to do her own shopping this one last time.'

'Hm, I'll send him a stiff email with instructions from head office. Have you done a handover sheet?' asked Dirk.

'Yes, I already gave it to him.'

'Send me a copy and I'll lay down the law.'

'Okay great.'

'I need you to come back via Johannesburg to update us on progress at Masaibu. Can you make us some sort of presentation? It should be an easy ride. You are doing a great job so far.'

'Thanks, Dirk. I'll chuck something together at home.'

'Have a nice time. Are you seeing that sister of yours?'

'She needs a babysitter, so I'm sure I will. You won't even notice I've gone,' said Sam.

'Ha! That's what you think. Bye.'

'Bye.'

Jacques had already occupied the back seat of the car when Sam got there. She threw her bag into the boot. It flew there with ease as it contained only the clothes that she needed for her visit to head office. She left her field gear in her room, thinking it might incentivize her to come back.

Having sealed her remaining tea bags into a zip-lock bag, she put them inside a plastic bag. She hooked the handles of the bag over the top of a hanger in the wardrobe so that they were dangling out of reach of insects. Her chocolate hoard finished, she had plans to replenish the supply in London. Sam shut the padlock on the bedroom door, an addition to prevent a repeat of the welcome she had received on her first day.

She jumped into the car almost overshooting her seat in her enthusiasm.

'Whoa, mind the suspension,' said Jacques.

'Are you insinuating that I'm fat?' said Sam.

Jacques examined her from head to foot in a way that made her feel as if she was frying.

'I don't want to die on the day I'm going home,' he said.

Ezekiel drove them down the main street and through the town out to the airport. He had removed the black film from the windows, which seemed at first like a great idea. However, it also meant everyone could see into the car. Sam had developed a film star status since the mortality rate at the hospital had plummeted, and they had to keep stopping the car to shake people's hands.

'Please don't leave us, Mama Sam.'

'I'm coming back, I promise.'

It was hard to fathom the difference between it and her initial welcome. Perhaps people just needed someone to care what happened to them, and she cared. More than she should.

'They can turn on you,' said Hans, when she discussed it with him. 'The hearts and minds method is a tricky balancing act. It can go wrong sometimes. And I should know.'

She was proud, even while she suspected it would end in a fall. No problem was insurmountable, with her ability for lateral thinking. Even pretend confidence seemed to work, despite her scepticism. Ezekiel's voice broke through her daydreaming.

'We have arrived, Mama Sam.'

Ezekiel took their bags to the door of the shabby shed that served as the airport building.

'Have a good rest. We will wait here for you. Safari salama Mama Sam.'

'Asante na wewe Ezekiel,' said Sam, thanking him for wishing her a safe trip.

The procedures for leaving the country were just as drawn out as those for entry. Sam felt as if someone had trapped her in a time warp like the one in the film Groundhog Day, which she had seen with her parents before coming out to Lumbono.

Jacques took it all in good humour, teasing the women in customs and making them blush and jostle.

'Don't forget our lipsticks,' said one.

'Would I dare?' said Sam, making them laugh.

'What's that about?' said Jacques.

'Oh, just girl stuff.'

Mad Mark stood planted on the tarmac like a dead tree with a bees' nest on top. He had the look of a man who had a pornographic newspaper to finish.

'Let's go,' he said. 'Time's a wasting.'

Sam recognised his stock departure phrase. It didn't take long to get used to something. There was no sign of any freeloaders hanging around on this trip. The small aircraft had a smoother take off without mysterious bundles in the hold.

Soon they were flying over Lake Albert where the air became turbulent as moist air rose into the sky. It threw Jacques against Sam who pushed him off with mock horror.

'There's no need to throw yourself at me,' she said.

'It's desperation,' he said. 'I've been away from home for three months.'

'I've never asked you if you were married.'

Mad Mark snorted.

'You're too late,' he said. 'Jacques has a lovely wife. She's French. Oh là là!'

'That's nice,' said Sam, but it wasn't. So much for playing the long game. It explained why he ran away every time he found himself alone with her. Probably instructions from '*her indoors*'. She sighed.

'That was a big sigh,' said Jacques. 'Are you sad to be leaving Masaibu?'

Sam couldn't help giggling. 'No. Are you?'

'I'm so happy I keep falling out of my seat.'

'There you go,' said Mark.

Philippe watched the jeep pull away from the office door. Even a confirmed hypocrite like him could not be bothered to wish the occupants a good trip. As soon as they were out of sight, he let himself into Sam's office using his set of keys and sat behind her desk. It was pristine.

He tutted and opened the drawers in her desk finding only paperclips, Sellotape and a book about beetles along with a variety of ballpoint pens from different hotels in South America. There were no files or notepads, nothing of any value to him. Sam had locked the filing cabinet.

He tried to start her computer, but she had protected it with a password. Sam's interfering had disrupted a nice income he had going from the local workers and his wife was on the warpath. He had not expected the money to dry up and hadn't warned her beforehand about Sam's arrival.

How was he to know? Charlie Okito had told him that she was harmless. But she was about as harmless as a leopard up a tree. She dropped on schemes without warning, suffocating them by the throat before anyone had a chance to react. She

174

mesmerised the security guys who followed her around like puppies, especially that Jacques fellow masquerading as French. He smelt like a Belgian, and they were scum.

Philippe picked up the telephone to ring Charlie and put his dirty shoes on Sam's desk, kicking a framed photograph of her parents onto the floor. He left it lying there, the glass cracked and splintered. By the time Sam got to Johannesburg, her career at Masaibu would be over. It was time he moved back into his office.

Charlie Okito replaced the phone in the receiver. Triumph was written all over his face. That weasel Philippe had come good. The arrogant bitch running Masaibu was on borrowed time. He thumped the table causing his coffee to flood into the saucer.

'Sara!'

His secretary sidled into the room with the air of a woman who expected to be groped. He gesticulated at the mess.

'Get me some more coffee and clean this up.'

She leaned over to get the cup and winced as he put his hand on her arm.

'About time we had another lunch, no?' he said, oblivious.

After she left, he found his address book in his briefcase and searched for the number of a journalist on the main Goro newspaper.

'I've a scoop for you,' he said.

The airport hotel was basic but clean. Both Sam and Jacques were taking flights early the next morning and its location near the runway made it the obvious choice. Sam had been looking forward to having dinner with Jacques and flirting a little to see what happened, but he was taken and knowing that, the plan lost its gloss. Anyway, Mark joined them, which knocked most topics on the head. They couldn't even talk about work.

She stayed in her room and ate a couple of bananas, feigning a headache. Her room smelt of cigarettes and DDT which threatened to produce a genuine one. She lay on the shiny counterpane reviewing her first rotation at Masaibu. Overall, things had taken a definite turn for the better, but serious problems still existed and rebellion lurked below the surface calm.

Some people, especially Philippe, would never come onside. She suspected that Charlie Okito was egging him on but there was no way of proving it. As manager of the Goro office, he was well placed to interfere, and it seemed reasonable to assume that he had skin in the game. Proving it would be problematic.

And then there were the terrible twins. Both were attractive in a disturbed kind of way, but she knew nothing about their pasts. There could be horrible truths hidden behind the gruff exteriors. Maybe them keeping their distance was a blessing.

The next morning, she stumbled down at dawn to share a taxi with Jacques to the airport. The sun was creeping up the sky throwing tree shadows on the front wall of the hotel. Sam pressed her sunglasses closer to her face and slumped in the back seat with him.

'Tired?' he said.

'Washed out. You?'

'After dinner with Mad Mark? You guess.'

They checked in at the scruffy counters and made their way to the business class lounge. *Were the Consaf travel department aware that there were other classes on an aeroplane?* Not that she minded. Plenty of different choices tempted them from the breakfast bar. Sam had some scrambled eggs and smoked salmon with a large cup of tea, made with her own bag. Jacques picked at some fruit. Her look of disdain was comical.

'I must look after my figure,' he said, smoothing his hands over his stomach.

'You'll get the squits. Not recommended for long-haul flights,' said Sam, grinning.

He finished the fruit and sipped his coffee, peering at her over the brim of his cup. Uncomfortable under his scrutiny, his eyes threatened to burn holes in the back of her skull. *What was it with him? Why couldn't he be a simple thug like Hans?*

All too soon, Sam's flight boarded. She stood up and stuck a hand in his face holding it out on the end of a stiff arm. He cocked his head to one side as if considering his counterattack, but, instead, he grabbed her hand in a bone-crushing shake. She refused to flinch, smiling a goodbye and rubbing her hand only when out of sight.

Chapter 21

S am opened the door to the street and held it open without looking.

'What's he done this time?' she said.

'Nothing,' said Simon, affecting to saunter in.

She blocked his path, trying not to be intimidated by his physical presence. Despite herself, she breathed deeply before speaking, inhaling his intoxicating odour, the mix of cologne and pheromones heady in the air.

'What are you doing here? How dare you come to my flat?' she said.

Simon reeled backwards, a hurt expression on his face.

'But you opened the door. Aren't you glad to see me?' he said.

'I was expecting Hannah. And don't be ridiculous. I would prefer never to see you again.'

'So, you have feelings for me.'

'Not the good kind. Why aren't you with her?' said Sam.

'She's thrown me out,' said Simon.

'And you thought you'd come here instead? Are you on drugs?'

'Don't be like that. I assumed you'd forgiven me,' said Simon, with a hangdog expression.

'I've forgiven Hannah. You, I'll never pardon. Get out.'

'Can't I have a coffee first?'

'No, you can't. Who told you I was back?' said Sam.

He gazed at her, a long lazy examination that made her feel naked. He stretched out a hand and touched her cheek, a gesture she used to treasure. She almost fainted as waves of the old desire threatened to overcome her.

'I knew. I could feel y...'

'No, you bloody couldn't. Go on. Out,' she said, shoving him.

What was she thinking? She couldn't. Hannah had a baby. No matter what had happened in the past, she would not relive the misery of Simon's wavering interest. She pushed him back through the entrance and out onto the street, slamming the door in his face. She leaned against it panting with exertion and fright. He whimpered outside like a lost dog.

'Go away,' she shouted with all her might.

'You don't mean it. I'll be back.'

And he was gone.

Sam sat on the hall chair with a thud, knocking a pile of junk mail on the floor which she kicked in frustration. She held her head in her hands and tried to slow her heart rate. Tears were queuing up to explode, but she forced them back in. *I won't let him ruin my time at home. He is history. But how could she forget him when he was the father of her sister's child and kept turning up to upset her emotions?* Life was so cruel.

Dirk was drinking a cup of Miriam's extra strong brew when the telephone rang. He wasn't expecting a call, and he regarded it with suspicion. He picked up the receiver and listened.

'Dirk? Are you there?'

'It's me, Charlie. What's up?'

'That woman you hired.'

There was undisguised loathing in Charlie Okito's tone of voice but Dirk affected not to notice.

'Which woman? But you liked your new secretary. Quite a lot from what I can make out.'

'Not her. The one at Masaibu,' snapped Charlie.

'Sam Harris? She has a name.'

'Well, I won't have to remember it for much longer,' said Charlie.

'Already? Is this necessary? What's she done now?'

'She's a racist.'

'I don't believe it. You'll need to do better,' said Dirk with disdain.

'I have proof. There's a nasty story in the newspaper about the racist South African mining company starving its workers.'

'What? This is crazy. I'm aware you want to get rid of her, but it's not the right time.'

'You've no idea how dangerous she is,' said Charlie.

'She tells me everything before she does it. How dangerous can she be?'

'I'll fax you the file. Believe me, we have to act now.'

'Goodbye, Charlie.'

Simon's visit had the effect of driving Sam to drink. When she was convinced that he had gone, she walked to the local corner shop at the end of her road along a pavement illuminated by a flickering street lamp. The murky yellow light threw threatening shadows on the road only increasing her anguish, and a cold north wind cut through her anorak.

She bought a bottle of cheap red wine and a packet of Camel lights, a sure-fire recipe for an evil hangover. Then she walked back fast with the bottle in the pocket of her anorak, the hood pulled up over her head in case Simon was still hanging around.

Once inside, she locked the front door and put the chain on, not to keep him out, more to shut the door on the emotions which threatened to overwhelm her. There was another solution, apart from getting drunk, to distract her from the incident, and that was to look at her photographs of Fergus taken in stealth mode when they worked together in Simbako.

Like many commitment-phobes, Fergus was not keen on leaving any trace behind and he used to shy away when she tried to take his photo. This didn't discourage Sam who got a few good ones with her telephoto lens while he worked on the diamond exploration pits. Staring at these photographs was as close to looking at porn as she ever got, with their closeups of his naked upper body and golden lion curls on his lower belly.

Sipping a glass of wine while gazing at his masculine form and remembering being held in his arms, swimming in a sea of passion, Sam could soon forget all about Simon. She blew smoke out of the back window of the flat into the night, leaning on the windowsill and gazing into the light pollution that had replaced the stars in Masaibu.

The problem with drinking a bottle of wine when you are almost teetotal is that you get much drunker than you intended and do things you know are stupid but need an excuse to do, anyway. Sam dialled Fergus's number. She was tingling with anticipation. *Surely, he would be glad she was in London? Even commitment-phobes hardly ever refused the offer of sex on a weeknight.*

'Yes?' A young woman's voice. Groggy with sleep. 'Hello, is anyone there?'

Sam dropped the receiver back on the cradle. She stared with horror at the telephone and then ran to the toilet to be sick.

***

'I can't believe it,' said Morné, screwing up his face and knitting his eyebrows together so that they almost touched. He rubbed his face with his hands and grimaced.

'It's true, I'm afraid. Philippe Mutombo, the HR manager at Masaibu, has put together a dossier which seems to prove it beyond doubt. Worse still, Charlie claims that an article has appeared in the Goro Daily News calling Consaf a safe harbour for white supremacists,' said Dirk, shrugging.

'Have we got a copy?' said Morné.

'Not yet. The phone lines were down again, but he has promised to fax me a photocopy of the article as soon as he can.'

'I'm not at all happy with this.'

182

Morné crossed his arms. Dirk stood his ground. Morné was notorious as a procrastinator.

'But we can't stand by and ignore it,' said Dirk.

'No, of course not, but she seemed like such a nice young woman. It doesn't fit her profile at all. Hasn't she worked in lots of multicultural environments before? I don't remember any negative comments on her references.'

'Me neither, but we must do something. The standing of Consaf in Lumbono is at stake,' said Dirk.

'In that case, it wouldn't do to let this go unchallenged. What's your plan?' said Morné.

'I had already asked her to come by on her way back from leave and give us an update on progress at the project. We can use the opportunity to interrogate her face to face.'

'Okay, but we must give her the right of reply. You seemed to think that she was doing a fantastic job up until now.

'She was. I...' Dirk trailed off.

'I'm loath to fire her unless we have to. There are no suitable replacements and we are making progress at last.'

'Nonetheless...'

'Yes, I know. Fine.' Morné groaned. 'Get her in here.'

Sam spent the rest of her break avoiding Hannah and Simon. She found refuge in her parents' house where the pair only went if invited, Sam's father having little tolerance for Simon's ways, his loyalty to Sam absolute.

'Will I ever find someone nice?' said Sam, slumped at the kitchen table, picking at a piece of coffee and walnut cake, her second.

'Sit up, dear. That's bad for your back,' said Matilda Harris, playing for time.

Sam subjected her to a glare with her troubled green eyes. Her mother's face softened as she read the suffering behind the question.

'Not everyone is that lucky. Perhaps you are meant for other things.'

'Like what? Spinsterhood?' Sam jabbed at the cake with a fork. Her mother reached over and moved the plate out of her orbit.

'There's nothing wrong with being unmarried. Look at your aunt Lottie. She's the happiest woman alive in her own little house with total control of the remote for the television.'

'But I don't want to be alone all the time.' Sam's shoulders slumped.

'At least you can choose when you are single. Married women almost never have a minute to themselves, and I should know. If it's not your children crying or hungry, your husband needs attention too. Are you sure that's what you want? You're independent and single-minded. Marriage might be too much for you.'

'I don't want to get married, exactly. I want someone to love,' said Sam, sniffing.

Sam's forlorn expression almost broke her mother's heart.

'You'll find someone again. What about that Fergus character? You liked him and from what you said, he liked you back. Why don't you call him?'

Sam dissolved into sobs.

'I did. There was a girl there. He said I was the one, but he chose someone else.'

'My poor darling.' Matilda Harris sat at the table and put her arm around her daughter's heaving shoulders. 'You don't know that. Maybe you dialled the wrong number. Anyway, if he didn't choose you, he has terrible taste. You're unique and one day someone who appreciates your soft heart and your kind soul will sweep you off your feet. Until then, you must be brave and keep kissing frogs. There's someone out there. I promise.'

Chapter 22

S am stopped talking, tailing off as the antipathy directed at her became obvious. She expected a positive reaction from the board after her presentation but a sea of blank faces met her gaze. A hot rush of blood suffused her features turning her into a traffic light on red. *What the hell was going on?*

She travelled to Johannesburg with high hopes that her progress at Masaibu would convince even the most fervent opponents of her appointment. To her surprise, Consaf had booked her in economy. Consaf never booked their senior managers in tourist class. She would have brushed it off, presuming there had been no free seats in business, if she hadn't also been demoted to the ground floor in the hotel. It didn't add up.

Her performance at Masaibu was stellar by any standards. She had even surprised herself with the effectiveness of her simple techniques, and the best thing was that no one lost their job. Resentment bubbled below the surface in a few cases, but even they would step into line when they understood that the old ways had gone forever.

The board must acknowledge the improvements in safe working practices, the reduction of deaths at the hospital, the increase in metres drilled per shift, all done at a reduced cost which had been achieved since she arrived. It was there in black and white on the transparencies she demonstrated to the board. But there was no reaction.

The strong light from the overhead projector made her face even hotter as she fiddled with the transparencies. *What had she expected? A round of applause? Why was everyone glaring at her?* Morné got to his feet.

'Thank you. I think we can all agree you've made remarkable progress at Masaibu so far. However, some issues have come to light that suggest a darker side to your presence there.'

What? Who did they think she was? Darth Vader?

'It has been brought to my attention that your behaviour has been below the standards expected of our managers in remote sites.' He coughed and flushed.

Her mind went blank. She couldn't imagine anything for which she should apologise. *Unless they were furious about her overspending on the safety equipment?* But she recuperated the funds from savings in other budgets. The conundrum paralysed her with indecision, so she stood there waiting. No one spoke.

Finally, she said, 'I'm sorry. I don't understand what you are talking about.'

Devin Ryan put his briefcase on the table and stuck both hands into it, sifting through the papers like a police diver looking for a murder weapon in a pond. The triumphant look on his face faded as he failed to find whatever he was looking for.

'For God's sake,' said Paul Hogan, reaching into his own briefcase at his feet and producing a photocopy of the front page of a newspaper which he threw across the table at Sam. She picked it up, hand shaking. It was upside down but the French headline was clear enough. It screamed out in big bold capitals: Manager of Masaibu Project is a Colonial Racist.

A horrible sensation crept up her back, and hot and cold with waves of shame flooded over her. She turned it around so she could read the rest of the article, dying inside under the accusing glances. *What on earth had precipitated the article? Why did a journalist in the capital city research an unimportant incident? And how did they find out about it in the first place?*

'When was this published?' she said, playing for time, her face burning.

'Last week. Front page news.' Charlie Okito's indignant voice came over the speaker phone from Goro. 'I'm firefighting here but I don't know how to answer the criticism. Someone has to pay for this with their job.'

His tone changed for the last phrase. Self-satisfied or gloating now. They had played her. She was staring down at the table trying to compose her thoughts. When she didn't comment, Morné Van Rooyen, the CEO, took over.

'The fact is, we've received reports of your racist behaviour direct from camp as well as being reported in the newspaper. One of the local geologists reported you for demoting him from his room and making him share with junior people. You have prevented the manager of the kitchens from going to Uganda to shop for the provisions and are using a white provider instead. She says that you are a racist too. It's all in the file. What do you say to this? It seems pretty damning,' said Morné, knitting his eyebrows.

All of Sam's pleasure at her progress with the project and her visit to Johannesburg, to receive praise and advice from the board, had evaporated. *God damn it, I'm going to cry.* She pressed her

188

nails into her arm to distract herself. *Think woman, think. There must be an explanation for this.*

'I'd like a glass of water.' she said, playing for time. 'Can I see the file?'

Ryan sneered at her and shoved it hard across the shiny table. Sam almost caught it as it fell, but it opened in the air and the pages scattered onto the floor. No one offered to help her collect them but she didn't care; it gave her time to think. She shuffled the pages and put them back into the file, smoothing it onto the table, taking her time while she tried to slow her thundering heart rate.

'Do you want an iron?' said Paul Hogan.

Sam did not dignify his question with a reply. She tried to focus on the newspaper article that danced before her shocked eyes. Someone had written it in hysterical, accusatory French, but she read a few more paragraphs before she found the cause of the headline. "Workers are being starved by this colonial racist witch. She refused them food and sent them home hungry. This is a denial of basic human rights".

The fog of panic cleared from Sam's mind in an instant. It was a setup. Philippe was the obvious candidate for this and Okito's motives were crystal clear. She had got too close to the truth, and he was getting rid of her before she discovered it. There had to be more to the cover-up than skimming off money from vegetable bills and workers' salaries.

There was an oppressive silence in the room and Sam could feel triumph emanating from Ryan and Hogan. She smothered a smile and took a gulp of water, wiping her mouth with the damp paper napkin acting as a coaster.

She raised her head and stared straight across the table into Ryan's eyes. He smirked at Paul Hogan who gave him a discrete thumbs-up. He held her gaze and raised an eyebrow. She winked at him.

189

The look of shock on his face told her all she needed to know about his motives.

'This is a very serious matter, Sam. It's a firing offence. We can't risk our reputation in Lumbono.' Morné Van Rooyen placed both of his hands on the table, fingers splayed

'I'll say it's serious. I've got government ministers calling me asking me for an explanation. We must act. Sam has to go.' Charlie Okito's voice crackled across the room.

Dirk Goosen was sweating; big patches appeared on the armpits of his shirt. He shot a worried glance at Sam. She winked at him too. His face showed confusion, amazement even.

'Sam, you must speak. How do you explain this article? These accusations from Philippe Mutombo? We need to decide,' said Van Rooyen.

'The decision is a foregone conclusion. She hasn't got a leg to stand on,' said Ryan.

'Actually, I've got plenty of legs,' said Sam. 'The journalist who wrote this article must have an axe to grind against the company. Or whoever fed him the story.'

The line from Goro crackled, but Charlie Okito didn't comment. They could hear him lighting a cigarette.

'Prove it,' hissed Hogan.

'My pleasure,' said Sam, her heart rate returning to normal as the facts became clearer in her mind. 'As you may know, circumstances have forced me to move the Masaibu budget around to finance pressing matters of health and security in camp. For instance, when I arrived there, the cooking was being done outside over fires with no regard for hygiene or safety. I ordered the refurbishment of an empty building to house the kitchen...'

'You've already told us this,' said Hogan.

'Now then, Paul. Let her speak. She has a right to defend herself,' said Morné.

'Thanks,' said Sam, gaining confidence. 'When the building was ready, we scheduled the changeover for a Saturday morning as being the least disruptive time for it. The local staff only work a half day on Saturday and are not entitled to a midday meal but they've got in the habit of being fed. It's not expensive and creates goodwill.'

'What relevance does this have to the article?' said Dirk.

'I met with Ngoma Itoua, the head of the Union, and alerted him that it wouldn't be possible to feed the local men their lunch because of the move. He agreed to tell them and asked me if we needed help with the move, which I accepted. We planned an agreement to pay overtime and provide snacks instead of lunch and we shook hands.'

'That's it?' said Van Rooyen.

'That's all,' said Sam. 'No one starved. The new kitchen is now functioning perfectly.'

'So, how did a journalist based in Goro get his hands on this story?'

'Ah, that I can't help you with,' said Sam, and smiled at Ryan, who shrank back in his seat.

'What about the HR complaints?' said Hogan. 'Are they invented too?' He was pink with indignation and his cheeks wobbled like jelly on a spring.

'The first is my fault,' said Sam. 'While Alain, the chief geologist, was on holiday, I sent the decorators into his room because it was shabby and run down. He is an excellent technician, and I wanted to reward him for his good work on the project. He came back a day early and found his stuff moved to the junior quarters. I was busy all day, cleaning the hospital with the rest of the workforce, so he couldn't find me.

'He's a good geologist, but he's a hothead. He must have gone to HR and filed a complaint without waiting for an explanation. I have to admit that I haven't won HR over yet so I guess that Philippe, the manager, sent it straight to headquarters without informing me.'

'Why would he do that?' said Morné.

'I'm sure he had his reasons,' said Sam. 'I'm not flavour of the month with a few of the staff. I am disrupting their money-making schemes and imposing order. Push back is a normal reaction.'

'And the kitchen manager?' said Dirk.

'Ah, Mama Sonia. I found out she was diverting the food bought in Uganda into her own restaurant and replacing it with the local, inferior quality produce. So, I rang up Stoddard, the suppliers in Uganda and talked to the owner, a Mr Singh, about shipping our supplies to the project. Since they already have a delivery route passing near our project, it was simple to organise. And Mr Singh is not white, he's a Hindu.'

'Why hasn't she been fired then?' said Van Rooyen with his hands on his hips.

'I believe she's Philippe's cousin,' said Sam.

'Is there any hope for the project? It sounds like a cesspool,' said Ryan, who had undergone a complete change in attitude.

'We've made progress, but it's not a quick process,' said Sam. 'I'm trying to reward good behaviour and change the culture without firing anyone. There are people who would be fired anywhere else, but the labour laws make firing almost impossible. I'm doing a workaround to avoid legal repercussions. I want the board to trust me and give me more time.'

It had been fascinating to watch the reactions of the directors as they realized the article in the newspaper was planted by someone in Goro. It didn't take much imagination to guess who was responsible. Even Devin Ryan sat there with his mouth open like a surprised hamster when Charlie Okito swore to find out who was behind this outrage in Goro, before slamming down the phone in disgust, leaving them all listening to the dial tone emerging from the phone hub in the centre of the table.

When it became clear that the other charges were also without foundation, some directors became contrite. Paul Hogan stunned her by muttering a few apologetic phrases.

'Damn bad show, that article. Should've known it was a setup. Didn't agree with you going out there, but I have to admit, you've surprised us all.'

And Devin agreeing. She couldn't decide which was more amazing.

But Dirk said nothing. It hurt her feelings and raised her suspicions about him, especially when he put his arm around her cradling her breast at the side in full view of the board. She wanted to pull away, but it was difficult to do without making it obvious and making a fuss was not an option in that company. She gritted her teeth.

'Okay, Sam, thanks. We need to discuss this.'

Morné opened the door for her and as she passed him, he whispered 'good show' in her ear. The door shut behind her and she could hear shouting. She hid in the toilet cubicle at the end of the row, trying to calm down. Her heart hammered in her chest and her shirt was wet with sweat. She tried to slow it down by controlling her breathing. As she was on the way out, two women entered the toilet, one of them was swearing.

'For fuck's sake, that filthy man just copped a feel in the boardroom.'

'In the boardroom? He has no shame.'

193

'He grabbed my bottom. You'd think butter wouldn't melt in his mouth with his nicey, nicey character.'

'Dirty Dirk. Yuck.'

Sam suppressed a squeak of horror. So, it wasn't just her. But he had been so supportive. She waited until they had gone and then washed her hands and sat on the seats outside the toilets trying to collect her feelings.

Her horrendous experience in the boardroom had overturned her conviction she was doing a good job. The bile directed at her had been shocking. *Had she been racist? Were her preconceptions of Lumbono colouring her decisions?* Her hands shook with shock and she dropped her shoulder bag on the floor. A pair of feet appeared in front of her. Sam looked up to see Miriam pursing her lips.

'You're as pale as a ghost,' she said. 'Come and have lunch with me.'

Lunch. Nice fresh fish appealed to her and made her acknowledge just how hungry she was. Sam needed food to help her process the morning's proceedings.

'Yes, please. I'm starving,' said Sam.

Chapter 23

They walked to a French bistro around the corner from the company building. Sam glanced around looking for anyone she recognised before sliding into a booth. They ordered their food and sipped a soft drink. A strong gin and tonic would have gone down better, but Sam needed to stay sharp.

'Dirk says you dodged a bullet today. It horrified me that they attacked you like that with no warning,' said Miriam.

Sam tried to speak but her voice stuck in her throat. Tears filled her eyes, and she shook her head in embarrassment.

'It was awful,' she said, choking over her sobs. 'They called me a racist.'

Miriam passed her a tissue and waited until the storm subsided.

'And are you?' she said.

'No, of course not,' said Sam.

'There are various agendas at play here. I'm not surprised they tried to throw you out. Masaibu is a cash cow for someone who doesn't want you to find out,' said Miriam, avoiding Sam's inquiring glance.

'Do you know who it is?'

'I have my suspicions but no proof. Even if I was sure, I couldn't tell you. I need this job. They'd fire me if I blew the whistle. That's why they hired you.'

'If I find out, they fire me, and if I don't, they still fire me?' said Sam.

'That's about it. Why do you think they hired a consultant? Everyone knows how toxic Masaibu is. Take the money while they are paying.'

Miriam patted Sam's arm. The food arrived, and they ate with gusto. Sam had ordered crispy French fries and a piece of poached salmon with a fresh salad. The food was so delicious the women stopped talking altogether.

When they had finished, Sam wiped the dressing off her plate with a piece of crusty bread.

'Yum. That was great,' said Sam. 'Saved my life.'

'They always do great food in here. I'll ask for the bill. Dirk will wonder where we got to,' said Miriam.

They sipped their coffees.

'Are you any closer to the truth out there?' said Miriam.

'Maybe. There are so many moving parts. I've dealt with some minor instances of fraud without too much hassle. I try not to draw attention to the culprit while I'm targeting him. It's like pinning a butterfly to a board without killing it first,' said Sam, frowning.

'I don't envy you. It must be hard knowing that almost everyone wants you to fail.'

'In a way, it makes it easier. I trust no one.'

'Good girl.'

That surprised Sam. *What about Dirk?* But she didn't ask. Her knowledge of his behaviour had already clarified the origin of the graffiti in the toilet. He was no longer the perfect boss. *Was there more to his dark side?*

The bill arrived and Sam snatched it before Miriam could pick it up.

'You don't have to do that, Sam. I'll put it on expenses.'

'That's okay. I owe you lunch after all your support.'

Sam skimmed the bill to see if they included service.

'Did you order some asparagus?' she said.

'No. I can't eat it.' Miriam patted her stomach.

'There's a portion of asparagus on the bill.'

She swivelled around and caught the eye of the waiter who was loitering in anticipation of payment.

'Excuse me, waiter, we didn't order this asparagus. You need to remove it from the total.'

The waiter raised an eyebrow and prepared to refute her claim. Sam held his eyes with a glassy stare. He reconsidered and stomped off to the till with bad grace.

'You got him there,' said Miriam. 'They're always doing that.'

'Doing what?'

'Billing you for things you don't get. I'm afraid it's a national hobby.'

A blinding flash filled Sam's head. Her hand shot to her mouth stifling a gasp.

'What is it?' said Miriam.

'Oh, nothing. I'm just shocked.'

Trust no one. Not even Miriam? Better to have no exceptions.

By the time they got back to the office, Sam's whole outlook had changed with the revelation she had in the restaurant. The scam was sucking the life out of Masaibu, but she could nip it in the bud. She needed proof and there was a simple way of finding out if she was right; she must scrutinise the Masaibu accounts. If she could obtain a copy to review, it should confirm her suspicions.

She left Miriam in her office and headed for the lifts.

'Hi, Sam. Where are you going? We should have a talk,' said Dirk.

Damn, Dirk had seen her. She tried to be nonchalant.

'Um, I'm just going to accounts. They have some sort of issue with my bank details.'

'Accounts are in the opposite direction.'

'Oh, are they? I get so confused in here. Is it okay if I come and see you after I talk to them?'

'Sure, I'll be in my office.'

Sam set off towards accounts walking at speed towards the lifts where she pressed the up button. The lift came almost immediately, and she jumped in, selecting the button for the third floor. Dirk waited until the doors close and returned to his office.

***

Joseph Kaba supervised his men as they shouldered the oily, black AK 47s leaving smears on their camouflage jackets. Some of them had axes with dull metal blades which they had stuffed down the gap between their belts and trousers. They grinned at each other, their teeth white against their black skins, and slapped each other on the back.

Excitement grew as the moment for leaving came closer. A large army truck bombed into the yard, smoke issuing from its exhaust.

'Right you lot, listen up,' said Kaba.

The ex-rebel troops gathered around their leader bristling with intent.

'Be careful in there. Stay together and shoot anyone who turns up. We don't want any witnesses.'

'What do we do with the booty, sir?'

'Pile it up near the roadside and cover it with vegetation. Then, move off and wait for the truck at the rendezvous. Questions?'

'When will you pay us?'

'When they pay me.'

A roar of laughter shook through the troop and they turned to clamber aboard the truck sitting along the sides and on the wheel hubs. The driver pulled a canvas cover over the metal frame above their heads provoking a storm of protest. Kaba put up his hand to silence them.

'No one must see you going in or coming out. Secrecy is essential for success. Keep your heads down and no opening the back until you arrive.'

He waved off the truck and entered his headquarters shaking with excitement. This was quite a coup. If they succeeded, he could leave the country and buy a house in the south of France.

He had no intention of paying the men more than the minimum but they did not understand the value of the pink ivory and got as much thrill from the kill as from the payment afterwards. That was what war did to men. They missed the murder and mayhem of guerrilla war. He was doing them a favour.

❧❧❧❧❧❧ ❦❦❦❦❦❦

The wooden floor in the accounts department vibrated under Sam's footsteps and echoed around the cavernous room. Someone had painted the blank walls in a shade of magnolia that threw a yellow pallor on the faces of the row upon row of people with their heads bent low over computer keyboards and ledger books. Piles of receipts teetered on desks too small for them.

Sam gave thanks that she was not chained to a desk in the same company for years. The events in the meeting had shaken her, but there was no time to dwell on the result. It was unlikely they would fire her now, and she had to do some digging while she got the chance.

A tiny woman, who appeared to be a relation of the raisin, peered over her desk at the noisy visitor. An ancient cardigan with moth holes almost swamped her and two scrawny legs appeared at the bottom as if by magic balancing in a pair of high heels with a charity shop air about them.

'Yes?' she said with an unmistakable air of impatience, glaring at Sam over the top of a pair of spectacles held together at the nose with tape.

'What a lovely brooch,' said Sam, having searched in desperation for something nice to say about this dried old fruit.

The raisin blushed and put her hand on the brooch in a tender gesture. Her closed face opened like a grubby flower blooming.

'Oh, thank you. It was my mother's. My name's Doris Magana. What can I do for you?'

'Nice to meet you, Doris. My name is Sam Harris. I'm the general manager at the Masaibu project. I need to see the annual accounts for the last couple of years.'

'The project accounts? Oh, I don't know. This is most irregular.'

The petals closed again. Sam didn't panic.

'I won't take them away, I promise. I want to check some orders so that I know how much I need to budget for next year. Please help me. I'm new to this.'

The old lady put her head on one side and narrowed her eyes.

'Okay, but you must sit opposite me in that desk over there so I can keep an eye on you.'

200

In no time at all, the woman had found the files and placed them on the desk in front of Sam. They were organised into sections which made it simple to find what she was looking for. She skimmed the pages and found the items under the maintenance tab, an order for spares for the heavy machinery identical to the ones that Frik had given her. The amount was a hefty eighty-five thousand dollars and change.

Sam couldn't take it in. Frik had told her that the machinery had never arrived. Either the money was being siphoned off somehow in the capital or the spares were purchased and then resold. Either way, the size of the fraud was staggering, and this was only one order out of hundreds. The local scams being run in Masaibu were small beer compared to this.

'How do I know if these orders were filled?' she said.

'Any orders in those files were authorised at head office, and the money sent out to the account in Goro. The manager in Goro pays for all the goods used in the country so they pass through the accounts of the country office and are written off against tax on any future exploitation we carry out,' said Doris.

'Who has copies of those accounts?'

'The originals are in the Goro office, and they send us a summary report at the end of every tax year.'

'Do you have them here?'

'Yes, but they won't be any use to you. All the expenses are lumped into the categories in the files you have there so individual amounts can't be worked out. They carry out an audit over there and we get a copy of the report for our files.'

Sam was in a quandary. *No wonder Charlie Okito wanted her out. And who else was implicated? It*

201

was inconceivable he didn't have an inside man in Johannesburg. But how would she find out what had happened to the money?

She needed a contact in Goro but she had no idea where to start. Miriam told her not to trust anyone and that meant Dirk too. *Surely, he couldn't be involved?*

When she had bookmarked the largest orders made through Goro, Sam persuaded Doris to let her photocopy them.

'I couldn't possibly remember all that stuff. Be a dear and help me,' said Sam.

Doris shuffled off and copied them all with an air of defiance that seeped out of her repressed pores.

'There you go. Let me know if you need anything else,' she said.

'Thank you so much. You are a star. By the way, I'd appreciate it if you could keep this quiet,' said Sam. 'I don't want the men thinking I can't do the job.'

'Don't you worry about that, dear. Your secret is safe with me.'

'You could say I had an issue with my bank details,' said Sam.

'I could.'

❧❧❧❧❧ ❧❧❧❧❧

The elephants were restless in the gathering gloom. The larger males stood on the outskirts of the group while the females and youngsters fed on the lush grass in the clearing. They stuck their trunks in the air and tested for suspicious odours, but there was no warning of the incoming disaster until the first soldiers appeared at the edge of the meadow holding lit torches.

The oldest female sounded the alarm, and the troop tried to move off into the jungle. More soldiers stepped forward barring their way, herding the elephants with the flaming torches along the old road which led to the edge of the forest. As the elephants approached the main road, panic spread, and they turned to face their tormentors. There was a standoff for several seconds and then they stampeded towards the rebels.

'Fire at their legs. Don't damage the ivory,' shouted the leader of the men, as they all crouched to shoot.

The sound threatened to burst their eardrums as a cacophony of squeals of fury and of pain combined with the bursts of machine gun fire. Several elephants escaped through the ranks of the rebels, one male killing a man by running him through with a tusk and throwing him high into the branches where he dangled from his rucksack like the victim of an unopened parachute.

The noise of elephants crashing through the undergrowth faded away, and the men moved from their positions slinging their guns over their shoulders. In front of them, a horrific scene emerged as elephants lay dying unable to get up on their crippled legs. Large dark pools of blood coalesced into a ghastly maroon lake around the disabled creatures.

The rebel troop stared in awe at the carnage. Bodies resembled large grey rocks dumped on the road and sprayed with red paint. The leader pulled his axe out of his belt and leapt on top of a corpse. He swung it at the jaw, biting deep into the bone.

'Get a move on,' he said. 'Someone come and pull on this tusk while I free it from the bone.'

The men hesitated. Members of the herd still writhed and snorted on the ground. A baby elephant slipped and fell over in the viscous liquid seeping from their bodies, bleating for help until one man aroused from his stupor and knocked it out with his rifle butt.

'Just shoot the ones that are moving. Come on. We've work to do.'

Sam walked back to Dirk's office with a swagger that betrayed her buoyant mood. All idea of losing her job had vanished. It occurred to her that she had some powerful blackmail material on her hands should she choose to use it. She was getting closer to the truth, and more pieces of the puzzle had now fallen into place. She had the framework, now she had to identify the architects. They'd soon learn what it meant to tangle with Sam Harris.

Chapter 24

Sam arrived back at Masaibu three weeks after she left, the business class ticket to Entebbe from Johannesburg a sign that they had restored her standing. She had taken her leave of Dirk with a certain coolness after her close shave at the hands of the board. He hadn't exactly leapt to her defence.

'They've given you a second chance,' he said.

'That's big of them,' said Sam.

'Don't get on your high horse. The evidence appeared pretty damning,' said Dirk.

'But they fabricated it and you didn't stand up for me.'

'I didn't know you well enough to assume your innocence. They were blaming me for recommending you. I was under the cosh. Can't you appreciate that?' said Dirk, throwing his hands up.

'Sure. But I consider myself to still be on my first chance since I didn't do anything wrong,' said Sam.

'Semantics. Get back to Masaibu and show them how wrong they were okay?'

'Sure, but next time, please check your facts with me before you join the crowd. I need someone in my corner and I thought it was you,' said Sam.

'It's a deal. Let's get this job finished then. Good luck,' Dirk said, avoiding her eyes.

'I'll do my best,' she said, meaning it.

Miriam was waiting in the lobby to see her off, wearing a purple lipstick that matched her perm. Sam remembered her promise to the women in the customs' shed.

'I need to buy some lipstick. Is there a discount store nearby where I can buy in bulk?' she said.

'You're trying to seduce the baddies?' said Miriam with a smirk.

'No, I'm going to bribe the ladies in customs,' said Sam.

'Ah. Don't say bribe. They'll have you back in front of the board before you can unpack your suitcase.'

'Gift, that's what I meant. Just kidding.'

'There's a place off the highway to the airport. Tell the driver to stop at Magic Mall. It's cheap and nasty in the main, but you can get nice makeup there,' said Miriam, who gave her a hug and whispered in her ear. 'Be careful out there. You don't have many friends.'

'Didn't I tell you about the French Foreign Legion boys?' said Sam, with a wicked grin. 'They provide for all my needs out there.'

Miriam giggled but Sam had left, shoving the revolving door with all her might and being thrown out on to the street with her suitcase at the feet of the startled driver.

'Magic Mall first please, and then the international terminal at the airport.'

After the usual bumpy journey across Lake Albert, Mad Mark dropped Sam off at the Masaibu terminal. Before her was the usual test of endurance in customs and immigration. Now that she had the right visa in her passport the officials had little reason to delay her and her cheerful demeanour appeared to break their will.

The ladies in the customs room didn't even open her suitcase after she handed over the contraband purchased at Magic Mall. She could still hear them squealing with delight as she got into the jeep after being greeted by an ecstatic Ezekiel, who she restrained from hugging her.

'Shikamo Mama Sam, you came back.'

'Yes, I must be out of my mind, but here I am,' said Sam, sighing.

'You were not out of my mind, Mama Sam.'

'Well, that must be it then. I blame you.'

This produced a massive smile which threatened to swallow him whole.

'Home James,' she said.

They drove through town without stopping. Sam wore a big hat and sunglasses and sank down in her chair so no-one could spot her in the front seat. Improving community relations after the ordeal she'd just been through made her shudder.

Hans and Jacques occupied their usual places on the balcony in front of the office building as Ezekiel drove up to the accommodation. Sam waved at them from the door of her prefab but made hand signs for going to sleep and went straight in. To her relief, the sitting room was spotless, and the padlock was still on her bedroom door.

She dug the key out from the bottom of her rucksack pocket where she had dropped it on leaving for her break and snapped the lock open. The door swung open, and she peered in.

Her room looked untouched, and she relaxed before ripping off the bottom sheet just in case. The mattress did not contain any unwelcome visitors, so she remade the bed pulling the mosquito net down from its binding until it covered the mattress. Sleep was not instantaneous, but Sam was stubborn and soon extinguished her racing brain.

Ota Benga, the pygmy, licked his fingers one by one. The prize of the sweet honey negated all the risks he had taken to gather it at the top of a tall tree deep in the forest. He pried a bee sting out of his shoulder and rubbed it with a salve he had wrapped in a leaf stashed in his ancient shorts. The honey dripped down the sides of the plastic container he was using, made out of a cut-off water bottle.

He finished checking for stings and then trotted off down the narrow path in the forest keeping his head low in case rangers spotted him. They didn't frequent the area he had been to because of its remoteness, but they took out their frustrations on any pygmies they found hunting in the forest.

The evening was cool, but clouds of mosquitos drifted on the breeze. He stopped to search for a bush whose leaves they used as a repellent and rubbed them all over his body. The swarm lifted and floated away in search of someone else to bite.

As he neared the exit, a strong smell of iron stopped him in his tracks. He stood upright testing the air with a bewildered expression. A lament floated through the forest, the cry of a baby elephant, but no adult answered its call. Elephants did not abandon their young, even when they were dead. Something had happened to the mother. Perhaps he could bring some fresh meat home as well as the honey.

Ota followed the odour through the forest. Alarm replaced bewilderment as the smell grew so strong that it stuck at the back of his throat, the iron making his tongue dry. A deep foreboding made his ribs tighten around his heart. Then he stepped into a small clearing where a scene of unspeakable horror waited.

꧁꧂

Philippe did not bother to look up when Sam entered her office the next morning. The expression of frank surprise on his face when he deigned to glance at her was worth many board meetings. He choked on the boiled sweet he had been sucking, going purple with exertion as his airways fought to force it out of his mouth. It popped out onto the desk and lay there shiny and sticky on a document he had been reading.

'You're back?' he said. 'I mean, already. How?'

'Get out of my office. Now. You have two minutes or you can keep walking to the front gate.'

Philippe gathered his papers together huffing and puffing with indignation. He stomped past her in a good pantomime of hurt feelings, but the metaphorical steam coming out of his ears told her how he felt about her return. Charlie Okito must have omitted to tell him that their plan to remove her had backfired. Perhaps he wanted to land Philippe in it to deflect attention from the obvious subterfuge of the newspaper article.

Whatever the reason, it was clear her return was not a complete surprise to everyone. No one else commented except to ask her how her holiday had been. The only person who appeared as stunned as Philippe was Mama Sonia who spent the whole of breakfast looking like a slapped cat.

'You'd swear she wasn't pleased to see you back,' said Hans, laughing into his coffee. 'She wouldn't win any Oscars for acting.'

'Moussa told me she marched into his office last week and demanded he cancel the Stoddard's delivery,' said Jacques.

'What did he do?' said Sam.

'He told her they had a contract and she would have to wait until next year.'

Jacques tried not to smile and stuffed a piece of toast in his mouth which he aspirated. Hans slapped him so hard on the back it flew across the table and landed in Sam's tea.

'Yuck. That's disgusting,' she said, wrinkling her nose, but it was hard not to gloat.

After the morning meeting, she shut herself into her office. She took the photograph frame from the rubbish bin and shook out the broken glass. The photograph of her parents was undamaged so she balanced it on her desk and made a note to ask Moussa to get a piece of glass cut to replace it.

She reached into the zipped pocket of her rucksack and removed the photocopies Doris had made her from the Masaibu accounts. She smoothed them out on her desk and put a pile of books on top to make them stay flat.

She started her computer and made a spreadsheet into which she entered all the data on the missing orders. There were thirty-seven major payments totalling over two million dollars. She put her hand to her mouth, her eyes wide with shock. *Two million dollars? Bloody hell. No wonder they tried to get rid of her. But who?*

Charlie Okito was the prime suspect in Goro, but she didn't have any proof yet. Also, someone else must have signed the orders in head office in Johannesburg. Was it possible that they signed them without checking that someone made the purchases? She was the first manager to live on site. No one ever bothered to come out to the project and check the inventories. It was easy to get away with a massive fraud.

She must get leverage and find out who was pulling the strings in Johannesburg. She didn't doubt that there were people in the know in Masaibu but who? If she wanted to find out what was going on, she needed someone to trust her enough to tell her the truth. Back to the drawing board then. *What was she missing?*

Chapter 25

O ta Benga stood at the gates of the campsite. The guards shouted at the pygmy that he must leave, but he would not move, resolute in his demand to see the boss.

'Ninataka kumwona,' said Ota.

'Go away. The boss will not see you,' said the guard.

'Mama Sam.'

They tried to manhandle him down the street but he ducked under their arms, ran towards the gate and under the barrier scampering straight into the arms of Hans, who was coming to inspect progress on fixing a new fence around the site. Ota flailed around trying to wriggle out of Hans' grasp.

Hans held the man at arm's length with his legs cycling in the air. Jacques emerged from the hut and recognised Ota.

'Put him down. Ota is the pygmy's representative from the stakeholder meetings. What does he want?' said Jacques.

'They say he wants to see Sam,' said Hans.

'He is within his rights. I doubt he'd be here if it were not of vital importance. Anyway, look at the state of him. He's shaking.'

'Oh. Sorry about that.'

Hans placed Ota back on the ground and gestured towards the office. The pygmy shook himself and followed Jacques up the road without a backward glance.

Sam was leaving for lunch when Jacques arrived with Ota. Her stomach growled in protest as she shook Ota's hand and pulled up a chair for him and Jacques.

Ota remained on his feet, his eyes wide, and garbled, a mixture of French, Swahili and Pygmy dialect. He sweated with effort, great beads falling around him onto the dusty floor. Stings or bites covered his skin but Sam couldn't work out if that had anything to do with what he was trying to say. Something terrible had happened in the forest but what?

'I'm so sorry, Ota. I don't understand. We need someone to translate,' said Sam

'What about Mbala? She's here today working with Dr Ntuli on the list of supplies needed to keep the hospital clean,' said Jacques. 'I'll get her. Why don't you fetch some food for Ota? He is swaying with hunger.'

Sam made Ota sit down and drink a sweet coffee from Jacques' flask. Then motioning him to stay where he was, she crossed to the canteen and loaded a plate with meat and rice for him, grabbing a banana to keep her going.

She returned to her office with the meal, covered by a napkin, where she found Ota sniffing the beetles that were laid out on the dado rail.

'Those aren't snacks,' she said, in her best schoolmarm voice, making him jump back and drop one on the floor.

She offered him the plate. Ota took it and hoovered the food up in an instant using his fingers. He then licked the plate clean before handing it back to her rubbing his stomach in appreciation.

213

The door opened and Mbala entered with Jacques. She addressed the pygmy in Swahili.

'Ota, you are welcome to our house. What is wrong at the forest? Is your family safe?'

'Safe, all safe, but there has been a massacre. Only the baby survived,' said Ota.

'A massacre. I don't understand. How are they safe if someone has killed them?' said Mbala who put her hand up to stop him talking while she translated for Sam.

At that moment Hans came in and caught the gist. 'What's the problem? A massacre of the pygmies? That's illegal apart from anything else. They are a protected people.'

'I don't think it's them that were attacked. Ota's confusion and distress have made him incomprehensible,' said Mbala.

'We must find out today, but first we should eat in case we don't get back tonight,' said Hans.

'Eat?' said Sam.

'I'm not going anywhere before I eat. Neither should you. I'm sure Ota will join us for seconds. He looks better already,' said Jacques.

'Okay, but quickly,' said Sam, whose guts were churning, her hunger replaced by dread. *Bloody army guys. Always thinking about logistics.*

They travelled in two cars. Hans and Sam shared the smaller, more mobile jeep and drove ahead of the bulkier car containing Jacques, Mbala and Ota. Hans used the horn whenever someone tried to intercept the car to chat. The startled residents jumped out of the way when they took in Hans' expression.

They took just over half an hour to reach the path to the pygmy village. Ota jumped out of the car and trotted away without waiting for everyone else. They all followed him, single file. Sick with trepidation, Sam placed her feet one in front of the

214

other on the path concentrating only on the act of walking.

By the time they got to the village, the whole population had assembled in front of their round huts, fear and incomprehension written on their faces. A strange bleating sound emanated from one hut.

'What the hell is that?' said Sam.

Hans shrugged. He turned to Mbala.

'Ask them,' he said, but she didn't need to.

'The elephants. They've killed many. The forest is full of blood.'

'Massacre.'

The bleating started again. Sam gestured towards the hut.

'Bébé,' said Ota.

'Christ. A baby elephant? It will die if we don't get it some milk,' said Jacques.

Sam found her legs and staggered to the hut. She peered through a crack in the door. A hairy trunk searched the crevice to sniff her. The infant bleated again. Her heart threatened to break.

'We need to ask Jean Delacroix. They know what to feed it. Can you go with Mbala and find him? He should be in town today helping the environmental team teach the ladies how to grow broccoli,' said Sam.

'And you?' said Jacques.

'Hans and I will go with Ota and find out how bad this is. We need to count the elephants. I must take photographs as evidence.'

'But Sam...'

'I have to do this. There's no choice. Hans will look after me.'

Jacques and Mbala headed back to town. Ota jumped into the jeep with Sam and Hans gesticulating and mouthing strange words as it threw them around on the terrible road. Soon the car entered the dark coolness of the forest. They did not have to drive for long before Ota made them stop the car and get out.

There was a smell of death in the air. Sam tried to breathe through her mouth but the iron clung to the roof of her mouth. She was drowning in blood way before she waded into it. The dead elephants resembled a field of boulders dropped by a glacier. Their corpses had sunk nearer the ground as the life force ebbed away into the soil but the large grey bodies still intimidated with their extraordinary size. They exuded sadness and fear.

Sam got close to one big male and could see an axe leaning against his bloodied head. The skull was split and torn where the killers had hacked at it to prise the tusk loose. Hans came up behind her and put his hand on her shoulder making her jump. She turned to him to say something, but the words got stuck in her throat. Tears coursed down her cheeks as he pulled her into his massive chest.

'You shouldn't have come. This is too much,' he said. 'Those bastards. Some of these elephants are almost one hundred years old and someone has cut them down for money.'

His voice was ragged, and he clung to Sam like a drowning man. 'You've got to take photos. I'm sorry, I know you don't want to but we must get the evidence. I'll take the axe with us. Maybe we can get fingerprints or something.'

Sam nodded, struck dumb in horror. She moved between the bodies taking photographs of the carnage. Their tails were missing, hacked off at the root.

'Jesus,' she said, 'The bastards took trophies.'

'We need samples in that case,' said Hans.

'Samples?' Sam almost vomited.

'For forensics. If we find the tails, we can prove they belonged to this herd. I will come back tomorrow with Jean.'

'But where are the tusks? They can't have taken them out yet. The baby elephant would have died after a short time alone. Two days perhaps?'

'You're right. If we couldn't get here in the small jeep, there is no way they could get a lorry through. They must have stored them nearby.'

Hans straightened up and crossed to Ota who was sitting on one body as if in a trance.

'Ota.' His voice echoed across the glade. 'We must find the tusks.'

Ota moaned, a broken man, but Hans shook him and mimed the carrying of the tusks on his back and the resulting fatigue.

'Where is the road?' he said. 'La route?'

Ota pointed through the trees.

'You track the men. Cherche les coupables.'

Hans raised his hand to his brow and mimed looking at the ground and picking up twigs. Ota sprung from his gruesome seat and onto the ground. He grabbed his spear. Moving to the edge of the glade, he made a circuit, crouching so low he was almost invisible. He stopped, his body rigid, and he picked up some leaves from the forest floor sniffing them with concentration, his eyes shut.

Suddenly, he stood bolt upright and pointed into the forest indicating that they should take the road and meet up with him on the outside.

'That makes sense. They have stored them nearer the road for easy removal. We can meet him when he emerges from the forest,' said Hans.

Sam was already walking to the car. Ota set off trotting through the forest following the trail. Soon the shadows swallowed him.

They jumped into the jeep and took off towards the main road. Sam changed the film in her camera and stored the used one in its container. Her mood had changed to one of vengeance and the muscles in her cheeks became white balls.

The subtle change in his companion did not go unnoticed and Hans nodded at her in admiration and respect. Sam glowed. *He had picked up the change in her attitude, hardly surprising. Since he was a soldier, he must know all about revenge.*

Chapter 26

As Hans turned the car out of the forest and up the muddy track running alongside it, Jacques and Jean Delacroix drove up in the other vehicle. Signalling for them to follow him, Hans led them along the road as Sam kept an eye out for Ota in the gloom. They needn't have worried. His face grim and shoulders slumped, the pygmy stood in the centre of the muddy ruts in plain sight.

They pulled the cars into the side of the road and followed Ota to the tree-line. He trotted into the forest for about a hundred metres and stopped in a small clearing in front of a pile of what appeared to be tree trunks covered in palm leaves and other vegetation, and stacked between six holding posts hammered into the ground, three on each side of the pile.

Sam shrugged at Hans, but he headed towards the pile. He lifted the covering from one end. Dark red stains covered the ends of the trunk-like objects. Hans stiffened with suppressed rage as he recognised the tusks. Sam watched his chest heave as he steadied himself. *How could a man like that control his anger when her blood was boiling in her veins?* She shoved her hands into her pockets and bit her lip. *Bastards.*

Hans, Jean and Jacques cleared the camouflage from the tusks, exposing their pinkish hue to the light. Sam steeled herself to take photographs at each stage, including objects against which to gauge their scale. Hans put his hand on her shoulder. She turned to face him; her distress unhidden.

'We must burn the ivory,' said Hans.

'Ivory doesn't burn, or at least, it does, but it takes days,' said Jean. 'It's almost impossible to destroy.'

'What else can we do?' said Sam.

'They have tried crushing it in the past but it doesn't work well either and these tusks are super hard,' said Jean.

'If we burn it for a day or two, that should destroy the value, don't you think?' said Sam. 'We only need to make it unsaleable.'

'That's true,' said Jean. 'But how do we find the culprits?'

'The pygmies can watch the site and report back to us when someone turns up to collect their booty,' said Sam.

'They must be careful. Whoever they are, these people are armed and ruthless,' said Jacques.

'Do we have any gasoline?' said Jean

'There's a canister in each car. Emergency supplies,' said Hans.

'Let's fetch them. Sam, stay here with Jean,' said Jacques.

The two men set off through the forest leaving Sam and Jean standing together. Only the sound of leaves falling through the canopy disturbed the silence.

'Did you see the bodies of the elephants?' said Jean.

'Yes, I took photographs. It was like a scene out of a nightmare. The elephants had their faces and trunks hacked away to get at the tusks. And the smell...' Sam's voice broke.

'Are you all right?'

'Not really. I've got blood on my boots to remind me,' said Sam. 'How much is the ivory worth?'

'About two thousand dollars a kilo,' said Jean.

'That much? No wonder the elephants aren't safe.'

Sam approached the stack of tusks and stroked the pink ivory. She leaned her forehead against one post feeling its rough bark pushing into her skin.

'I can't understand why the people who buy it still think it's okay. Haven't they watched David Attenborough or any documentaries about poaching? Don't they know how intelligent and magnificent elephants are?' said Sam.

Jean grimaced. 'Culture,' he said. 'There's an emerging middle class in Asia who buy ivory as a status symbol. They don't care about elephants, only their tusks. Organised crime has become involved now. There's talk of them stockpiling the ivory to avoid any vetoes.'

'They'll come back and kill the others, won't they?'

'Yeah. Elephants represent mountains of money to the poachers. They don't think of them as sentient beings.'

'We've got to stop them,' said Sam.

'But how? The stakeholders don't want to use money for rangers,' said Jean.

'We need to show them the evidence of the slaughter. Surely, they'll agree to support them when they see the carnage.'

'They might. It's worth a try. How can I help?'

'Does your organisation have printing facilities?' said Sam, an idea forming.

'Yes, we have all mod-cons in Kampala. We can print posters.'

'If I give you the film with the photos of the massacre on it, how fast can you get them developed and made into posters?'

'Almost immediately, I should think,' said Jean, brightening.

'Soon enough for the stakeholder meeting next week?'

'Yes, if you give it to me now.'

'I want to get some photographs of the ivory stack on fire and then I'll rewind the roll and take it out of my camera.'

'Okay, that sounds perfect. No-one could fail to be moved by what you have seen today.'

The sound of branches being pushed aside interrupted their chat as Hans and Jacques arrived back at the clearing with two canisters of gasoline. They went straight over to the tusks and poured the gasoline on the top of the heap. The strong fumes entered Sam's nasal passages making her feel as if they were on fire too. Nausea rose in her throat.

'Has anyone got a match?' said Jacques.

✦✦✦✦✦✦ ✦✦✦✦✦✦

By the time Sam got back to her prefab, her head had cleared enough for her to appreciate the thrilling blanket of stars thrown over the dark town. The starlight cleansed her eyes after the horror of the carnage in the forest. Despite smoking two of Hans' cigarettes, the acrid smell of the burning tusks clung to the lining of her nose.

A cry of protest escaped her before she could prevent it. She roared with impotence and fury like a lioness whose cubs have been killed by a rival male. Anxious faces appeared at the windows of several prefabs, but she had gone inside to make tea, the only remedy she knew for her troubles.

Once inside, she curled up on the reclining chair and sipped a cup of tea so hot that it threatened

234

to remove the roof of her mouth. This job made everything else she had ever done look like sucking eggs. Not only was someone siphoning money from the project, but poachers were slaughtering elephants with impunity in the park Consaf was sponsoring. Added to that, the pygmies were being killed and even eaten by rebels because people thought they were subhuman. Somehow, she had to deal with these problems at the same time.

And then she remembered seeing the Asian man talking to Joseph Kaba outside the stakeholder meeting. *Could that meeting be related to the slaughter? What on earth could they have in common besides that?* He was the only Asian she had ever seen in Masaibu, and the markets for ivory were all based there.

She lay in bed tossing and turning but sleep wouldn't come. Images of the large grey bodies had seared into her eyeballs and the smell of blood kept coming back to her, dense and metallic.

Suddenly there was a knock on the door. Her heart leapt in her chest. She lay there quivering with fear. *Who would be at her door at this time of night? Maybe they would go away if she didn't answer.*

Again, she heard knocking, gentle, insistent. She dragged herself out of bed and felt her way to the door.

'Who's there?' she said.

'It's me, Hans.'

'Hans? What's wrong?'

She pulled the door open to find him leaning against the wall. He turned his head to her and she saw distress in his face.

'Come in,' she hissed, grabbing his arm and tugging him, terrified someone would see him, add two and two together and make twelve.

He stumbled into her sitting room and slumped into her reclining chair.

'Hey,' he slurred. 'This is like mine.'

Drunk.

'What are you doing here?' she said.

His face worked and he screwed it up as if trying to banish his demons, but when he turned to look at her, the sorrow showed.

'I miss her,' he said. 'Today, you reminded me of her again. I wanted to...'

He trailed off. Sam could see tears glinting on his cheeks. Her soft heart ached for him. She had never suffered a loss like that, but her empathy for him made her sad too. She felt her eyes filling with tears to see his huge frame shaking with grief.

Hardly knowing what she was doing, she got onto his lap and pulled the lever of the chair so that they were both leaning back. She put her head on his shoulder and her arm around his chest and held him while he wept.

He fell asleep eventually. Sam threw a rug over him and tip-toed back to bed. The relief he felt had crept through her pores and comforted her. She turned over and fell into a deep slumber. When she woke the next morning, he was gone.

Chapter 27

'It was bound to happen. Fucking savages.' Frik thumped the table with a massive fist. 'What did you expect?'

The racist overtone of his statement hung in the air challenging someone to disagree. Sam rolled her eyes to heaven.

'If the rebels are killing the elephants, someone is paying. We intend to hunt down the source of funds,' said Hans.

'I can give you a head start on that one,' said Sam. 'I remembered last night that I noticed Joseph Kaba having lunch with an Asian man in the restaurant run by Mama Sonia.'

'And what were you doing there?' said Hans, knitting his eyebrows together in fake jealousy.

'Having a rather delicious lunch with Jean Delacroix. I hear the standards have slipped since you disrupted her supply chain,' said Sam.

She winked at him and he threw his head back emitting snorts of laughter. It was such a relief to see him back to normal. His nocturnal visit already seemed like an odd dream.

'I also saw Kaba talking to the same man outside the last community meeting before I went on leave. It can't be a coincidence. There aren't any Asian businesses in town that I know of,' she said.

'But why are you so concerned about these elephants? They are wild animals,' said Ngoma Itoua. 'We need to focus on the people.'

'But that's just my point,' said Sam. 'If we keep the elephants alive, we can encourage tourism here, to create jobs for local people.'

'What about the mine? Consaf told people they will have jobs when they build the plant,' said Philippe. 'Someone asks me about the mine most days.'

'The mine? But we don't have a resource yet,' said Sam.

'What's a resource?' said Dr Ntuli, never one to shirk a silly question.

'It's a measure of the amount of gold in the ground. We have to find enough gold to fund the building of a plant, cover all the costs of drilling and make a profit,' said Alain.

'But Consaf have been drilling for years. How come they haven't finished yet?' said Kante.

'It's difficult to find enough gold in one place that's also feasible to take out. Most projects fail to become mines because there isn't enough metal in the ground to make it economic to take out. That's why it's so important that we have a backup plan, to ensure that there are always jobs for the people of Masaibu, even if there is no mine in the future,' said Sam.

The meeting dwindled to a close. Sam was left sitting on her own as the managers filed out. A black depression descended over her as she struggled to make sense of their reactions to the slaughter. Being worried about the fate of the elephants was a white person's concern, nothing to do with the local poverty and violence. *Was it racist to save the elephants while women were dying in childbirth?*

She lifted her head as the loud thud of raindrops hitting the zinc roof reverberated around the room, intensifying with every wave of rain that swept over the camp. Soon the whole place would be a quagmire and the daily fights over the heavy machinery would get worse.

Sighing, she got up and went to the front door of the office building. The rain was being driven in at an angle, hitting the floorboards of the verandah and splashing her work boots with dark stripes.

All day the deluge fell, yellow streaks of lightning racing across black skies. The gutters overflowed and leaves clogged the storm drains. Large pools of standing water sat waiting for the mosquitos to deposit their eggs. The frogs croaked their love songs and hopped into the grass, prey for waiting constrictors.

Sam took the chance to go through the musty files stored in the cabinets under the bookshelves in her office. She emptied them one by one, reviewing the contents before putting them into new folders with clearer labelling. Some pages were damp and had stuck together, but she dried them with a hairdryer, borrowed from a woman in the kitchen.

She could not find any evidence that the machinery had ever arrived at Masaibu, but proving the absence of something was a lot harder than it had seemed when she left head office, buoyed up by her discovery. The whole job was getting on top of her. It was always one step forward and two back. Her small victories appeared pyrrhic beside the enormity of the problems facing her.

She stepped outside, the last of the rain dripping off the zinc roof in warm droplets onto her tense back. The desire to hide in her room crept over her like a black cloud over a mountain. Then, she saw something glitter in the storm drain beside the office, like the flash of a kingfisher or a peacock's tail, iridescent.

She bent down to remove some leaves and gasped. Lying dead on its back was a beetle with shimmering blue wings, one of which had unfolded and was jammed open by a twig. She reached down and picked it up, straightening the wing and folding it back along the body.

It had been washed into the drain with several Rhinoceros beetles which had also drowned in the torrent. They lay in a tangle of limbs and horns over the grid covering the drain, their matt black carapaces shiny with water.

Gathering them together, she went back into her office and placed them to dry on the dado rail which ran around the office. The beetle book proved harder to find than she had imagined as it had wedged itself behind the drawer in her desk. She scanned the pages, looking for a photograph of the strange beetle she had found in the storm drain.

There it was, Colophon beetle, a genus in the stag beetle family, but hers was iridescent blue. These were black or brown and supposed to be endemic to South Africa, confined to restricted ranges of particular mountain ranges. She picked up the beetle again and examined it with more care. *Oh God, we have a rare sub-species of a beetle on our project.*

She put it back on the dado rail wrapped in tissue and groaned. As if she didn't have enough problems. She kicked the chair which skidded into the desk almost knocking the computer screen on the floor. *For fuck's sake, what am I going to do?*

Alain put his head around the door and his face fell when he noticed her expression.

'Oh, um, should I come back later?'

Sam looked around the office at the mouldy pages strewn all over the floor and the beetles on the dado rail. She was conscious of her swollen eyes and blotchy face. She sighed.

'No, that's okay. What's up?'

'It's not important, but I'm worried now. Did someone upset you?'

'No, I'm just...'

Despite herself, Sam started to cry. She had shoved the ambush in the boardroom to the recesses of her mind, trying to pretend it hadn't happened, but now the memories surged back suffocating her. Forgetting that he was one of the people responsible for the inquisition in Johannesburg, she recounted the horror of what happened in the boardroom, blow by blow, sobbing as she remembered the awful shock.

Alain listened without interrupting, which was just what she needed. Once the cork was out of the bottle, the anguish flooded out. Without intending to, she also told him about the discovery that someone had stolen a lot of money from the project, probably with collusion from head office. She gestured at the mouldy files, choking on her anger.

'There's nothing in here. It's so frustrating. I can't prove a thing even though it makes the schemes around here look like small beer. Someone doesn't want me to succeed but I can't fail, I refuse.'

She had finished and was clearing her nose with the force of a leaf blower. Alain couldn't look her in the eye. She felt embarrassed and flapped her hands at him.

'Well, there's also the business of the elephants and the hospital and so on. I let it get to me. I'm sorry you had to see this.'

'No, it's okay. I understand.'

But he pushed his chair back, and it fell on the floor where he groped for it, while watching her face and then backed out of her office muttering that he was busy, his expression panicked.

Sam felt even worse. Too late now. Better out than in and all that. Alain was trustworthy. He wouldn't spill the beans, not after the room thing. She collected the files together and put them back into the cabinets.

Jacques watched with curiosity as Sam foraged for dead beetles in the storm drains around the square. Engrossed in her task, she bit her bottom lip until it was crimson. She was bent double for several minutes and she rubbed her back muscles when she straightened up. He noticed the bags under her eyes and the slump of the shoulders as she walked across to the office building.

'What's up with Sam?' he said.

'She's a woman,' said Hans. 'Nobody can tell.'

'Something happened in Johannesburg. She hasn't been the same since.'

'Are you forgetting about the elephants?' said Hans.

'No, but she was down before then. And she's got worse.'

'You're soft on her. Get over it. We are not allowed feelings for clients. I thought we had an agreement.'

'What if I am? She's special. Anyway, I haven't gone near her.'

'She must be suspicious by now then. You make it so obvious that you are avoiding her.'

'Jesus, Hans, haven't you got anything better to do?'

'You asked.'

Hot shame enveloped Alain as he walked towards his cabin. He stopped and looked at the sky where the stars had vanquished the clouds and jeered at him. Philippe. It was his fault. He was the source of all the gossip and malice in camp that the boss in Goro received. Alain had never met Charlie Okito and never wanted to. Everything he had heard about that man made him either cross or afraid.

Alain swore out loud just as Bruno emerged from the canteen wiping his mouth on his sleeve and easing his belt over his plump stomach.

'What's up, brother?' said Bruno. 'You look troubled.'

'Can I trust you to be discrete?' said Alain.

'Is that a joke? Who listens to me?'

'Do you want to drink a beer with me in the shack outside the main gates? It's private there.'

'Sure. I'll meet you there in five minutes.'

When Alain invited him for a beer, Bruno had presumed they would talk about Alain's relationship with a woman his family disapproved of, something he had confided only to Bruno. But instead, Alain had told him of his shameful capitulation to Philippe, and the resulting witch hunt directed at Sam in head office. The domino effect of a small mistake appalled him.

'I had no idea. Why didn't they ask us if she is a racist?' said Bruno. 'We'd have set them right.'

'What do you think of her?' Alain asked him. 'Generally, I mean.'

'To tell you the truth, before she arrived, you lot treated me like a laughingstock. Mama Sam treats me like a professional. She respects my qualifications. I'm happy she's here,' said Bruno.

Alain flushed and swirled his beer around the bottle avoiding Bruno's eyes.

'I'm sorry. I got involved with that bullying too. I let myself be carried along by the crowd. It won't happen again.'

'That's okay. I shouldn't have allowed it. Sometimes it's easier to be a doormat than fight back,' said Bruno.

'I'd like to help her, but I have no power here and no contacts in Goro. The information she needs must be in the files kept in Charlie Okito's office, but how do we get it without alerting him?' said Alain.

Bruno had not answered, but guilt crept into his pores and permeated his being. *He held the key. Was he brave enough to use it?*

Chapter 28

Jean Delacroix was as good as his word. He turned up in Sam's office the afternoon of the stakeholder meeting in great humour.

'Ah, there you are. I've got the posters. And some stands to hang them on,' he said.

'Already? I can't believe it. You're a genius.'

'Yes, I am.' He grinned. 'Hey, you've got a great collection of beetles there. What's the one wrapped in tissue?'

'Oh, the same, I was trying to dry it out,' said Sam, pushing it out of sight.

'You know they'll smell terrible after a couple of days? You need to hang them outside on a thread so they'll dry without being eaten by ants.'

'But won't ants eat the insides and leave the carapaces?'

'They'll also eat connecting tissue and the legs will fall off.'

'Ah, okay. I'll hang them under the eaves so the rain doesn't get them. Do you want a coffee before we go?'

Hans swung the car into a space beside the meeting hall and helped Sam and Jean to unload the posters and stands from the back. They set them up inside the hall at the centre of the horseshoe-shaped table used by the stakeholders. Sam tried not to look at the gruesome images. Nausea threatened to overwhelm her as the odour of blood came back, suffocating her.

She smoked one of Jean's Gitanes outside the hall, blowing the smoke into the cool evening air.

'Are you all right?' said Hans. 'Only Jacques worries about you.'

Sam laughed. A short barking sound which sounded fake, even to her.

'And you aren't? Come on Mr Tough Guy, admit it.'

'I hadn't noticed, until he pointed it out,' said Hans, squirming, 'but your demeanour has been subdued.'

'Just busy,' said Sam. 'Masaibu by name, Masaibu by nature.'

It was Hans' turn to laugh, but he didn't.

By the time they entered the hall, most people had taken their seats. Animated conversations filled the air. Some people's faces wore expressions of disgust as they gesticulated at the posters. The mayor left his seat to shake Jean's hand and shepherded Sam to hers. He had an air of doom about him and couldn't meet Sam's eye. It occurred to her that Victor might have taken money from the perpetrators for turning a blind eye to the carnage. She shuddered and pushed the idea out of her mind.

With the usual formalities over, Sam stood up to address the meeting and caught sight of Joseph Kaba, who flicked at the flies congregating over his bag of biltong with some kind of whisk. She screwed up her eyes to focus on it and gasped. She grabbed the edge of the table afraid she might faint. Hans was at her side, in one swift movement, naked power on show as his muscles rippled with anticipation.

'Sam. Are you okay?' he said, spinning her around and grabbing her by the shoulders.

'Kaba,' she whispered. 'Look at his fly whisk.'

Hans glanced at Kaba who had not noticed Sam's distress and was flicking flies off his food with the air of a schoolboy trying out his new catapult. Hans turned back to Sam; his eyes narrowed like the slits on a pillbox.

'I can't believe it,' he said. 'The bastard is using an elephant tail. I can take him down if you want.'

The knuckles on the hands clutching her shoulders had gone white. She breathed deeply and put her own right hand up onto his.

'You're forgetting something,' she said. 'Watch soft power in action.'

For a split-second, Hans looked as if he would ignore her plea, then a smile passed across his eyes like a cat slipping through a fence. He sat down again.

Sam turned to face the now curious audience.

'I'm sure you noticed the posters on display in the hall this evening. They are shocking, but I intended them to shock. I took these photographs myself, in the forest reserve outside Masaibu ten days ago,' she said.

A spontaneous exclamation escaped from the attendees. Joseph Kaba, who had been feigning disinterest and slumped in his chair with

235

half-closed eyes, sat bolt upright in his chair as if transfixed. She continued.

'Poachers have entered the reserve and killed half of the herd for their tusks and, unless we do something, they'll be back for the rest.'

'But who would do such a thing?' said the representative of the shopkeepers.

'Someone with manpower and weapons,' said Hans, glaring at Joseph Kaba, who had recovered somewhat and glared back.

'But where are the tusks?' said Victor. 'Did you find them too?'

Sam let the question sink in with her audience before she answered.

'We not only found them, mayor, we burned them,' said Sam.

There was a crash as Joseph Kaba stood up and threw his part of the table across the floor, his glass shattering on impact.

'You had no right,' he roared, the veins on his neck standing out in fury. 'You'll regret this, you bitch.'

Before anyone could react, he stormed out of the building, slamming the door so hard that spiders fell from the rafters.

Sam flushed scarlet with triumph as all eyes turned back to her. *This was her chance to convince them. She needed to get money for the rangers or it was all in vain.*

'Now, more than ever, we need to fund extra rangers for the park. I'm begging you,' she said.

'We need all the money available to repair the road after the rains. There is no way we can pay for rangers right now.'

The mayor was apologetic but his relief was palpable. Kaba must have gotten to him. There was a murmur of agreement. No one defended her or the elephants. Sam was staring defeat in the face.

236

Then, Ota Benga, the pygmy, jumped onto the table and thumped his puny chest with his hand. He declaimed in Swahili. One of the shopkeepers translated what he said.

'The Pygmies can help. We are hunters and trackers, and we already live in the forest and know every inch. We can protect the elephants for you,'

'How will you protect them? With spears? They will mow you down with machine guns,' said Hans.

'They will not see us. We are the invisible people. If you give us radios, we can call the rangers if we see poachers. That way, you will not need any extra rangers, as we can be their eyes on the ground.'

'And what will you get out of this?' said Victor.

'We want to hunt in the forest as before, gather nuts and berries and take honey from the bees. It will not cost you any money. We need little. Oh, and milk for the elephant.'

'The elephant?'

'We saved a baby from the slaughter. It drinks a lot of milk,' said Ota.

There was silence. Ota Benga got off the table and nodded at Sam and Hans.

'You know where to find me,' he said.

He left the hall. There was the sound of the door shutting, and then a cacophony of comments, everyone talking over each over. The mayor held up his hands for silence.

'We will leave the matter with Consaf then,' he said.

'Please let me know if you spot any suspicious behaviour in town,' said Sam. 'I understand the priority for funding the road, but we must try to protect the elephants. Do you want to tell your children that they are extinct because you would not act to save them?'

The shell-shocked attendees filed out of the meeting, murmuring, most avoiding the posters with their eyes.

Sam and Jean stayed in the empty hall while Hans left to smoke a cigarette.

'Why don't you hire the pygmies officially?' she said.

'Hire them? What do you mean?'

'If WCO hired them to help the rangers, they could take prey instead of payment without fear of reprisals.'

He raised his head from his coffee and commented.

'They'd still need radios.'

'I'm sure Consaf could cough up the cash for a new transmitter and aerials and so on,' said Sam, who had no idea if this was true.

'I must speak to head office, and to Ota. It won't be an immediate decision. Let me get back to you,' said Jean

'What will the rangers think?' said Sam.

'Um, it could be a little tricky,' said Jean, wrinkling his nose.

'How so?'

'Well, some rangers are ex-rebels and they used to hunt the pygmies for fun.'

'They ate them, according to Hans,' said Sam.

'I didn't want to say so, but I have it on good authority.'

'Can we get them together for a negotiation?' said Sam.

'I think it would be more profitable to read them all the riot act. Negotiation will not work. We should just tell the rangers that the pygmies will work with them and lay down the ground rules for both groups. We can give them a week to think about it and to raise objections before a second meeting.'

'Perfect. Have you considered writing down working rules?'

'I have drafted some just now.'

Jean reached into his pocket and pulled out a sheaf of paper with hurried squiggles on it.

'Why don't you have a read, add your own, and get back to me with any suggestions before our next meeting?'

The next morning, Sam found Bruno waiting in her office with his habitual hangdog expression and an air of gloom that would have done justice to Eeyore. Sam refused to be drawn.

'What can I do for you today? How's progress on the refurbishments?' she said with a cheery grin.

Bruno fiddled with the buttons on his cuffs, avoiding her eyes.

'Work is good,' he muttered, but he didn't look up.

'Okay, I give up. What's wrong?'

Bruno glanced up as if gauging the likelihood of an angry reaction. Sam tried to keep her expression sympathetic, even though she was desperate for him to leave.

'Well?'

'I was talking to Alain. He told me you need help.'

Sam froze. *What on earth had possessed Alain to spill the beans to Bruno?* She fixed him with a stare.

'Did he? Help with what?'

'Um, the orders,' said Bruno, squirming.

'What orders?'

'He told me you are looking for proof that someone logged large orders from Masaibu, which are filed in the head office accounts, but the items never got here. Machinery parts and such like.'

He cringed as if waiting for a blow.

'Oh, well, I can't be sure. It seemed odd finding all the heavy machinery broken down when I got here, so I checked the orders at head office. I discovered that they had approved spare parts and sent the money to Goro. That's where it seems to have stayed.'

She hesitated.

'But I don't know what happened next. I'm not accusing anyone of anything,' she said.

Bruno raised his head and examined her face. His eyes bored into hers searing her soul. *A revelation. He knows something, but he isn't sure if he can trust me.* She held his gaze.

'What do you know?' she said.

'Do you trust me?'

Did she have a choice? She nodded.

'Give me the list,' he croaked.

Joseph Kaba had his head in his hands, his elbows planted on the desk in front of him. He moaned in fury and frustration. *What the fuck was he going to tell Chu?* He had blown the advance and now he had nothing to show for it. *It was that interfering woman who was to blame.*

There was a knock at the door which swung open with an ominous creak. Kaba looked into the grim face of Mr Chu, whose glare was scorching in its intensity.

'Some unpleasant rumours have reached me concerning our business arrangement. I need you to clarify the situation for me. Now.'

'I had planned on visiting you today. The...' stammered Kaba.

'I'm here now. What happened?' said Chu, red with fury.

'Those Consaf bastards found the ivory, and they burned it.'

'Just like that? Are you sure no-one told them where it was?' said Chu, glaring at him.

'A pygmy found the dead elephants and followed the tracks to the place where my men had hidden the tusks.'

'This is a disaster. I'll lose face if I don't deliver the ivory to my clients.'

Fear had replaced anger in Chu's tone.

'Half of the herd is still out there. We can hunt them down and kill them too,' said Kaba.

'What about the rangers?' said Chu.

'There are not enough rangers to cover the terrain. I have an informant who can tell us where they are on certain days. We need a meticulous plan like we had last time. We can do it. I guarantee it,' said Kaba.

'You guaranteed it last time.'

'Don't you think I know that? My debt to you is a matter of fact.'

'How soon?' said Chu.

'The town is on edge. It would be unwise to act straight away. Give it a couple of weeks to calm down and I'll plan the attack. We won't fail again.'

'Don't mess up.'

Chapter 29

The sun was splitting the stones when Bruno arrived in Goro. His cousin waited for him at the bus station. She stood with her back to the wall, hugging herself despite the heat, her face a mixture of emotions. Then she saw him and joy replaced them all, and she ran over to greet him.

'You've lost weight, Sara,' he said.

She glanced up at him, doubt in her expression.

'Am I ugly now?' she said.

'No, you're like a beautiful flower growing through a crack in the pavement.'

She smiled, a timid admission of pride.

'Let's go,' she said. 'I've made us a nice dinner, and we can have a quiet evening as no one is expecting you until tomorrow.'

She put a slim arm around his chubby waist and squeezed, making him blush with pleasure.

Sara's flat was near the bus station which bordered the slum area on the west of the city. She lived in one of the half-abandoned blocks of flats in an estate that had seen better days and was due for demolition. The building manager had removed the elevator from the shaft so they traipsed up seven flights of stairs. Bruno's heart threatened to give out; such was the stress of climbing the steps in the heat of the narrow stairwell.

Delicious smells swirled around the small room making Bruno faint with hunger. He sat on the small bed trying to fill himself up with the aroma of fish stew by taking in great warm lungfuls. Finally, Sara turned from the double gas ring with two large bowls of stew which she placed on either side of the rickety table, followed by a big saucepan full of rice.

Silence reigned as they ate. Bruno tried to eat slower than usual so that he would not finish too far ahead of his cousin. She laughed at him.

'Finish up and help yourself to more. I don't have a fridge. It will only go off if you don't,' said Sara.

Bruno lumbered over to the stove and poured the rest of the stew into his bowl. He was flushed with heat and mild embarrassment and sweat poured down his face. The flimsy paper serviettes on the table were not adequate to stem the flow, so he grabbed a towel Sara had laid on the chair for his use.

'How is work?' he said at last.

Her face creased with misery, and to his horror, she wept, tears falling in the remains of her fish stew. He reached over and gave her a handful of the serviettes, waiting while she recovered her poise.

'That bad, huh?' he said.

'I was so excited when I got this job. The salary meant I could move into my own room and have a private space just for me. I never expected to...' Sara wrung her hands.

'To what?'

'Charlie Okito, he's, he wants...'

Her voice broke again.

'Has he raped you?'

Bruno stood up unable to contain himself.

'Well, it wasn't rape, but I didn't want to. He says I will lose my job if I don't do it.'

A red mist descended over Bruno's vision as he imagined the scenario. He sat down on the bed and tried to calm down. His cousin came and sat beside him. She didn't speak.

'Would you like to get him back?' said Bruno.

She turned to him, her eyes glistening.

'What do you think?' she said.

'You'll lose your job,' said Bruno.

'I don't care. I can't stay either.'

'Is tonight too soon?'

The Ntezi project had recently upgraded their communications system, so they donated their redundant radios and the old receiver to Masaibu reserve. Dr Ntuli went to collect them and to do another couple of days safety training with their HSE team. He was becoming an asset with his own ideas and systems.

Sam left it to Jacques and Jean to train the pygmies in their use. As predicted, the rangers had not been receptive to the idea of working with the pygmies. Jacques pointed out it would reduce the number of hours they would spend meandering around the forest looking for poachers, inducing a tacit agreement to try out the scheme.

Sam arrived at the pygmy village just in time for the first trial run of the system. She listened as the radio operator explained how the messages got forwarded and the ranger's positions coordinated. They used several landmarks to make location easier. The poachers were not that discrete so once the rangers had a ballpark region, they could soon track them down just by listening.

She was standing in the middle of the village when a small grey train ran into the back of her legs and knocked her to the ground. The villagers were delighted and whooped with glee as Sam picked herself off the floor. A soft grey trunk probed her hair and ears, and then her pockets for treats. It emitted a squeal of delight as it withdrew the trunk curled around a banana. Sam melted.

'How's my girl?' she said and rubbed the elephant child on the head, getting knocked to the ground again. She cuddled the small grey body and wrestled it to the ground. It was miraculous. Such a tiny elephant should not have survived.

'How did they keep it alive?' she said.

'They sleep either side of her at night and keep her warm,' said Jacques. 'It's remarkable. And they have the special milk formula.'

Despite some teething problems, the pilot went well, with the rangers finding the location indicated by the pygmies without issues. The success of the trial led to lots of smiles and mutual congratulation which augured well.

'Let's see how it works in the real world,' said Jean.

'We won't have to wait long,' said Jacques. 'There are rumours a raid is imminent.'

Sara and Bruno approached the office building at midnight. A power cut was in progress, darkening the streets and driving people into their homes. Light from Bruno's torch picked out small bodies huddled together on sheets of cardboard, their wide eyes searching for dangers. Sara stumbled on a bottle which skittled up the pavement clinking over the dirt until it fell off into the gutter.

A dim light flickered in the lobby of the building which housed the Consaf office. A sleepy security guard smiled as he recognised Sara who approached his desk with an air of supplication.

'Good evening, Miss Sara. What can I do for you?'

'I forgot to finish something for Mr Okito. You know how angry he gets.'

'And this gentleman?' said the guard.

'He's a neighbour who walked me over from my house to protect me. These power cuts encourage dangerous people out onto the streets.'

'Okay, but he can't go up with you.'

'Please, I won't be long. It's pretty scary up there at night,' said Sara, pleading with her eyes.

'Fine, but it's your responsibility. Be as quick as you can. The lifts don't work on auxiliary power. You must use the stairs.'

Sara was already making for the door to the stairwell. Bruno stifled a groan. More stairs. The fourth-floor lights came on, brighter than expected, as the fluorescent tubes blinked into life, powered by the small generator. Sara led the way to the filing cabinets in a side annex.

'The cabinets you need are on the right. They file records by year. Take out the ones you want and we'll copy anything important,' said Sara.

A pile of folders teetered on the boardroom table. Bruno divided them in two and photocopied the list Sam had given him.

'It's simple. We're looking for the deposits of cash related to the list of items given to me by my boss. Even a few of them will be enough.'

The sound of paper rustling was the only noise to break the silence for the next twenty minutes apart from the buzz of the lights. Bruno grunted with approval twice before Sara spoke.

'Okay, what have you got? I've found five.'

'I've got seven. We need to confirm them on the bank statements to be sure,' said Bruno.

Sara retrieved the statements from another cabinet. It was child's play to match them up with the orders. She gasped and stepped back from the table.

'What?' said Bruno.

'The money. It came into the company account and was transferred out a couple of days later in all cases.'

'Where was it transferred to? The suppliers?'

'No,' she said, shaking her head. 'To Charlie Okito's personal account.'

'Oh my God. Sam was right. We need to photocopy these and get out of here. Can I see one of his statements from the same time?'

'I can't show you that,' said Sara, shaking her head.

'Please, it's so important.'

She fished out a statement and handed it to him. Bruno skimmed through the statement. He paused and reread the entry for the last day of the month. His legs turned to jelly, and he sat down.

'It's worse than I thought. He is taking a cut from the Ntezi Project as well. Look.'

'I don't want to know. I'll copy everything and let's get out of here,' said Sara.

But the copier wasn't working.

'It's the power cut. You must copy them tomorrow,' said Bruno.

'But what if Okito sees me?'

'You're not staying here after tomorrow. I'll wait for you downstairs. It will be okay. Just put them back after you copy them. He's sure to go out at some stage. Come on, we've got to get out of here,' said Bruno, looking around in panic as a noise reverberated in the stairwell.

Sara stuffed the papers in the bottom drawer of her desk and they left, locking the door on their

247

way out. The power came back on just as they exited through the lobby but there was no way of returning upstairs to the photocopier without arousing suspicion.

'I'll make the copies tomorrow. Let's go home,' said Sara.

The poachers left for the forest at dawn, armed to the teeth. Joseph Kaba sat up front in the lorry, puffing on a Cuban cigar he had stolen from a businessman he had murdered in Bukavu. The rich flavour of the smoke filled his lungs and soothed him. *If you want something done, do it yourself.*

He waited in the cabin of the lorry until his men had located the herd. It wasn't hard to spot them as they were creatures of habit and liked to drink from the shallow pool near the edge of the forest in the early mornings. They set up another ambush on the trail leading away from the pool and waited for the animals to return.

The forest came to life as they crouched in the shadows. Butterflies wafted through the shafts of early morning sunlight as the sun rose higher in the sky. Lizards adorned the trees like strange brooches following the warmth as it crept around the trunks. Damp legs begged for release as the cold rose up their combat trousers and cramped their calves.

There was a rustling in the bushes and suddenly, the air filled with the whistle and crack of bullets.

'What the hell is going on?' roared Kaba, who had been urinating a little way off and ran towards his men. 'Stop shooting immediately.'

He put his hands on his hips in fury before being pulled down into the mud by one of his men.

'It's the rangers, sir.'

'And how the fuck did they find us?' said Kaba.

'I don't know. They must be psychic.'

'Get me out of here, now,' said Kaba.

Three men smuggled him back to the lorry while the others took part in a fierce gun battle with the rangers. As they drove him away, Kaba could hear the shooting echoing through the forest. Humiliation seeped through his pores enraging him still further. He had never run from the field of battle before. *Someone would pay for this.*

Sara arrived at the Goro office the next morning leaving Bruno in a nearby café for some breakfast. To avoid arousing any suspicion, she let herself in at the usual time. On most mornings, Okito strolled in two or three hours later than her so she had at least a couple of hours for replacing the papers unseen. Despite this, she had a horrible gnawing in the pit of her stomach which wouldn't go away.

She rounded the corner of her alcove. To her horror, he was sitting on the edge of her desk smirking as she came in. *Oh God, had he found the papers in the drawer?* She tried to smile, pulling her lips back from her teeth.

'Good morning, my jungle flower. Have you got anything for Papa today?'

Before she could move away, he shoved his hand between her legs and pulled her towards him by cupping the back of her head in his meaty hand. His eyes searched her face looking for fear or revulsion.

Only her iron will enabled her to keep her expression neutral. She even raised her eyes to his and fluttered her eyelashes. Tilting her head, she said, 'What did you have in mind, boss?'

Okito licked his lips, desire written all over his fat face.

'Lunch. A long, long lunch,' he said.

'Oh no, I'm sorry. I can't,' said Sara.

His forehead furrowed like trenches in a field of black earth.

'You don't get to choose the day.'

'I've a doctor's appointment to check for diseases down there. I have itching.' She pointed.

Okito flinched and narrowed his eyes.

'Oh, okay. Tomorrow then. I'm going to lunch, anyway.'

'Tomorrow will still be fun.'

She used her little-girl voice. Okito grunted and returned to his office. Sara shivered. A line of cold sweat was making its way down her back. She sat at her desk and transferred the papers to her drawer. *Why had she ever let Bruno talk her into this? The risk was too great. Okito would murder her if he ever discovered the truth. But he would leave for lunch.* She steeled herself.

Chapter 30

Sam found Jean Delacroix sitting in her office after the morning meeting. He turned to greet her as she came in. His taciturn face creased with a grin so wide the top of his head looked as if it was detachable. The twinkle in his eyes conveyed the good news he was bearing.

'Good morning, Jean,' said Sam. 'To what do we owe the pleasure?'

'A great pleasure, I can assure you.'

He sat there like a skinny Buddha radiating smug happiness.

'Spit it out,' she said, irritated by his self-satisfied air.

'There was a gun battle in the forest yesterday. Three poachers are dead, and five are injured and were arrested by the rangers.'

'The pygmies came up trumps?'

'They sure did. It's amazing. I can't believe it.'

'Me neither.'

Sam shook her head. She wanted to jump and shout, but Jean would have taken the chance to hug her, so she stayed behind her desk, thumping it with both fists and screwing up her face in triumph.

'Are the elephants okay?'

'The rangers ambushed the poachers before they could fire a shot.'

'Wow. I'm speechless.'

'I've got to go. My boss wants to visit the pygmy village to see if we can offer them any help with their agriculture or other education programmes.'

'Sure. Thanks for dropping in. Do the security boys know?' said Sam.

'They were off on some kind of inspection when I came in so I don't think so.'

Their network of contacts would have told them by now.

'I'll tell them.'

'Bye then.'

He stretched his hand over her desk. She shook it briefly.

'You already made it clear how you feel,' he said. 'I won't try again. There's no need to be rude.'

Before she could apologise, he was gone.

Charlie Okito arrived back from lunch still feeling randy and thwarted, the risk of catching something shoved to the back of his mind. He wanted sex, now. But Sara was gone. He searched the whole office, his anxiety increasing. She looked shocked to see him in the morning but he had brushed it off. Now he wondered why.

The filing room was empty but someone had left the drawer of a cabinet open. That was unusual, she being so efficient. He wandered over to shut it and had a quick root around in the files. They were from two years previous, machinery orders from head office. *What was she looking for? The woman was an enigma.*

His lawyer arrived for a meeting and requested a copy of Okito's identity card. Seeing as Sara might be delayed at the doctor's for longer, he took it out of his wallet and crossed over to the photocopier. Someone had left it switched on. Sara always turned the machine off when she wasn't using it, to save the mechanism from power surges. Feeling uneasy he lifted the lid to place his card on the screen.

There was a document stuck to the underside by static. He peeled it off, his heart rate increasing. It was a bank statement that came from the same year as the machinery orders, and several of the entries were highlighted in yellow. *What the fuck was going on?*

He sat in Sara's chair and read the entries which she selected. They were all transfers from the head office and subsequent deposits into his personal account. Large amounts of money that he appropriated with the cooperation of Dirk and Philippe, who both received a cut from every payment.

A cold chill rose up his spine. He staggered to his feet and over to his desk where he picked up the phone and dialled.

'Dirk, it's Charlie. You'd better sit down.'

Morné spotted Dirk out on the balcony of his office. He had the air of someone who was deciding whether to jump or not. Morné crossed the floor dragging his bad leg behind him and stepped out onto the small outside area, affecting a relaxed air.

'There you are,' he said.

Dirk spun around. He wore a haunted look on his face. Around him, a small platoon of cigarette butts held the ground. He swallowed.

'Oh, you gave me a start,' he said.

'Everything all right?' said Morné, knowing it wasn't, but unwilling to pry.

'Yes, fine. Just distracted.'

'Is there anything I can do?'

'Do? No, nothing.'

'You should go home for the day. It's so quiet, you won't miss anything.'

'Okay.'

A shocking reaction. Dirk would never countenance such a suggestion under normal circumstances. He was as pale as the wall.

'Are you sure you're okay?'

'Yes. Quite sure.'

'See you tomorrow then.'

What the hell was going on?

Dirk blew the cigarette smoke out of the car window as he surveyed the massive hole in the landscape that had been excavated at the Big Deep Mine. Sheer cliffs remained where the original banking had long fallen into the bottom. The bottomless hole resonated with him as he measured the depth of his despair. He reviewed his conversation with Charlie Okito, looking for an out, but finding none.

'We're screwed. Someone's made copies of the bank transfers,' said Charlie, without preamble.

Dirk's legs folded under him and he slumped into his chair.

'What transfers?'

'Don't play the coy virgin with me, Goosen. You know.'

'How the fuck did they find out about it?' said Dirk.

'I don't know. Perhaps it has something to do with that busybody you hired to work at Masaibu.'

'Sam? But how on earth did she discover the truth? There's no evidence on site. You have all the accounts in Goro.'

'What about the accounts in Johannesburg?'

Dirk's stomach lurched as he remembered Sam's trip to accounts. He visited the department the next day on a pretext and asked the mousey Miss Magana what Sam was doing there. She told him that Sam was confirming her bank details and turned her back on him. He should have known. Women in solidarity together were more dangerous than a platoon of loaded rifles.

'Miss Magana rules that department with a rod of iron. There is no way Sam could have looked for the information without express permission from me, and I didn't give it.'

'Did Sam ask questions about the accounts?'

'No, she was too busy answering questions about her supposed racism. Your bright idea if I remember rightly.'

'Well, my new secretary is the fly in the ointment. She has disappeared with the evidence. Whoever arranged the theft will turn us in.'

'What about blackmail?'

'I doubt it. Too complicated with so many implicated. It's time to leave, Dirk. Take your money out in cash and run away somewhere nice without an extradition treaty. I'm leaving tomorrow. It's been fun.'

Click. The line went dead. Dirk hung up the phone and walked out to the balcony for a smoke where Morné prevented him from taking the quick way down. There was no way out. All his money had gone on two expensive divorces and sending

255

his children to university in London. There was nothing left. Anyway, he had nowhere to go.

He drove to the Big Deep where he started his career as a teenager on holiday work. It always soothed him. Now he would rest here. He flicked his cigarette out onto the ground, took a final swig of whisky from his flask, and drove his car straight at the wooden safety fence along the cliff.

※※※※※ ※※※※※

The next morning, Miriam knocked on Morné's door.

'Have you heard from Dirk? I tried ringing him at home but he has switched off his phone,' said Miriam.

'Have you looked on his desk? Maybe he left you a note.'

Miriam bustled over to Dirk's office. There was a whisky bottle on the desk and stains where he had spilt some trying to decant it into his flask. She rolled her eyes to heaven and tutted. Then she saw the letter.

Chapter 31

J oseph Kaba's vehicle arrived at the mayor's office in Masaibu, its tires screeching with the effort of keeping the car on the road, scattering a flock of chickens who were pecking at the body of a mouse in the gutter. A smell of burning rubber filled the air and a large welt was left in the mud beside the building.

Passers-by jumped back in alarm as the car came to a halt in the middle of the road, but no-one dared complain when the occupant got out, stepping over the puddles with exaggerated care for his crocodile boots. Kaba swore as he miscalculated and sank into the mud. He had a reputation for comic book violence that was well deserved and triggering him was all too easy. They gave the vehicle and its owner a wide berth.

Kaba stalked into the office building without the customary greetings and approached the secretary who cowered behind her desk.

'Where's the mayor?' he said.

'He's in his office,' she said, her eyes on stalks, 'but he has a visitor.'

'So?' said Kaba. 'Tell him, I'm here.'

She hesitated and bit her lip.

'Don't bother. I'll tell him,' he said.

The secretary lifted a hand in feeble protest but Kaba had gone, striding across the office leaving a trail of mud. He threw open the door and burst in to find the mayor having a coffee with a local shopkeeper who was a member of the stakeholder committee.

'Good morning, general. To what do we owe the pleasure of your visit?' said the mayor, his voice neutral.

The shopkeeper stood up. He edged around Joseph Kaba and towards the door. Kaba turned around and shoved him through the opening, slamming the door behind him, leaning against it and breathing with a vicious intensity. His nostrils flared, and he glared at the mayor.

Victor Samba held his gaze, but shrank back in his seat as Kaba approached the desk and shoved his face across it.

'This is your fault,' he said, poking his finger into Victor's chest. 'You did this.'

Victor reached up and removed the digit with a calmness he did not feel. 'I don't understand what you are talking about,' he said. 'Sit down.'

'You haven't heard?' said Kaba.

'Heard what?'

'We returned to the forest for the rest of the herd yesterday and the rangers ambushed us.'

'How did they know where you were? Was it the pygmies?' said the mayor.

'What do you mean?'

'They have been taken on to guard the forest and tell the rangers if any poaching is going on.'

'Fucking pygmies? Who organised that?' said Kaba.

'WCO got together with Consaf.'

'It's that bloody woman again. It's time we got rid of Ms Harris.'

'And how are you going to do that? Charlie Okito tried, but it's not that easy,' said the mayor.

'He's an idiot. There is only one way fix this. We'll take the camp.'

'You can't kill local people. I won't allow it.'

'You were happy to take my money before.'

'Elephants are not people.'

'So, get them out of there. You have until dawn, but on one condition.'

'What's that?'

'Have someone disable the cars. I don't want her getting away. I have plans for the bitch.'

'For God's sake, Kaba. We are not at war now. You won't get away with it.'

'Don't you dare interfere or you'll disappear too. I'm going to enjoy this.'

Kaba rubbed his balls in anticipation, making the mayor queasy.

'Get out of my office,' he said, quaking with anger.

'Oh, don't worry. No-one will know I involved you. I won't squeal,' said Kaba, sneering.

'Out.'

Victor Samba sat alone on his balcony. A large glass of whisky, with ice cubes as insubstantial as ghosts, rested on the table in front of him. Several small flies were struggling to get to the safety of the ice cubes like passengers from the Titanic. He stuck a match into the liquid and scooped them out, flicking it out over the balcony surround and down into the yard below.

Mbala appeared at his side and put her hand on his. He pulled his hand away as if stung but she was not intimidated.

'You must do something,' she said. 'Kaba will not stop at murder. You know what they do to women that they capture.'

Victor frowned and shook his head.

'It's none of your business, woman.'

Mbala took a deep breath and let it all out before speaking in a tone he didn't recognise.

'Don't you dare speak to me like that. I'm not one of your women.'

Victor's eyes widened.

'I didn't say...' he stuttered.

'Do you think I'm stupid? No, don't answer that. You bought me, so I'm a servant. What right have I to an opinion?' said Mbala.

She stood up and faced him, her countenance dark with fury. Victor did not answer.

'The daughter of Chief Fantu is not one of your filthy whores. I've a job now and my own money. I don't need you anymore.'

Victor's mouth had fallen open so wide she could see his tonsils.

'You think I didn't hear you talking to Joseph Kaba? You hypocrite. Sam has been good to us,' she said.

'Good? How did you work that out?' Victor stood up and knocked his drink flying. 'She's ruined me. Where do you think I got all my money before she turned up?'

'The state pays you plenty,' said Mbala.

'You don't know everything. They haven't paid me this year. Without the cuts of the hospital money and the kickbacks from Charlie Okito and Joseph Kaba, we would be in the gutter.'

'But...'

'But nothing. Are you so naïve?'

Mbala was silent, her face working in the shadows.

'So, you'll let her die? You're a monster,' she said.

She swept past him as he reached out to grab her, falling headlong on the boards as he stuck out a foot. He leant over her.

'You're not going anywhere,' he said.

It was late, and the camp deserted, by the time Sam and the security men could get together to discuss the previous day's happenings. Sam didn't drink much, but the air of celebration was catching and she felt like letting her hair down for a change. She had a couple of beers before making herself a big mug of tea.

'That's not a drink,' said Hans.

'Caffeine is a drug,' said Sam.

Hans clinked his bottle of beer against Sam's cup of tea, the steam rising off it in the cool evening air. Jacques reached over to do the same but missed. The air of satisfaction in the office of the security house was palpable. Hans lay back in his recliner, the laces on his army boots loose in the eyelets, and emitted a long sigh of relief.

'I didn't think I'd live to see the day,' he said. 'Rangers working with pygmies, it's extraordinary.'

'Jean Delacroix should get the credit. He's the one who laid down the law,' said Jacques.

'And threatened to withhold their salaries,' said Sam. 'Do you think the poachers will give up now?'

'I don't know. It's obvious that Joseph Kaba is behind this. He's not a man to take defeat lying down.'

'We need to be vigilant,' said Jacques.

There was a knock on the door. Mbala Samba staggered in, her face puffy and her eye black and swollen. Sam gasped and her hand flew to her mouth. Hans leapt to his feet and caught Mbala as she fell to the floor, lifting her onto the camp bed in the corner of the office.

While Jacques ran to the kitchen to get some ice, Sam knelt beside the bed and stroked Mbala's hair. Blood and dirt matted the hair where her weave had been pulled off.

'What happened?' said Sam. 'Who did this to you?'

But Mbala was mute, staring up at the ceiling to avoid Sam's eyes.

Jacques arrived back with the ice wrapped in a clean tea towel which he applied to the bridge of Mbala's nose. She winced, and cried out, but did not remove it. The minutes passed as only the rasping sound of her breathing broke the shocked silence in the room.

She tried to raise her head. Jacques put a cushion under it, and then a second one. Sam tried again. 'Who hit you?'

Mbala's jaw jerked into life. Her arms flailed about as she tried to sit up.

'Rebels,' she said. 'They'll attack at dawn. They are coming to kill you.'

'How do you know this?' said Hans.

'I heard Victor talking to Joseph Kaba.'

'Did Kaba do this to you?' said Jacques.

'No, it was my husband. He was angry with me. It does not matter.'

Despite the urge to dispute this, Sam held her tongue. Now was not the time for lectures.

'We must get away from Masaibu before they arrive. We can't defend ourselves against machine guns,' said Hans. 'Stay here with Mbala and we'll get the cars ready.'

The two men disappeared into the night leaving Sam shaken. She resisted the temptation to look out of the window but no sound broke the silence outside. Instead, she made tea for Mbala with three spoons of sugar for shock. *How could her husband do this to her?* Victor never showed Sam a vicious streak; on the contrary, he had been proactive despite his misgivings about her ideas.

Time passed with glacial slowness. Still the men did not return. Mbala had fallen into a deep sleep and Sam covered her with an old blanket before going to stand in the window of the office peering into the darkness for moon shadows.

Just when panic was grabbing hold of her, they returned. Both men were sweating and panting. Hans placed his hands on the table and took a couple of deep breaths.

'It's not good news,' he said.

Her heart tightened in her chest but she asked, anyway.

'Where are the cars?'

'Someone has slashed the tires and removed the spark plugs from all the vehicles,' said Jacques.

'Sabotage? Who would do such a thing? Have you asked the men?' said Sam.

'All the locals have left. Someone must have warned them,' said Hans.

'So, who's still here?'

'Frik, Alain, Ngoma, Dr Ntuli, and us. I told them to stay in their houses and lock the doors,' said Jacques.

'Can we smuggle Mbala out?' asked Sam.

'The guards have deserted too. Kaba's men are at the gates,' said Hans.

'What are they waiting for?'

'Their boss,' said Jacques.

'What can we do?'

Hans pulled up a chair and took Sam by the hands.

'Nothing. Sticks are no protection against machine guns,' he said.

'So, we will die?' she said to Jacques who looked away.

'Looks that way,' said Hans with a shrug. 'Would you like me to shoot you?'

'What?' Sam stood up and backed away, knocking the chair over. 'Are you crazy? Why would I want you—'?

But the penny had dropped. Rebel soldiers wouldn't miss the opportunity to rape a white woman. They had nothing to lose. And she had stopped them killing the elephants and getting their money. They were waiting for Kaba so he could have first dibs but after that...

'Goddamn elephants. I knew they were trouble,' she said.

'Only as a last resort,' said Hans.

'The police are supposed to protect us,' said Jacques. 'There's still time for them to come.'

A faint hope, and not one she would espouse.

'Okay, but only if you have to. And don't let me see the gun,' said Sam. *Fuck.* She swallowed a sob.

Chapter 32

Victor woke before dawn sprawled on the floor of his bedroom. His hangover was so severe he wanted to die. He rolled onto his back and thanked God it was still dark, and he wouldn't have to face the sunlight yet. He lurched to his feet and noticed the bed had not been slept in. Mbala. A hot flush of shame worsened the evil pain in his head. *Where was she?*

He searched the house with his heart hammering in his chest. *She was right. He was a monster. What if he had killed her?* Fear gripped him as he found a piece of her hair weave near the front door, still sticky with blood. But she was nowhere to be found. Leaving the house, he approached the shed where the servant boy lived and shook him awake.

'Where is she? Where is Mama Mbala?'

The boy's eyes were wide with terror. Victor raised his hand to strike him and then lowered it again. It would be like striking a puppy.

'Please,' he said. 'I must know.'

'Mama Mbala went to see the foreigners at the mining camp.'

Victor dropped him and the boy fell to the floor where he lay cowering. Victor was also frozen with fright and horror. Then he shook himself. They

265

would rape and kill her too. He had to stop them. *Oh God, what have I done?*

He wrenched open the door of the car and jumped in slamming it shut. The vehicle careered down the road into town, close to crashing on every corner. Victor's panic increased with every minute. The empty streets mocked and accused him. He leapt out of the vehicle and ran down the main street pounding on doors, shouting with all his might.

Kaba had not arrived at the camp yet. Unable to bear the tension in the office, Sam had gone for a walk with Hans and Jacques. Mbala refused to come, hiding in the bed under the covers. There was still a chance the rebels wouldn't find her. They wanted Sam.

Despite the ghastly circumstances, Sam couldn't help feeling proud of the changes since her arrival. The accommodation blocks were military in their neatness.

'You'd have made a great soldier,' said Hans.

'The Legion doesn't know what it's missing,' said Jacques.

The newly painted kitchen block lured them in and they made tea with some of Sam's precious supplies.

'You're letting us have a tea bag? You're going soft,' said Hans.

Sam did not mention the elephant in the room. She punched his arm.

'Don't be cheeky or you won't get one.'

It was an effort to maintain the jovial mood, and soon they sank into silence sipping their tea, each of them deep in their thoughts.

Loud cheering at the entrance gate broke their contemplation.

'Come on,' said Hans.

'We need to face Kaba,' said Jacques. 'Maybe we can change his mind.'

Sam could not speak. Mute with fear, she had to force her stiff limbs to move towards the gate. She walked between the two men who closed ranks so that their shoulders touched and bumped hers.

As they approached the gates, Kaba's men shouted and leered and made gestures at Sam that left her in no doubt of the outcome were they to enter. Hans put Sam out in front of himself and Jacques. They stood so close to her back she could feel the heat of their bodies. It was comforting.

Kaba had been sitting in his car outside the gate, in no hurry to get out. He had the upper hand and intended to enjoy it. He threw his legs out first and heaved himself vertical, smoking a Cuban cigar clamped in his teeth. His men slapped him on the back and offered encouragement with lewd hand signals as he strolled into the camp and planted his feet wide in front of Sam.

Sam's face was ghost white, but she did not flinch.

'General Kaba. You're welcome to Masaibu Project. How can I help you?'

Kaba hesitated. He glared at her but she did not react. She waited.

'You've got a fucking cheek,' he said finally. 'Give her to me and I'll let you live,' he said to Hans.

'If you want her, you'll have to take her,' said Hans.

He removed his Glock from his waistband and took off the safety catch. Sam jumped at the sound but she didn't look over her shoulder. A hornet drifted by, trailing its long body behind it, causing

267

them all to duck. Kaba shook his head in disbelief and beckoned his men through the gates.

The rebels took their guns off their shoulders and checked they were ready to fire. The pungent smell of sweat and unwashed bodies filled the air. Then they lined up behind Kaba, their lips drawn back from their teeth, and lifted the guns to their shoulders. Jacques stepped forward and took Sam by the hand. His grasp was warm and strong.

Then Hans put his arm over her chest and pulled her to him. She could feel his heart beating, fast and strong. She took a deep breath and let it out, gazing up at a lone cloud that was drifting lost in the now blue sky. Time stopped and Sam shut her eyes.

Suddenly, there was a commotion behind the rebels. A roaring of voices that got louder and louder. Some shots rang out, and Sam winced waiting for the coup de grâce, but none came. The mayor was pushing his way through the ranks of Kaba's men, shooting in the air and leading about five hundred townspeople who were all armed with an assortment of weapons, mostly AK47s, the gun of choice in African nations.

The bedraggled army flowed into the camp and lined up in front of Sam and the security men. They outnumbered Kaba's troops by four or five to one.

'Go home, Joseph,' said Victor. 'No-one will die today.'

'She is mine,' said Kaba.

'She is ours,' said Victor. 'You are finished here. I have alerted the army to your presence. If you and your men leave today, you may get away.'

'You must be joking,' said Kaba, looking around for support, but his men were slipping away like black shadows. He spat on the ground, spun on his heel and marched off with his remaining followers.

People who had remained in camp, overnight emerged groggy-eyed in time to witness the celebrations of the jubilant local people as the troops melted away with their leader leaving Sam, Hans and Jacques frozen in position.

'What's going on?' said Alain, who was the first to appear.

'A little local difficulty,' said Jacques.

Hans still held Sam tight to his chest as if he was afraid to let go. Alain stared at them with his head tilted to one side in question. Hans released her and stood back embarrassed.

'Sorry, I forgot,' he said.

'That's okay,' said Sam, who had been paralysed by shock, and not even noticed, only the sensation of being safe.

'That was close,' said Hans.

'I thought we were toast,' said Sam.

'We need to find out who sabotaged the cars,' said Jacques. 'Philippe's a prime candidate but he wouldn't know where to find the spark plugs on a vehicle.

'It's also unlikely that he would stoop to getting his hands dirty with real grease,' said Sam.

'Leave it with me. Someone will tell me,' said Hans. 'It's likely they were offered a king's ransom to carry it out. Bygones should be bygones in this case,' and he stomped off to assemble the security men.

Sam did not argue. The drama had arisen and passed so rapidly she wondered if it had been a nightmare. She could still feel Jacques' hand enveloping hers as Hans' heart thundered into her back. The adrenaline coursing around her system heightened the sensation and made her feel sick. *This is not an appropriate time to feel lust.*

'Are you okay?' said Jacques. 'You were amazingly brave. I don't think I've ever met a woman like you.'

'I didn't have a choice,' said Sam. 'I was too afraid to run away.'

269

'Courage is being scared to death and saddling up anyway,' said Jacques.

'Who said that?'

'John Wayne.'

They both giggled. Absurdity is the best cure for adversity.

Things returned to normal within hours. After the rebels left, the mayor picked his wife up in his plump arms and kissed her with a tenderness that did not compute after the violence to which he subjected her. Mbala did not protest, and even smiled, as Victor carried her out to the waiting car.

Having nothing better to do, Sam held a staff meeting which was remarkable only by the mundane nature of its contents. She refused to answer questions about the rebels and concentrated on the continuing problem maintaining the ancient vehicle fleet.

As the managers left to go to their offices, Alain put his hand on her arm.

'Are you really okay? What happened out there?' he said.

'It's over now. Just another day in paradise.'

Chapter 33

A week later, Bruno rushed back to camp from his break, desperate to give Sam the evidence she craved about the widespread corruption in the Lumbono projects. He had spent the whole of his time at home fretting about the papers in his possession. His attempts to inform Sam about developments in Goro were thwarted because the rebels had cut the telephone lines to Masaibu camp, and it took almost a week for them to restore communications.

His agitation increased on hearing about the abortive attack on Masaibu. The occupants of the camp were gossiping like a hive of bees about the goings-on. It was hard for him to take in as he was still stunned at the speed of events which took place in Goro after he photocopied the statements.

Charlie Okito left Goro the day after he telephoned Dirk Goosen, fleeing to the South of France where he owned a small villa in the outskirts of Cannes. Unaware Charlie had absconded, Sara left for Senegal to join a friend who was making shea butter from Karité fruits and needed a trusted helper with whom to run the business. There was no way of knowing if she would stay safe in Goro as Charlie Okito could have organised a revenge attack on her, so she stayed away.

Bruno walked straight to Sam's office on his arrival and found her frowning at a beetle walking along the top of her computer screen, his claws slipping on the shiny surface. When she raised her head, he saw the strain written on her face. He hesitated.

'Bruno, welcome back. Did you have a good break? I thought you weren't back until Friday?'

'I found something important. It couldn't wait.'

Sam groaned. *Would the problems never stop?*

'I don't understand. What sort of thing?' she said.

'Papers, bank statements. You were right. Charlie Okito siphoned massive amounts of money from the company,' said Bruno.

'How did you get these papers?' said Sam, clenching her hands.

'From the office, I...'

Sam gasped. 'The office? You went to Okito's office. Are you crazy? These people are dangerous.'

'I don't care. I'm sick of them running my country into the ground. I wanted to help you like you helped me.'

He stood his ground, defiant and plump, almost comical. Affection for this unlikely warrior overcame Sam's shock at his actions.

'Wow. You're a hero. Well done,' she said.

'Thank you, Mama Sam,' said Bruno, blushing and avoiding her eyes.

'I was just about to call Johannesburg as communications have been cut off for a week since the rebels paid us a visit. The lines have just been restored. I expect you heard about Kaba coming here?'

'Just now. I can't believe it. You are lucky to have survived. Joseph Kaba is notorious.'

'Not anymore. He left for Bukavu with his tail between his legs. They say he has acquired a cobalt mine over there.'

272

She reached out to him.

'Okay then. Show me what you've brought.'

Bruno handed her the rolled-up sheaf of paper which would not lie flat on her desk. Sam put rock samples on the four corners of the top document and balanced her head between her hands. She whistled as the contents of the first statement became clear, but she did not react as he had expected. Instead, she bit her lip and read them between big sighs.

She raised her head.

'You took a huge risk but it was worth it. I can't quite believe it. This is all the proof we need of a massive fraud. You're a genius.'

Bruno flushed and looked at the ground.

'That's not all, Mama Sam,' he said. 'Charlie Okito has left the country. He emptied the company bank account on his way to France.'

'Jesus, what has head-office said?'

'I'm not sure if they are aware yet. There is no one left in the office to tell them. The Johannesburg office may be assuming that the lines are out of order,' said Bruno.

'Listen, what you did was fantastic and foolish at the same time. I'm grateful to you, but I need to call head office right now and you shouldn't be involved.'

Bruno lumbered to his feet.

'That's okay. I need to have a shower. You can tell me what they say later.'

Sam made herself a cup of tea and ate some stale biscuits while rereading the explosive contents of the documents on her desk. She compared the entries with the list she had brought from South Africa and the truth crystallised in her head. It was her duty to tell Morné Van Rooyen what his managers were up to. This would not be an easy conversation.

She pulled the telephone towards her and lifted the receiver to her ear. They had done a good job fixing the line and dial tone returned. Holding the receiver between her shoulder and her chin, she pinned the address book open with one hand and dialled with the other. Just when the phone connected and rang, the receiver slipped out onto the floor. She grappled around and lifted it to her ear.

'Hello? Who's that? Sam, is it you?'

'Miriam? Hi. How are you?'

There was the sound of a nose being blown and Miriam came back on the line.

'Not good. There's terrible news about Dirk.'

'Has he had an accident?'

'Nobody knows what happened, but he drove through the barriers at the Big Deep and he's dead.'

She wailed. Sam couldn't speak at all. *Dirk dead? What was going on?*

'I'm so sorry. I know you worked with him for ages.'

'Fifteen years,' said Miriam, sobbing. 'Hang on, Morné's just come in. I'll pass the phone to him.'

'Hi, Sam. I gather Miriam gave you the news. Everyone is in shock here. Dirk was a legend in his own lifetime at Consaf,' said Morné.

'How awful for you all. What would you like me to do?'

'I'm going to come on a visit. Would that be okay? We need to talk and I don't think this is the right place for that conversation.'

'Just let us know when you are arriving and we'll pick you up at the airport,' said Sam.

'Miriam will fax you.'

He was gone. Sam replaced the receiver with a shaking hand. She left her office to find Hans and scrounge a cigarette. *Dirk was dead. What on earth had happened? From what Miriam said, he had committed suicide. Could it have something to do with the papers that Bruno removed from Charlie Okito's office in Goro? Miriam told her to trust no one. Had she included Dirk in that warning?*

She decided not to tell Hans and Jacques about the manner of Dirk's death in case they had a conflict of interests with their management. *Who knew who else was involved in the scam? Morné's visit would be an important milestone for the project. That should keep them busy.*

Dirk's death hit Sam much harder than she had expected. *Why didn't he run away like Charlie Okito? Perhaps it was the shame of being discovered?* It just didn't add up, but there was no way of finding out. She brooded on the conundrum and became withdrawn, embarrassed and even sad at the results of her triumph. Not even the terrible twins, Jacques and Hans, could make her smile.

She trudged around the project like a wet weekend affecting everyone's mood, but she wasn't the only one. Philippe, the sole remaining vestige of resistance in Masaibu, had capitulated. He slunk around camp and cringed like a beaten dog when Sam was near. A man who would have crowed from the roof tops, if Kaba had had his way, he now acted as if his days were numbered.

Morné's visit was an excuse to get in some special food from Uganda. The freezers were groaning with beef and pork steaks and Sam reviewed menus with over-excited cooks who relished the visit of the boss as a chance to show off their skills. She took a dim view of being told that the big boss was coming at last. Where she had imagined that she was the big boss, she had only been keeping the seat warm for Morné Van Rooyen.

'It's the culture,' said Jacques. 'You are a woman. They will never accept that you are the boss. They are expecting a man to take over. You can't win.'

'Ungrateful bastards,' said Sam, her bubbling sense of resentment breaking surface for once.

'It's not their fault.'

'I know. I just hoped they would appreciate me by now but it seems, unless I grow a penis, I'll never make the grade.'

'Don't do that. I'd find it very hard to fancy you with one.'

'So, you fancy me now.'

'I didn't say that.'

But he blushed and changed the subject. *Another conundrum.*

Frik and Bruno were constant visitors to her office in the days before the visit, discussing inconsequential improvements and paint colours. She hadn't the heart to discourage them. They had formed an unlikely friendship which was touching in the way that a newly formed couple is; their sideways glances of approval and shared jokes made Sam feel jealous.

Alain kept his head down, working on the new resource estimate with some junior geologists. He did not seem able to talk to her anymore. *Had he known something about the attack?* She wouldn't have blamed them for staying in their houses. Kaba's beef was only with her.

Just when she was at the end of her tether, she had another nocturnal visit from Hans. He knocked on her door as she was going to bed. She only wore a t-shirt and a pair of knickers, so she peeped out through the curtain to see who it was. Hans was standing outside with a bottle of whisky hanging from his hand. It caught the light and glinted with purpose at her.

She should have told him to go away, but the tables had turned. Now it was she who needed comfort. She pulled open the door and put her hands on her hips.

'And what do you want? Do you know what time it is?'

'I'm checking on my troops. Morale is low. It's my job,' he said, stilted by his fading bravado.

'Morale is low,' Sam agreed. 'Come in.'

He poured them a whisky and she sat in the recliner with her legs drawn up under her t-shirt while he perched on the uncomfortable sofa.

'We're worried about you,' said Hans. 'Is it the elephants?'

'Oh, everything. Just struggling. This job is hell.'

'But you're finally winning.'

'I wouldn't say that. Dirk killed himself and it's my fault,' said Sam.

'You didn't tell us that. How is it your fault?' asked Hans.

'I found the papers that proved he was stealing from the company with Charlie Okito.'

'So? It's his fault then. You didn't kill him. He killed himself,' said Hans, angry.

'I have no one to talk to. It's so hard.'

'Don't you have a boyfriend?'

'He's afraid of commitment and has shacked up with a teenager.'

She shrugged.

'He's a fucking idiot. You are magnificent, brave and intelligent. He must be a fool.'

Hans had risen and he stood over her. His face softened and he leaned over and stroked her face. His touch made her weak. She still didn't fancy him, but his desire leaked out of his fingers and infected her.

'Let me show you how a real man appreciates a woman like you,' he said. 'Please.'

Sam shrank back into the seat. *What?* Hans drew back.

'You think I am ugly,' he said, sad.

'No, you are magnificent too. I just didn't think of you like that. We're colleagues.'

'Sex is not a big deal between adults. I think you'd enjoy it. I know I would.'

A smile crept across Sam's face. She remembered his heart beating against her back in the standoff with the rebels, and despite herself, she felt aroused by his passion. She longed for the escape of a roaring orgasm in the arms of a strong man, which would obliterate all the sorrow and leave her floating in the stars.

'No one must know,' she said, flushing. 'You must never refer to it again.'

'You kept my secret. I'll keep yours. I won't tell anyone. Not even Jacques,' he said, hand on heart.

'Especially not Jacques,' she said, stretching out her arms.

Chapter 34

Morné Van Rooyen stepped out of the airport building at Masaibu with the air of someone who had been solicited in the street. He smoothed his moustache and glared at her.

'What is wrong with these people? Don't they have any respect?' he said.

'Did they ask you for lipstick?' said Sam.

The stare she received told her all she wanted to know about his mood. He had come on a flying visit, scheduled to spend only two nights in camp. One of the treasured menus would have to be cancelled. He sat in the front seat of the jeep, relegating Sam to the back, and opened the window 'for air'. The breeze that blew into the back of the car carried his stale odour.

Sam wrinkled her nose in disgust. The big boss had taken advantage of one perk offered by the awful airport hotel in Entebbe. Any normal person would have showered, but perhaps there was no water in the hotel. She had to stay rational and open to all ideas about the project even if they were from a man smelling of sex. *Yuck.*

'Sir, perhaps you could close the window as we drive through town,' said Ezekiel.

'No need. I don't mind people talking to me.'

'They'll see Mama Sam in the car and we'll have to stop. The people love her.'

Sam smirked. Ezekiel winked at her in the car mirror as Morné forced the window back up, winding the handle with jerky movements.

As luck would have it, Hans was standing at the main gate when the car pulled up. He waved them through, disappointing Sam who was dying to see how Morné would react to the guards examining his underwear. She showed Morné into his accommodation in the guest cabin. He wrinkled his nose at the musty air but didn't comment.

'I'll see you in the office then,' said Sam. 'It's the building at the far end of the square with the verandah.'

'I'd rather see the project first.'

'Okay, just let me know when you're ready. My office is at the front so I can see you coming out.'

Morné grunted.

Sam had not known what to expect from Morné's visit but his attitude toward her was worrying. *Was this something to do with Dirk's death?* Having not been aware of Bruno's plan to raid the Goro office, she had been as shocked as anyone to hear of Dirk's demise. No doubt Morné would tell her. She wandered back to the office and waited for him to appear.

The tour of the project only increased Morné's obvious annoyance. The praise heaped on Sam by her workforce, most of which she had to translate from French, induced curt nods and changes of subject. Even the now-functioning heavy machinery lined up for the occasion by a proud Frik did not elicit more than faint praise.

Sam offloaded Morné in the geology department, afraid she might punch him if left unsupervised. Alain took him to the core shed and on a circuit of the drill sites while she went to have a cup of tea with Hans.

'Where's the big boss?' said Hans.

'Alain is showing him the exploration work.'

'Has he told you why he's here yet?' asked Hans.

'No, I guess it's something to do with the implosion caused by Charlie Okito.'

'How did they find out about him?'

'I don't know. Probably something to do with the accounts.'

'What about Dirk? Weren't they friends? Dirk's sudden demise can't have been easy for him.'

'Yes, troubles do seem to come in threes.'

'That's only two.'

'Don't remind me,' said Sam.

Lying to Hans after what they had shared made her feel uncomfortable, but Miriam's warning had taken full effect. She wanted to protect Bruno at all costs.

By the time Morné turned up, Sam recovered her equilibrium and was organising her collection of beetles by size into a caravan along the dado rail, the biggest first.

'Haven't you got anything better to do?' said Morné.

'Ah, you're back,' said Sam, letting the barbed comment float over her head. 'I hope you're pleased with our progress.'

'We're years behind on the drilling and the resource calculation is months away.'

'It's true we are playing catch up, but now the project is working smoothly again, I'd like

281

to set some more ambitious targets for our next exploration programme.'

'I think you've done enough damage already, don't you?' said Morné.

Sam stiffened and her throat constricted.

'I don't understand,' she said. 'What damage? I have—'

'You've caused the death of one man and the disappearance of another, ruining the perfect scheme to get bribes into the hands of the government without the IMF interfering.'

Sam felt her insides turn over and twist into a knot. A cold hand gripped her heart.

'Bribery? What are you talking about?'

Morné sighed. 'For God's sake. You don't think we expected you to run the exploration project successfully, do you? You're supposed to be the fall guy, but you just wouldn't stop digging. Everything is ruined.'

'The project's a scam?' said Sam.

'From top to bottom. And now you've wrecked it.'

Morné let this sink in.

'But Dirk was taking his cut too. Why did you allow that?'

'He wasn't the only one profiting from some tax-free cash. Until you came along, everyone was happy.'

'You picked me to fail.'

'What a disappointment that turned out to be.'

Morné laughed and tugged at his moustache as if he expected it to peel off.

'You're a right royal pain in the arse.'

'So, what happens now?'

'Do you have to ask?'

The bitter disappointment of leaving just when the sky turned blue seeped through her being, laced with bitter resentment at her treatment by Morné. *Just another corrupt bastard. Why should he get away with his plan after all her work to normalise the project?*

Almost worse than losing her job was the knowledge they had selected someone from head office to replace her and run the project remotely. They would destroy all her work and Philippe would soon reign supreme again. Something had to be done, and she had a fool proof idea to precipitate the project's downfall. Morné suffered from the need to be important, the clever one in the crowd. He wouldn't be able to resist the chance for one-upmanship, especially if it put Sam in her place.

While he was at breakfast, she placed the rare Cape Beetle on the table in his cabin just before his meeting with Jean Delacroix. *Just add beetle and stand back. Dirk would have appreciated the notion of Morné being hoist with his own petard.* She raised her mug of tea to Dirk's memory. He had chosen her because he thought she would be useless, but without him, she would never have had the job in the first place.

As she expected, Morné arrived at the meeting in Sam's office waving the beetle in the air. Having fired Sam, his mood had changed to one of triumph. He didn't notice Jean Delacroix standing behind the door hanging up his rain jacket.

'Look what I found. Better than any of your dull efforts, Sam.'

Jean pushed the door shut and tried to take the beetle from Morné who held it up in the air.

'Can I see that?' said Jean.

'And who are you?' said Morné.

'Oh, he's Jean Delacroix, the WCO representative in Masaibu. He has been helping us protect the elephant herd,' said Sam.

'Nice to meet you, Morné. That's an unusual beetle.'

A tremor of excitement disrupted Jean's voice and too late, Morné threw it in the rubbish bin beside Sam's desk.

'It's just a filthy beetle. Probably covered in dangerous bacteria. I wouldn't touch it if I were you.'

Jean was not listening. He crouched on his haunches and reached into the bin, picking the beetle up by the carapace and placing it on the desk. The iridescent blue body of the beetle dazzled Jean, who peered at it muttering 'wonderful' and 'amazing'.

'Do you have the beetle book I gave you?' he asked Sam, who was already rooting in the drawer for it. She didn't look up as she handed it over, terrified she might give herself away. Jean leafed through the book and stopped at the section where Sam had bent over the corner of the page to make it easier to find. He went back and forwards examining the photos of the species. Morné shifted in his seat.

'Is this necessary?' he said. 'We have important matters to discuss.'

Sam bit her lip and stirred her tea with a pencil. Finally, Jean looked up from the book.

'You have discovered a new species of beetle,' he said.

'Oh, I'm sure they're common as muck,' said Morné, looking to Sam for confirmation. But Sam was staring out of the window, pretending some workers carrying a plank were distracting her. Her insides were bubbling with glee.

'Cape beetles are rare. They only live in specific locations in South Africa on the tops of small elevated plateaus. They are a protected species,' said Jean.

'Protected? But you said this one is a new species so it can't be on a list already,' retorted Morné.

'I don't think you understand. All work must cease on the project until Consaf carry out an environmental impact study for the species. We must establish the range and populations before you perform any more work.'

Morné's jaw dropped onto his chest. Sam could almost hear the clang.

'Oh my, how unfortunate,' she said.

'Can I take it?' said Jean. 'I must show it to the others at WCO. They'll be so thrilled.'

'Of course,' said Sam.

Chapter 35

M orné left the same day, hitching a lift on a Consaf flight taking Ntezi employees out on leave. He didn't speak to Sam again after the meeting with Jean Delacroix. *Did he realise she had played him?* Sam was not a vindictive person, but she had had enough of Consaf and Lumbono and the endemic corruption. In fact, she was sick of the whole enterprise and all its shabby protagonists.

If the mayor's wife had not been at the project, he would not have stopped Kaba and his men from taking her. The people of Masaibu showed no gratitude for her efforts to improve conditions. It was like trying to fill a leaky bucket. The more she did, the more they wanted. It exhausted her.

The stakeholders meeting presented the ideal opportunity for her to inform the local community of her departure. She saw no point in apprising Victor Samba of developments. The last thing she needed was a fake display of unhappiness and insincere farewells. The job had depressed her and she wanted to go home.

There was no sign that the meeting would be any different to those that had gone before. Hans and Jacques both came in the car with her to the hall, citing security concerns.

'I thought Kaba had taken over a cobalt mine,' she said.

'You never know,' said Jacques.

'It's our duty to keep you safe,' said Hans.

Sam rolled her eyes and swallowed the response that rose up her throat.

'I'm so lucky,' she said.

For once, no one was waiting outside the building for the meeting to start.

'Are you sure the meeting is on?' said Sam. 'It looks quiet.'

'I'm sure,' said Hans. 'It was raining earlier this evening, maybe they went inside for a change.'

Sam shrugged.

'Let's get it over with,' she said, and pushed open the double doors to find a sea of people waiting. The air smelled like a wet bar of soap and the ladies were all wearing their full regalia of wax print dresses and matching headdresses. The sea parted and Hans pushed Sam through the crowd to a trestle table at the top of the hall. Spontaneous applause broke out.

'What's going on?' said Sam.

'You'll see,' said Jacques.

They installed Sam behind the table with Victor Samba and other important stakeholders. Behind her stood Jacques and Hans, smug looks on their faces. The mayor rose from his chair and the hubbub in the hall died down.

'Welcome, Mama Sam. Tonight, the women of Masaibu have a presentation for you,' said Victor, in his best mayor's voice.

Before Sam could protest, or question this statement, about forty women shuffled forwards and formed a phalanx of bright yellow and orange, which looked as if someone had lit a fire in the centre of the hall. A stout woman placed herself in front of the group and counted out loud in Swahili.

287

As the women burst into song, the hairs on Sam's arms stood on end. They sang as a unit, their rich voices filling the hall and rattling the roof.

The sound was so rich that the audience were brought to tears. Sam could feel her marrow shaking. A young woman appeared on the periphery of her vision carrying a bunch of wilted wildflowers tied with a pink ribbon. She presented it to Sam without ever looking her in the eye while the singing raised the rafters.

The mayor leaned over.

'Do you understand what they are singing?'

'No, I'm afraid not.'

'It is a song they usually sing for politicians or important men who visit the town. Would you like to know what they are saying?'

Sam hesitated and nodded.

'God has chosen Mama Sam to be our leader,' he said, smiling. 'They think he sent you to help us.'

Guilt flooded through her, mixed with pride, making her feel wonderful and awful at the same time. *Why hadn't someone said something before? She had never expected an ambush like this, never suspected that she had broken through. Oh God, she had just killed the project when it was about to fly.*

The singing had stopped. The eyes of the town were on her, concern replacing glee as renegade tears escaped from her eyes and rolled down her cheeks. She pulled herself together.

'Thank you so much. That was the proudest moment of my life,' she said. And she wasn't lying. Somehow, she got through the meeting, the speeches from different parts of the community, the update on the pygmies surrogate parenting of the elephant, the complaints about the new uniform rules.

When everyone had left, she pulled the mayor aside.

288

'Victor, they have fired me.'

'Consaf? Are they crazy? What happened? You cannot go.'

Sam shook her head.

'I cannot stay.'

'When do you leave?'

'Tomorrow. They want me out of here as soon as possible.'

'It's a disaster.'

'No, it's just a new beginning. You know what to do now. The elephants are the key to your future. Don't rely on Consaf.'

'We will miss you.'

Sam shook his hand and returned to the sanctuary of the space between her two security men. She wanted to weep or shout but instead she scrounged a cigarette and stood outside and smoked it with them. The mayor joined them, but no one spoke.

It was more difficult than she had imagined to leave the project. The physical act of folding her clothes and filling her suitcases drained her. Hans came to see her 'to make sure she left', but he failed to convince her, especially when he wrapped her in his long arms and held her for a minute sniffing her hair as if he wanted to remember the smell of her.

'I'm going to miss you, Sam Harris. You made my life more bearable again,' said Hans.

She was unable to reply, only gulping and shoving him out again before he made her cry.

Her precious tea bags were donated to Alain who shook her hand and would not let go. Bruno wept, his cheeks wobbling and had to be comforted by Dr Ntuli. Frik couldn't pretend, offering her a final cigarette before fleeing to the sanctuary of his workshop. Even the girls in the kitchen made her a special breakfast.

The only people who were ecstatic about her departure were Philippe and Sonia, who spent hours in his office discussing their tactics without any idea that Beetle-gate had happened. Neither of them came to see Sam off, for which she was grateful.

Victor and Mbala had said their goodbyes the night before to avoid alerting the townsfolk.

'They won't let you leave,' said Victor. 'You are ours now.'

'I always will be,' said Sam. 'You saved me. I'll never forget it.'

Mbala couldn't speak but lowered her head to Sam who did the same, their foreheads touching in mutual homage.

'Keep the hospital clean,' said Sam.

Ezekiel had cleaned the jeep in her honour and they drove through town to the airport with Hans and Jacques in the back. Sam waved and touched hands momentarily with people in the street, but Ezekiel did not stop. They pulled up to the scruffy airport building in the battered jeep. A dog lounging on the warm mud outside the door moved out of the way with ill-concealed annoyance.

Ezekiel jumped out of the vehicle and took Sam's bag out of the back. He grunted as he heaved it through the door and into the loading area at the back of the building.

Sam slid off the seat and landed in a puddle almost falling over. Hans and Jacques pretended they hadn't noticed and fought their way through some leaving clichés.

'Been a pleasure working with you,' said Hans.

'Let's do it again sometime,' said Jacques.

'Come here,' said Sam, and grabbed Jacques in a hug. He did not object or freeze, hugging her back with genuine warmth. Hans waited, looking at his boots. He offered her his hand when it was his turn. Sam shook his hand but pulled him in close before he could release his grip.

Standing on tiptoes, she whispered in his ear. 'You held my life in your hands. I'll never forget it. Thank you.'

Han straightened and gulped, his big Adam's apple like a lift too big for its shaft.

'It was an honour to work with you,' he said, his voice breaking.

Afraid she would cry, Sam headed for the airport door. A synchronised crunch of gravel alerted her to their action, and she risked a glance over her shoulder. They were standing at attention in full military salute. She dropped her rucksack on the floor and gave them a shy salute back, then she walked through the airport where the staff stamped her passport with ceremony.

Mad Mark, the pilot, waited at the battered metal roll-up door leading to the runway, her suitcase at his feet.

'Let's get out of here,' he said. 'Time's a wasting.'

<<<<>>>

The next book in the Series is **The Bonita Protocol**

Thank you for reading my book. If you enjoyed it, won't you please take a moment to leave me a review at your favourite retailer? Thank you

Other Books by the Author

Individual books in the Sam Harris Adventure Series

The first book in the Sam Harris Series sets the scene for the career of an unwilling heroine, whose bravery and resourcefulness are needed to navigate a series of adventures set in remote sites in Africa and South America. Based on the real-life adventures of the author, the settings and characters are given an authenticity which will connect with readers who enjoy adventure fiction and mysteries set in remote settings with realistic scenarios.

Set in the late 1980s themes such as women working in formerly male domains, and what constitutes a normal existence, are examined and developed in the context of Sam's constant ability to find herself in the middle of an adventure or mystery. Sam's home life provides a contrast to her adventures and feeds her need to escape. Her attachment to an unsuitable boyfriend is the thread running through her romantic life, and her attempts to break free of it provide another side to her character.

Fool's Gold - Book 1

It's 1987. Newly qualified geologist Sam Harris is a woman in a man's world - overlooked, underpaid but resilient and passionate. Desperate for her first job, and nursing a broken heart, she accepts an offer from a notorious entrepreneur Mike Morton, to search for gold deposits in the remote rainforests of Sierramar. With the help of nutty local heiress, Gloria Sanchez, she soon settles into life in Calderon, the capital. But when Sam accidentally uncovers a long-lost clue to a treasure buried deep within the jungle, her journey really begins.

Teaming up with geologist Wilson Ortega, historian Alfredo Vargas and the mysterious Don Moises, they venture through the jungle, where she lurches between excitement and insecurity. Yet there is a far graver threat looming; Mike and Gloria discover one of the members of the expedition is plotting to seize the fortune for himself and is willing to do anything to get it. Can Sam survive and find the treasure or will her first adventure be her last?

Hitler's Finger - Book 2

The second book in the Sam Harris Series sees the return of our heroine Sam Harris to Sierramar to help her friend Gloria track down her boyfriend, the historian, Alfredo Vargas.

A missing historian, a vengeful journalist, some unhinged Nazis and a possible pregnancy. Has Sam gone too far on her return to Sierramar?Historian, Alfredo Vargas, and journalist, Saul Rosen, have disappeared while searching for a group of fugitive Nazi war criminals. Sam and her friend Gloria join forces to find them and are soon caught up in a dangerous mystery. A man is murdered, and a

293

sinister stranger follows their every move. Even the government is involved. Can they find Alfredo before he disappears for good?

The background to the book is the presence of Nazi war criminals in South America which was often ignored by locals who had fascist sympathies during World War II. Themes such as tacit acceptance of fascism, and local collaboration with fugitives from justice are examined and developed in the context of Sam's constant ability to find herself in the middle of an adventure or mystery. Sam's home life provides a contrast to her adventures and feeds her need to escape. Her continuing attachment to an unsuitable boyfriend is about to be tested to the limit.

The Star of Simbako - Book 3

The third book in the Sam Harris Series sees Sam Harris on her first contract to West Africa to Simbako, a land of tribal kingdoms and voodoo.

A fabled diamond, a jealous voodoo priestess, disturbing cultural practices. What could possibly go wrong?Nursing a broken heart, Sam Harris goes to Simbako to work in the diamond fields of Fona. She is soon involved with a cast of characters who are starring in their own soap opera, a dangerous mix of superstition, cultural practices and ignorance (mostly her own). Add a love triangle and a jealous woman who wants her dead and Sam is in trouble again. Where is the Star of Simbako? Is Sam going to survive the chaos?

This book is based on visits made to the Paramount Chiefdoms of West Africa. Despite being nominally Christian communities, Voodoo practices are still part of daily life out there. This often leads to conflicts of interest. Combine this with the horrific ritual of FGM and it makes for a potent cocktail of conflicting loyalties. Sam is pulled into this life by her friend, Adanna, and soon finds herself involved in goings on that she doesn't understand.

The Bonita Protocol - Book 5
An erratic boss. Suspicious results. Stock market shenanigans. Can Sam Harris expose the scam before they silence her? It's 1996. Geologist Sam Harris has been around the block, but she's prone to nostalgia, so she snatches the chance to work in Sierramar, her old stomping ground. But she never expected to be working for a company that is breaking all the rules.

When the analysis results from drill samples are suspiciously high, Sam makes a decision that puts her life in peril. Can she blow the lid on the conspiracy before they shut her up for good?

The Bonita Protocol is the fifth book in the Sam Harris Adventure series. If you like gutsy heroines, complex twists and turns, and heart pounding action, then you'll love PJ Skinner's thrilling novel.

Digging Deeper - Book 6
A feisty geologist working in the diamond fields of West Africa is kidnapped by rebels. Can she survive the ordeal or will this adventure be her last? It's 1998. Geologist Sam Harris is desperate for money so she takes a job in a tinpot mining company working in war-torn Tamazia. But she never expected to be kidnapped by blood thirsty rebels.

Working in Gemsite was never going to be easy with its culture of misogyny and corruption. Her boss, the notorious Adrian Black is engaged in a game of cat and mouse with the government over taxation. Just when Sam makes a breakthrough, the camp is overrun by rebels and Sam is taken captive.

Will anyone bother to rescue her, and will she still be alive if they do?

Concrete Jungle - Book 7 (series end)
Armed with an MBA, Sam Harris is storming the City - But has she swapped one jungle for another?

Forging a new career was never going to be easy, and Sam discovers she has not escaped from the culture of misogyny and corruption that blighted her field career.

When her past is revealed, she finally achieves the acceptance she has always craved, but being one of the boys is not the panacea she expected. The death of a new friend presents her with the stark choice of compromising her principals to keep her new position, or exposing the truth behind the façade.

Will she finally get what she wants or was it all a mirage?

All of the books are available in paperback. Please go to your favourite online retailer to order them.

Sam Harris Adventure Box Sets
Sam Harris Adventure Box Set Book 1-3
Sam Harris Adventure Box Set Book 2-4
Sam Harris Adventure Box Set Book 5-7

The Green Family Saga (under the pen name of Kate Foley)

Rebel Green – Book 1
Relationships fracture when two families find themselves caught up in the Irish Troubles.
The Green family move to Kilkenny from England in 1969, at the beginning of the conflict in Northern Ireland. They rent a farmhouse on the outskirts of town, and make friends with the

O'Connor family next door. Not every member of the family adapts easily to their new life, and their differing approaches lead to misunderstandings and friction. Despite this, the bonds between the family members deepen with time.

Perturbed by the worsening violence in the North threatening to invade their lives, the children make a pact never to let the troubles come between them. But promises can be broken, with tragic consequences for everyone.

Africa Green – Book 2

Will a white chimp save its rescuers or get them killed?

Journalist Isabella Green travels to Sierra Leone, a country emerging from civil war, to write an article about a chimp sanctuary. Animals that need saving are her obsession, and she can't resist getting involved with the project, which is on the verge of bankruptcy. She forms a bond with local boy, Ten, and army veteran, Pete, to try and save it.

When they rescue a rare white chimp from a village frequented by a dangerous rebel splinter group, the resulting media interest could save the sanctuary. But the rebel group have not signed the cease fire. They believe the voodoo power of the white chimp protects them from bullets, and they are determined to take it back so they can storm the capital.

When Pete and Ten go missing, only Isabella stands in the rebels' way. Her love for the chimps unlocks the fighting spirit within her. Can she save the sanctuary or will she die trying?

Fighting Green – Book 3

Liz Green is desperate for a change. The Dot-Com boom is raging in the City of London, and she feels exhausted and out of her depth. Added

297

to that, her long-term boyfriend, Sean O'Connor, is drinking too much and shows signs of going off the rails. Determined to start anew, Liz abandons both Sean and her job, and buys a near-derelict house in Ireland to renovate.

She moves to Thomastown where she renews old ties and makes new ones, including two lawyers who become rivals for her affection. When Sean's attempt to win her back goes disastrously wrong, Liz finishes with him for good. Finding herself almost penniless, and forced to seek new ways to survive, Liz is torn between making a fresh start and going back to her old loves.

Can Liz make a go of her new life, or will her past become her future?

Mortal Mission – a mystery set on Mars (under the pen name of Pip Skinner)

Astronaut Hattie Fredericks's dream is realised when she is selected for the first crewed mission to search for life on Mars, but her presence on the Starship coincides with a series of incidents which threaten to derail the mission. The Mars mission encounters heated opposition from the religious right, but they're not the only ones dreading positive results.

After a near-miss while landing on the planet, the world watches as Hattie and the crew struggle to survive. But worse than the harsh elements are their suspicions that someone is trying to destroy the mission.

When more crew members die, Hattie doesn't know who to trust. And her only allies are 35 million miles away. As the tension ratchets up, violence and suspicion invade both worlds. Will Hattie's dream turn into a nightmare?

If you love your space exploration with a tinge of mystery, you'll enjoy this book.

All of the individual books are available in paperback at your favourite online retailer

About Author

The author has spent 30 years working as an exploration geologist managing remote sites and doing due diligence of projects in more than thirty countries. During this time, she has been collecting tall tales and real-life experiences which inspired her to write the Sam Harris Adventure Series chronicling the adventures of a female geologist as a pioneer in a hitherto exclusively male world.

PJ has worked in many countries in South America and Africa in remote, strange and often dangerous places, and loved every minute of it, despite encountering her fair share of misogyny and other perils. She is now writing these fact-based adventure books from the relative safety of London but still travels all over the world collecting data for her writing.

The Sam Harris Adventure Series is for lovers of intelligent adventure thrillers happening just before the time of mobile phones and internet. It has a unique viewpoint provided by Sam, a female interloper in a male world, as she struggles with alien cultures and failed relationships.

PJ's childhood in Ireland inspired her to write Rebel Green, about an English family who move to

Ireland during the beginnings of the Troubles. She has written a follow-on in the same Green Family Saga called Africa Green which follows Isabella Green as she goes to Sierra Leone to write an article on a chimpanzee sanctuary. She is now writing a third in the series, Fighting Green, about Liz Green's return to live in Ireland.

PJ has just finished Mortal Mission, a mystery set on Mars under the name of Pip Skinner.

She is now mulling a series of Cosy Mysteries, or a book about... You'll have to wait and see.

If you would like updates on the latest in the Sam Harris Series or to contact the author with your questions please got to the website: https://pjskinner.com

Printed in Great Britain
by Amazon